# IN CASE YOU
# DIDN'T KNOW

SAMANTHA CHASE

Editor: Jillian Rivera

Cover Design: Uplifting Designs/Alyssa Garcia

# ONE

"Success." Mason Bishop looked around the room with a satisfied grin. Sure, he was alone and talking to himself, but he was alone in a place of his own and it was beyond exciting. It was something he should have done a long time ago, but...here he was.

Collapsing down on his new sectional, he studied his surroundings with a sense of accomplishment. Had he known how satisfying it was going to feel, he might not have moved back in with his family after he finished college five years ago. Hindsight and all. Relaxing against the cushions he realized that as much as he hated the way things had gone down a week ago, it was exactly the impetus he needed to get him here.

Of course the fact that his cousin Sam kept poking at him because he still lived with his parents helped moved things along, but...

As if on cue, his phone rang and Sam's name came on the screen.

"Hey!"

"So?" Sam asked giddily. "Is it glorious? Please tell me it's glorious!"

Mason couldn't help but laugh. "I just put the last of the boxes in the trash so I haven't had the time for it to feel particularly glorious yet, but..."

"Okay, fine. Pretend, for crying out loud. You're in your own place and it's filled with your own stuff. Doesn't it feel great?"

It would be fun to keep needling each other, but to what end? "You know what? It does," he said with a big grin. "I slept here last night but there were boxes and crap everywhere. Now everything is put away and...yeah, I guess it is kind of glorious."

"There you go! Now don't you feel like a complete idiot for waiting for so long?"

"Weren't you living with your mom up until a couple of months ago?"

"Dude, that was totally different. I'd been living on my own up in Virginia for years.  It was only when I was forced to move here that I *chose* to live with my mother. Apples and oranges."

"Maybe."

"No maybes about it," Sam countered. "And now Shelby and I are living together and it's awesome."

"You sure that's a good idea? Moving in together so soon? Her father's a pastor. The gossip mill must be going crazy with the news!"

"Thanks. Like I needed the reminder," Sam deadpanned.

"And?"

"And what?"

"C'mon, are you telling me there's been no backlash? No one spouting how you're living in sin and whatnot?"

Sam let out a low laugh. "Oh, they spout it all the time, but we're good with it. We both know this is it for us and if anyone really starts hassling us, we're more than okay with going to the courthouse, making it legal, and shutting everyone up."

Mason was pretty sure his jaw hit the floor. "Are you serious? Making it...? Who are you and what have you done with my cousin?!"

That just made Sam laugh harder. "When you know, you know. And with Shelby...I know."

And damn if he couldn't hear his cousin's smile.

It was enough to make a guy sick.

"Wow...just..." He let out a long breath. "I never thought I'd live to see the day."

"Yeah, well...me either. But like I said, she's it for me. But I appreciate the uh...concern." He laughed again. "That's what that was, right? You being concerned?"

"Um...yeah. Sure. We can call it that," Mason said with a snicker. "We're family and we just look out for each other, right?"

"Yes, we do. But enough about me. Weren't we talking about you and the decisions you're making for your own life?" He paused. "You know I was seriously just thinking of your own sanity, Mason. Every day I watched you die a little more while under your parents' thumbs."

"I know and now that it's done, I can't believe I didn't do it sooner—like as soon as I graduated college."

"Hell, I'm still surprised you opted to move back here at all."

Raking a hand through his hair, he looked up at the ceiling. "I tossed around the idea of moving somewhere else, but...believe it or not, I like it here. I see all the things I want to do and help change. And if it means I have to live under the watchful eye of my folks, I'll live."

"They'll get hobbies eventually, right?" Sam teased.

"God, I hope so."

"They will. And either way, this move is going to be great for you. Trust me."

He didn't need his cousin to tell him that. He already knew it.

He could feel it too.

Last night when he'd carried in the last box and closed the door behind him, Mason felt like he had taken his first free breath.

Sad, right?

"I do trust you and I know the time was right because everything fell into place. The house–even though it's only a rental–is the perfect size for me. In a couple of years, I might be ready to buy a place, but for now this works."

"If you'd make a damn decision on the bar Pops left you, you know you could have afforded something of your own. I mean, why are you holding on to this place? Let it go already!"

Yeah, everyone had been in his face about The Mystic Magnolia and Mason had to admit, the whole thing still stumped him. Everyone else got an inheritance that made sense except him. Granted, he never felt the closeness to Pops his sisters or his cousins did, but to be left a decrepit old bar just seemed like a slap in the face.

Although–if he were being honest–he'd admit there was one *tiny* reason he was still holding on to it...

"I'll deal with it when I'm ready," he stated, unwilling to let his mind wander any more than it already had. "The lawyer said there wasn't a rush. Everything is being handled–bills are being paid and all so...I'm still trying to wrap my brain around it all."

"You mean why Pops gave you the place only old locals go to?" Sam teased. "And I mean *old*! No one under the age of sixty-five goes there!"

"Okay, that's not *that* old..."

"C'mon, fess up. Pops took you there when you were younger, didn't he?" Sam prodded. "The place must hold some significance to you and that's why he felt like you should be the one to have it."

"Why would I go to a bar with my great-grandfather? That's just...it's weird, Sam."

"Some could say it was like bonding, but whatever."

"Look, Pops never took me to The Mystic Magnolia or any other bar so...I'm stumped."

"Did he give you a letter? I thought we all got letters."

Rubbing a hand over his face, Mason let out a long breath. "He said a lot of things in my letter but none explained why he thought I should get that place."

"Really? Huh...that's strange. What did he say?"

Ugh...this really wasn't something he wanted to talk about right now. He was feeling all good and proud of himself and was ready to order a pizza. The thought of being able to kick back and enjoy it here in his new place was awesome. But now his cousin was crapping all over his good mood.

"Look, you um...you wanna come over for some pizza?" he said, hoping to change the subject. "I was just getting ready to order one when you called."

Luckily, Sam could be easily distracted.

"Wish I could, but rain check, okay? Shelby and I have dinner plans with Jake and Mallory. You wanna join us?"

The laugh escaped before he could stop it. "Right. Why

wouldn't I want to be the fifth wheel at dinner? I think I'll pass."

Catching his meaning, Sam laughed. "Yeah. Okay, I get it. Are you going to the benefit concert tomorrow night?"

"Shit," he murmured. "Is that tomorrow?"

Sam chuckled. "Yup. I think your mom bought out the entire VIP section."

He groaned. "Of course she did." He paused. "Wait, the Magnolia Amphitheater has a VIP section? Seriously?"

"Sure. Most places do."

"Still, that place isn't all that big–like 2,500 seats max."

"And that has to do with VIP seats...why?"

He groaned again. "Never mind. It doesn't really matter. We'll all be there so...wait, who's playing?"

"A couple of bands, I think. I didn't pay much attention either, but they're all somewhat local."

"Go have dinner and tell everyone I said hey and I'll see you at the show tomorrow."

"Yeah, sure. Sounds like a plan. Have a good night."

"You too."

After he hung up, Mason stretched his arms out along the top of the sofa cushions and smiled. He could order some pizza and maybe invite some friends over, instead of his parents and the brutal conversation he'd normally had with them over dinner. It was always about what other people his age were doing or who had just gotten engaged or who would be a suitable spouse for him. Seriously, he loved his parents but their obsession with his life had gotten out of control.

The breaking point was ten days ago.

He had come home from work to find his mother drinking wine with a woman he'd never met before. Leslie...something. Mason had figured she was involved in one of his mother's many charity projects and said a brief hello, then went to go change so he could go for a run.

That's when it all went wrong.

"Mason, sweetie," his mother said in her best Southern drawl. "You can't go for a run. You have dinner reservations in thirty minutes with Leslie."

The rage he felt in that moment was like nothing he'd ever felt before. In the past, he dealt with being introduced to women his parents thought would be a good match for him and being asked to take out their friends' daughters, but this was the first time he had been so blatantly ambushed in his own home.

Forcing a smile onto his face, he looked at Leslie and said, "I'm so sorry you were misled, but...I already have plans this evening." When he turned to leave the room, his mother had jumped to her feet and started to berate him for being rude.

"Rude?" he snapped. "You made dinner reservations for me with a stranger without talking to me about it and *I'm* being rude? This is it! I'm not doing this anymore! You have interfered with my life for the last time!"

The argument went on for hours and even though his father came home and tried to calm things down, it was too late. The damage was done. Mason had walked to his room, packed a bag and walked out.

And hadn't talked to either parent since.

He spent a week staying at Magnolia on the Beach—a small local hotel—and frantically combed the real estate ads looking for a place to live. The house was a complete godsend and when it was available immediately, he knew it was meant to be his. Furnishing it was a breeze since his cousin Mallory, who owned the local decor place, helped him and then his sisters both took turns bringing some of his things from home over to him. They could be total pains in the ass at times, but he was thankful for them right now.

It was quiet and for a long minute he sat there and enjoyed it and then...not so much. He wasn't used to the silence at all. Suddenly the thought of sitting home eating pizza wasn't quite so appealing, but then again, neither was going out to a bar or going out to eat alone.

Maybe he should've been the fifth wheel.

"This is ridiculous," he murmured coming to his feet. He'd lived in this town his entire life. Surely he could go out and grab something to eat, maybe run into a friend or two and kill some time before coming back here alone.

Or maybe...not alone.

Hell, he could finally bring a woman home instead of either going to her place or going to a motel!

The idea had merit.

But then...it didn't.

Honestly, he was tired, sweaty, and hungry. There was no shame in admitting that a quiet night in his own home was really what he wanted. Still, now he didn't want pizza, he wanted something with a little more substance. Feeling like he had a bit of a plan, he walked with purpose into his new en-suite bathroom to shower so he could go out and grab something to eat before settling in for the night with some Netflix.

* * *

"I THINK my virginity is growing back."

"Engine grease under your fingernails isn't very attractive, Scar. Maybe that's why guys aren't banging down your door to ask you out. But that's just my opinion."

Scarlett Jones looked down at her hands and frowned.

*Damn.*

With a shrug, she walked back into her bathroom to rewash her hands. Yeah, she wasn't a girly girl. She grew up working in her father's garage alongside him and her three brothers and it turned out, she really had a gift for working on motorcycles. If the engine grease and the smell of gasoline on her didn't turn guys off, the fact that she was fiercely independent did.

Did it bother her? Yes.

Enough to make her quit? No.

Glancing up at her reflection, Scarlett couldn't help but wonder what was wrong with her. In just about every other aspect of her life, she was confident–sometimes overly so. She was smart and caring and always willing to help out anyone in need. Everyone was always saying how great she was.

And yet, she hadn't been in a relationship in a long time.

Like...a really long time.

Hence the fear of her virginity growing back.

Turning off the water, she shook out her hands as she continued to stare at herself in the mirror. While there wasn't anything particularly remarkable about her, she was bold enough to know she was attractive, long, wavy brown hair, dark brown eyes, and if she did say so herself, a pretty kick-ass body. So why couldn't she seem to attract a decent guy?

"You're not pissed at me, are you?"

Reaching for a hand towel, Scarlett pulled herself from her thoughts and looked over at her best friend Courtney. With a smile, she replied, "Nah. That would be a pretty stupid reason to be mad. I had grease under my nails and you were just pointing it out. No biggie."

Only...it did bother her.

Not that Courtney pointed it out, but that it was there in the first place and she hadn't noticed it.

And it probably wasn't the first time.

"Are you sure? Because you just sort of got up and walked away."

Scarlett tossed the towel aside before holding up her hands and wiggling her fingers. "To get rid of the grease!" With a small laugh, she walked past Courtney and back into her bedroom. "Okay, where are we going tonight? Do I need to change?"

Looking down at herself, she seriously hoped not. She was comfortable. For the most part, they stuck to the local pubs and going out in jeans and a nice top were fine. But lately, Courtney had been wanting to broaden their horizons and that meant dressing up more.

Courtney walked across the room and flopped down on the bed with a dramatic sigh.

*That can't be good*, Scarlett thought, but waited her friend out.

Busying herself with straightening up her room, she mentally prayed her friend would just say what was on her mind.

"I think I want to move," she finally said and Scarlett immediately gasped in shock.

"Wait...why? Where would you go?"

Sitting up, Courtney flipped her hair over her shoulder and sighed again. "Anywhere. I'm just never going to do anything or meet anyone if I stay here. I'm over small-town life."

They'd had this conversation multiple times and for the most part, Scarlett was used to it. Walking over, she sat down on the bed beside her. "Okay, what brought this on?

Last weekend we went out and had a great time and I seem to remember seeing you make out with Mike Ryan." Then she winked. "And I distinctly remember watching you wave goodbye to me as you left with him."

Courtney fell back on the bed. "Yeah, and it was good and the sex was good, but...it's like it's always the same guys! We've been hanging out with the same people we've known since elementary school!"

"That's not true. We're heading into the peak tourist season! You know it's going to be crazy around here for the next six weeks or so. Maybe you'll meet someone..."

"You don't get it, Scar. I don't want to be the girl the tourists hook up with for a quick weekend fling or the girl the locals pass the time with until they can hit on the tourists! I'm just...I'm ready for a change!"

"Okay, okay," she soothed, falling back next to Courtney. "How about this...let's just go out tonight and grab something to eat and then we'll pick up some ice cream on the way home and have a mellow night. How does that sound?"

"Boring," Courtney said with a pout. "And the exact reason why I'm done with small-town life."

"Hey! I'm kind of taking offense to that! I know I'm not the most exciting person in the world, but..." Sitting up, Scarlett immediately bounced off the bed.

"You're right, you're right, you're right," Courtney said, standing up. "That was uncalled for." She gave Scarlett a long hug before pulling back. "I'm just in a funk and I'm bored and...don't listen to me. I'll get over it."

And the thing was, Scarlett knew she would, but it didn't mean she could just ignore the situation either.

"Look," she began cautiously, "I'm bored too. It's not

like a whole lot of exciting stuff happens around here or that I've got all kinds of interesting things going on..."

"Now that's not true. You could be doing so much more if you would just share your hobby with..."

"Lalalalala!" Scarlett cried out before stopping to glare at her friend. "I swore you to secrecy and you promised never to bring it up!"

Courtney looked around the room in confusion. "Who's going to hear me? It's just the two of us!"

There was a slight chance she was being paranoid, but there was no way she was going to tell anyone other than Courtney what she'd been doing in her spare time.

"Fine. Whatever," she murmured. "Can we go grab something to eat now? I'm starving."

And yeah, there was a little snap in her voice that she instantly regretted.

They walked out of the bedroom and Scarlett picked up her purse and keys, then followed Courtney out the door.

"So not the fun night I was hoping for," she said under her breath. At her car, she paused and apologized. "I'm sorry I snapped at you. That was wrong of me."

Courtney–ever the drama queen–merely shrugged.

Awesome.

"You want to go to Café Magnolia or The Sand Bar for burgers?"

"Ugh...I know their burgers are legendary, but why won't they change the name of the damn place? It's not very appetizing to go eat somewhere that has the word 'sand' in its title."

"So you want to go to the Café?"

"I didn't say that," Courtney was quick to amend. "I mean, we both know a girls' night requires burgers."

"And fries," Scarlett said with a grin as they climbed into her car.

The Sand Bar was like most of the businesses in Magnolia Sound—an institution. It had been around for at least twenty years and was in need of a renovation, but business was too good to close down and get it done. When the hurricane hit a little more than eight months ago, it seemed like the logical time to finally freshen the place up. Unfortunately, old Mr. Hawkins simply fixed the roof, replaced a couple of windows and declared The Sand Bar open again just a week after Hurricane Amelia blew through.

"I'm getting the bacon cheeseburger, fries, and possibly onion rings," Courtney declared as they drove along Main Street. Turning her head, she grinned at Scarlett. "And I think you should share an order of fried pickles with me."

Her stomach hurt just thinking about all the food, but she kept that to herself. Fried pickles definitely weren't her thing, but she'd eat a couple and move on. "Sure. Why not?"

The parking lot was crowded, but that wasn't anything new. The location was prime—on the beach side of the street—and it had indoor and outdoor seating, live entertainment, and a full bar. Honestly, Scarlett never cared much for coming here to drink, though. She was all about the food. Once they parked and started making their way toward the front entrance, she was more than ready to eat.

Courtney worked her way through the crowd and managed to find them a small booth in the corner.

"How do you do that?"

"Do what?"

"Always find us a place to sit?"

"It's my lone superpower," she said dryly as she flagged a waiter over. Once their orders were placed, Courtney began scanning the room. "I swear, even the tourists are the same."

Scarlett looked around and frowned. "How can you tell?"

"Because we've been doing this for what feels like forever. Maybe there will be some different faces at the concert tomorrow. You're still coming with me, right?"

Their server came back and placed their drinks down and Scarlett eagerly reached for hers. There was no way she could admit she wasn't looking forward to the concert, but she still needed a little sweet tea to bide her time.

"Nice delay tactic." Courtney knew her too well. With a weary sigh, she asked, "Tell me why you don't want to go."

"I don't know. The amphitheater is small and the crowds are going to be crazy! We're going to be up in the nosebleed section and packed in like sardines! And on top of that, it's going to be ninety degrees out! Call me crazy, but that is not my idea of a good time."

"Why are you like this?" Courtney whined. "It's like you just refuse to have fun!"

"That's ridiculous! I have fun all the time! I just don't find it enjoyable to stand around and sweat when I don't have to!"

"You work in your dad's garage and it's always hot in there! Every time I've ever seen you there, you're sweating!"

"And that's because I have to be there!" she cried with more than a little frustration. "When I'm there, I'm working. I work, because I need money! And sometimes that means working in a building with little to no air conditioning!"

"Scarlett..."

"I'm forced to sweat for work so why would I choose to

get sweaty on a night out when I'm supposed to be having fun?"

"Look, we both know you don't have to work at the garage. You choose to."

"I need the income..."

"Yeah, yeah, yeah...I get it. You use the second job to feed your hobby supplies," she said with a hint of sarcasm. "You work too much and you're always saving and you live frugally. It's admirable."

"But...?"

"But...you are way too uptight! No one is thinking about it being hot out, Scarlett! We're all like 'Yay! Concert!' Why can't you do the same?"

"When have I ever simply followed the herd, Court? That's not me."

"Okay, fine. It's not, but...can't you just do it this once? C'mon! It's going to be so much fun! For one night can't you forget about your jobs and be a little carefree? You might actually enjoy it."

So many comments were on the tip of her tongue–most of them snarky–but Scarlett opted to keep them to herself. It was easy for people like Courtney to be carefree and not obsess about finances. And while she didn't begrudge her friend having a family who always was and probably always would be financially stable, there was also no way for her to fully understand the anxiety that plagued her daily.

Growing up poor–and knowing that everyone you knew wasn't–wasn't something you got over. From the time Scarlett first started school, she knew she was different. Besides never having anything new for herself, she was dressed more like a boy than a girl. Looking back now she could almost laugh about it, but back then, it was beyond painful. Her father had done the best he could and she loved him for it. She just wished someone had stepped in and tried to explain to Dominic Jones that raising a daughter was very different from raising sons. Her brothers were all fine–in their own annoying ways–all three of them. But they were boys who were raised by a strong male role model.

They'd also had more time with their mother before she died from colon cancer when Scarlett was four. Kandace Jones had fought hard to win her battle with the deadly disease, but it was too much for her. There were days when her memories of her mother were so strong it was as if she were sitting right there with her, and other days it was like she couldn't remember a thing. Those days were devastating.

Still, her father had struggled to raise four kids on his own and apparently it was easier to treat them all equally–like boys–rather than figuring out that Scarlett wanted nothing more than to be treated like a girl.

Something she still struggled with.

Maybe that was another reason why she couldn't seem to find anyone she was interested in dating. It was hard to find the balance between being the girly-girl she longed to be and the tough-as-nails mechanic she presented to the world.

A damn dilemma indeed.

Although if anyone who didn't know much about her dared to look in her closet, they'd only see the girly stuff.

Way too much of it.

"Hey," Courtney said with a growing smile. "Just when you thought there were no new faces in the crowd..."

Scarlett turned her head and tried to see who her friend was talking about. "Who are you looking at?"

"I don't think I've seen him here before. I mean...I suppose it's possible, but I always heard he tended to hit bars and restaurants out of town—especially since we graduated."

Frowning, Scarlett continued to scan the crowd. "So it's someone we know?"

"Oh, good Lord. I think he got even better looking..."

Now her curiosity was seriously piqued. Still, not one face in the crowd looked familiar and with a huff of frustration, she faced Courtney again. "Who the hell are you talking about?"

"Mason Bishop," she replied before taking a sip of her beer. "He's a little too pretty for my taste, but still, you have to appreciate a fine-looking man." Putting her drink down, she looked at Scarlett. "What's with the face?"

Doing her best to put a relaxed smile on her face, she replied, "What do you mean?"

"You were practically scowling. Why?"

With a shrug, Scarlett reached for her own drink and wished it were alcohol. "I really wasn't."

"Yes, you were. Now spill it. What's up?"

If there was one thing Scarlett was certain of, it was that Courtney would continue to badger her until she answered her.

So she did.

"Guys like Mason? They're what's wrong with the world!"

Courtney's eyes went wide. "Um...what?"

Nodding, she looked over her shoulder and glared briefly when she spotted him. When she turned back to Courtney, she explained. "Everything comes easy to guys like him. Like it's not enough that he comes from one of the founding families here in town, but his folks are wealthy and successful, his sisters are both super nice and pretty, and he looks like a damn model!"

"Scarlett..."

"No, I'm serious! Do you remember what he was like in school?"

"Uh...yeah..."

"Mr. Popularity! Captain of the baseball team, student body president, homecoming king, prom king...ugh! It was enough to make me sick!"

"Okay, if I didn't know him, I'd agree with you. All those things combined are a bit much. But Mason was always a nice guy, so..." She shrugged. "It's just who he is, Scar. What's the big deal?"

Rolling her eyes, she was about to go off on a rant when their server returned with their food. With a muttered thanks, she opted to reach for her burger and take a huge bite instead.

And damn...as far as distractions went, this was the best one yet. It was almost enough for her to forget what they were talking about.

"You should probably get to know him before you get so judgy," Courtney said as she picked up her own burger. "I bet if you spent some time talking to him..."

"Oh, I know him, Court. Back in middle school we were lab partners for a short time. He was semi-decent and kind of nice, but once high school hit, it was like he didn't even know me. So...I stand by my earlier opinion, thank you very much."

"Look, I get you have issues with people you think lead a privileged life...

"You have no idea."

Courtney gave her a hard stare before she continued. "However, sometimes you have to remember that looks can be deceiving and you have no idea what goes on behind closed doors."

Doing her best to appear bored, she reached for an onion ring. "And sometimes it's all exactly as it seemed. Sometimes shiny happy people are exactly that–shiny happy people with no substance."

"Well damn."

With a shrug, Scarlett took another bite of her burger and pushed all thoughts of Mason Bishop completely out of her mind.

## TWO

Everything felt weird.

Mason glanced around and found that their VIP section had what felt like an invisible wall down the middle. His parents were on the far-right side of the section, dancing awkwardly to the rock music that was playing, while he positioned himself on the far left.

He groaned even as he mentally shook his head. Eventually he'd get over his anger, but right now he felt like a fraud being here. Georgia Bishop wanted the entire town to think all was well and perfect within the family and he was helping her perpetuate that. Luckily, the music was a good distraction and along with the family, there were about twenty-five of their closest friends sitting here–or standing and dancing here–with them. So it wasn't like he had to directly interact with his parents.

Finishing off the last of his beer, he grimaced. He could flag down the server who was assigned to their section and simply order another drink, but it was hot and he was distracted and not particularly into being here. The music was great and all around him everyone was having fun, but...he just wasn't feeling it right now. Glancing around, he saw how the amphitheater was full to capacity and if he wanted to stroll out to the concession area, he could probably do it without having to wait in a long line. However, leaving the security of their little corner of the venue meant leaving the comfort of the fans.

*Do I want a drink more than I want to be cool?*

That was the million dollar question.

The band was only into the third or fourth song of their set and Mason had to admit, the time was perfect to go and wander around–no crowds, no lines, and he could be back here drinking a cold beer with a fan blowing on him in a matter of minutes. Out of the corner of his eye, he saw their server handing drinks to his cousin Mallory and her fiancé Jake.

*You could have your cake and eat it too, dumbass, if you just order your drink here.*

Yeah, yeah, yeah...he could, but for some reason he felt restless and just wanted to get out of the crowd and move around a bit. It was stupid but being here with his family right after finally getting some freedom and distance from them just irritated him. Granted, it wasn't like he was here with them and only them, but...still. He had a whole grabbing-the-world-by-the-balls attitude because of his new-found independence, so sitting in a specially-sectioned space just for his family seemed to be in direct contrast with that.

*And...I'm going to the concession area!*

His cousin Sam caught his eye and Mason simply motioned that he would be right back. With a wave, he made his way out of their box and up the aisle toward the gate he had originally entered through. About ten feet from the gate, the hot air hit him like a wall, but he chose to ignore it and continued up the aisle.

He waved at some friends, had more than a couple of women give him a flirty smile and wave, but none of it was enough to make him stop and linger. Being social was the last thing he wanted right now and even though he could admit it, he didn't feel good about it.

This was who he was–Mr. Friendly, Mr. Personality, Mr. Everybody's-Best-Friend...Ugh. It was exhausting. It wasn't always that way, and for the most part, he was a friendly and sociable kind of guy. He enjoyed hanging out and talking with people. But lately it just took far too much effort and he had to wonder why.

Probably because his mother's crazy behavior had him on his guard everywhere he went.

And even though he was a grown man who was living on his own, this was a small town and everybody knew everybody. There was still a part of Mason that wondered if his mother had people spying on him so she could try to sneak some social-climbing debutante into his path.

He snorted at his own wild imagination.

*Paranoid much?*

Still, he was on guard whenever people approached him and stayed that way until he could determine if they were talking to him because they wanted to and not because they were directed to.

And what made it all that much funnier was you'd think he was one of the damn Kennedys or Rockefellers with the way people treated him. Granted, the Bishops were a wealthy family and very prominent in the community, but this was a fairly small community! He had no doubt that if someone transplanted his folks into the middle of Manhattan or L.A., they would not measure up to their own hype!

Either way, the people of Magnolia Sound treated Mason and his family with a bit of awe and respect that he never quite understood. And why so many people wanted to be a part of their family was a complete mystery to him.

Walking through the gate, he stopped and smiled. There were multiple food and drink counters and none had more than a handful of people waiting. Deciding he could finally take a breath and relax, he opted to hit the restroom first, then grab a drink before heading back to his family's cordoned-off section of the world.

* * *

"THIS IS AMAZING! Oh, my gosh, the band sounds so good!"

Scarlett smiled at Courtney even as she fanned herself with the concert program to try to cool off.

It wasn't working.

Their seats were literally in the last row with their backs to the wall and even though the venue was small, they were far enough from the stage that she had to squint a bit to see the guys in the band clearly.

Then her squint turned to a glare when she caught sight of the VIP crowd.

*Look at them—with their fans and their food and drinks being brought to them like they own the damn place...*

Okay, maybe she did have a chip on her shoulder that she was getting tired of, but old habits die hard, right?

It didn't seem fair how most of the people here had to walk and get their own refreshments while fanning themselves with wrinkled and wilted paper while the high-society snobs practically had people fanning them and feeding them grapes.

"I love this song!" Courtney cried out and Scarlett had to admit, she liked it too. She just needed to focus on the music and not on how unfair life was.

Reaching for her bottle of water, she was about to take a sip when the drunk guy next to her elbowed it out of her hand while he was attempting to dance.

Awesome.

Now her pants were wet and her water was gone.

Muttering a curse, she moved around Courtney and explained how she was going to get a drink and offered to get one for her too. With a wave, she wandered down what felt like a mile of stairs and made her way out to the concession area. By the time she made it there, her pants were practically dry but she opted to run into the ladies room to freshen up. When she stepped out five minutes later, she scanned the concession area to figure out what she wanted to get.

And that's when she saw him.

Mason Bishop.

He was standing all alone and sort of doing the same as her–looking around with an utter lack of enthusiasm.

For a minute she almost felt a kinship with him.

Then, pushing thoughts of him aside again, Scarlett squared her shoulders and made her way toward one of the kiosks that only sold water and soft drinks. Looking down, she rummaged through her tiny purse to find some cash and walked solidly into someone.

"*Oof!*"

Her eyes widened when she realized who she had run into.

Dammit.

For some reason, her stupid heart decided to skip a beat and when the smile on Mason's face dawned with recognition, she had no idea if she'd be able to form a single word.

"Scarlett, right? Scarlett Jones?" And yes, his voice was just as sexy as the rest of him.

Double dammit.

Her throat was suddenly dry and when she forced herself to meet his gaze, she felt like the same insecure thirteen-year-old girl she was when she last had a conversation with him. Forcing herself to clear her throat, she nodded. "Uh, yeah. Hey."

No doubt the smile she was currently trying to pull off was awkward but Mason didn't seem to mind.

"So, how've you been?" he asked with genuine interest and Scarlett had to wonder why he even wanted to have a conversation with her. Why couldn't he simply say "excuse me" and walk away?

Clearly she was taking a little too long with her response because he arched one brow at her but his smiled never faltered.

Wait...did he have dimples?

*Gah!* Why was she being so weird about this?

"Good," she finally said. "And you?"

He shrugged as his hands slid into the pockets of his cargo shorts. "Good. Yeah, I'm good too." Turning, he looked over his shoulder briefly and then back to her. "You enjoying the concert?"

She shrugged. "It's a little too warm out to truly enjoy it, but the music's good."

Mason nodded and Scarlett realized there wasn't really much else to say. They had done the polite chit-chat thing and now she really needed something to drink and to get back to her seat so Courtney didn't think she just ran off.

"Well...I just came out here to grab a bottle of water. I guess I'll see you around," she said and turned to walk away.

"Hey!" he called out even as he fell in step with her. "Where are you sitting?"

It was quite possibly the worst thing he could have asked. Scarlett felt herself tense up but refused to shy away from answering him.

"Back row," she stated, almost as if she were daring him to make a lame comment.

Nodding, he replied, "Great view from up there! And you probably don't have to deal with people banging into you from all sides."

The boyish grin was still in place, dimples and all, and it was almost hard to be annoyed with him.

Almost.

"You're down in the VIP section, right?" she asked, crossing her arms across her chest because...obviously she needed to make some sort of social stand.

With another nod, he shrugged. "Yeah. My folks thought it would be fun to have us all down there."

For a minute, she was confused. It seemed like he wasn't all that thrilled to be down there and he certainly wasn't bragging.

Weird.

"So, what are you doing slumming it up here?" And yeah, there was a snap in her voice that almost made her cringe.

*Why are you being so bitchy?*

"Uh...what?"

"You've wandered to the wrong side of the tracks, Bishop. Don't they have butler service down there for your group? Champagne and caviar and whatnot?"

Now he was the one to look confused and for the first

time, his smile started to fall. Tilting his head slightly, Mason studied her. "Is there...I mean...do you have some sort of problem with me?"

Where did she even begin?

"Look, it's not you, per se," she began. "I'm just wondering why you'd be up here with the common folk when you can be catered to, that's all."

Scarlett was fairly certain he'd figure she was some sort of nut job and walk away.

But did he?

No.

If anything, his smile was back in full-force and he laughed.

Hard.

"You want to know something funny?" he asked.

With a careless shrug, she replied, "Not particularly."

"Aww...come on. Aren't you even a little curious?" He nudged her with his shoulder and he was so much bigger than her that Scarlett nearly toppled over. Mason's hands immediately reached out to steady her and she was quick to move away. She was already having a hard time remembering why she shouldn't like him and even the brief touch of his hands on her skin had her wanting to almost rub up against him.

*Bad, Scarlett!*

"Well?" he prompted teasingly and she couldn't help but let out a small laugh even as she rolled her eyes.

"Yeah, sure. Tell me something funny."

His laugh was low and a little gruff and a lot sexier than she thought a laugh could be. "That almost sounds like a dare, Jones."

Now it was her turn to arch a brow at him. "Jones? Seriously?"

He shrugged. "Seemed appropriate."

"Was that what you thought was funny?" It was meant to sound like she was impatient, but really, she was enjoying the banter.

Mason leaned in close again. "No, but now it kind of is."

"Get to the point, Bishop," she said and this time, Scarlett was pretty sure she sounded flirty, not intentionally flirty, but it just came out that way.

And it seemed to please Mason.

"I guess I deserve that one," he said and then paused for a moment. "So here's what's funny–I was sitting down in the VIP section and thinking how ridiculous it all was. Is it convenient not to have to get up and come up here for refreshments? Sure. But for the most part, it seemed pretty pointless to me."

"And pretentious," she added unapologetically.

With a hearty laugh, he nodded. "That too." They stood like that–sort of watching each other with smiles on their faces–for less than a minute before Mason asked, "What are you doing after the show?"

There was no way to hide her surprise. Guys like Mason Bishop never showed any interest in her and she had to wonder why he even was. She knew she hadn't been particularly friendly and, other than her one flirty comment, she didn't think she had encouraged him at all.

"I thought maybe we could go grab a drink and catch up," he said, clearly trying to prompt her to respond.

A couple of people started walking around them to grab some beverages and as if of one mind, they both moved away from the kiosk and toward the brick wall that stood in front of the restrooms. It was suddenly quieter and Scarlett knew she was going to have to say something–she couldn't stand there mutely much longer.

"Um...thanks, but...I can't," she finally said.

"Oh," he said, and it was obvious he was disappointed. "Are you here with someone?"

She wasn't going to play dumb and act like she didn't know what he was fishing for. "I'm here with my friend Courtney."

"Baker?" he asked.

"Yeah. How did you know?"

He shrugged again. "We had some classes together and I thought I remembered the two of you being friends."

Wait...what? He noticed *and* remembered that?

"Uh...yeah, so I'm here with her and I probably should get back to up to my seat and..."

"Don't go," he said, moving in shamelessly closer. Scarlett could feel the heat of his body, could smell his cologne and all thoughts of going back to her spot in the nosebleed section were forgotten. "I mean...what's the hurry?"

Scarlett tried to think up something witty to say, but her mind was a complete blank.

Okay, that wasn't totally true. She was thinking about how in a perfect world she could have just said yes–that she'd love to go out with him after the concert. Or better yet, that she could just go back to his celebrity section and watch the rest of the show together.

"C'mon," he said, interrupting her thoughts. "If you won't go out with me later, hang out for a bit now."

And then she completely embarrassed and horrified herself.

She giggled.

God, she hated women who did that.

She was one step away from twirling her hair and Scarlett knew she needed to get herself under control.

"Have a drink with me," he prompted.

"I really just wanted some water."

"Then we'll have water."

Her laugh this time wasn't quite so girly, but there was a huskiness to it she didn't recognize either. "You can drink whatever you'd like. You don't have to be lame just because I am." Standing this close to him, she could smell the beer on his breath so she knew he was most likely out here to grab another one.

"I don't think you're being lame, Jones," he said playfully, being a total flirt. "I think it's hot as hell out here and it's probably the smarter choice than what I was thinking."

"Well...I try to be practical."

*Wow. Way to sound appealing, dork.*

His grin was downright boyish and if she wasn't mistaken, he moved a little closer. Only...she didn't feel crowded by him. If anything, she wished she were bold enough to do the same.

"Practical can be good," he commented. "But sometimes it's fun to be a little...impulsive."

*Oh my...*

Swallowing hard, she nodded. "Are we still talking about beverages?"

And yeah, that totally wasn't her voice.

Mason let out a low groan and slowly licked his bottom lip and Scarlett couldn't believe how incredibly attractive she found the move. Her eyes traced the movement and when she looked up and met his steel-blue eyes, she felt like everything around them faded away–the crowds, the noise, the music–and all that was left was the two of them.

It didn't seem possible and her first thought was how she was just feeling this way because it had been so damn long since she'd been with a guy. But the longer they continued to look at each other, the more she realized it had nothing to do with how much time it had been—it was all him. All Mason. And as much as she wanted to be annoyed by that fact, she couldn't seem to make that happen. Whatever was happening was happening, and she was more than willing to let it.

What was the harm in hanging out with him for a bit? Hell, what was the harm in flirting? It wasn't as if this were going anywhere and there was no one around to tell her he was out of her league or to remind him how he shouldn't be hanging around with someone so beneath his social status. Right now they were just a man and a woman maybe having a drink and a little conversation.

Flirty conversation.

She could do that, right?

For a little while, she could be the girly-girl no one thought she could be and have the full attention of one of the most eligible bachelors in town. How hard could it be?

Doing her best to relax, Scarlett smiled up at Mason. "So, we were going to have an impulsive drink, right?"

His grin was slow and sexy as hell. "Well, that would have been my request for after the show. But since you have plans..."

She shrugged. "Then I guess we should do it now before we both miss the entire concert." Her tone was light and carefree and she had to admit, it felt good.

"Stay right here," he said anxiously before sprinting over to the drink kiosk. Scarlett wasn't sure how he did it, but he managed to be back with two bottles of water in less than a minute. It was almost as if the small crowd parted for him and let him skip to the front of the line.

And seriously, that wouldn't surprise her at all.

"Thanks," she said, accepting the drink from him. "But you seriously could have gotten something else."

"And risk taking too much time away from the little we have?"

Rolling her eyes, she couldn't suppress her laughter. "Dude, seriously? That has to be the cheesiest line ever!"

Luckily, he laughed with her. "Oh, I don't know about that. I think I could come up with a few more if you gave me the chance."

Her curiosity got the better of her and she wanted to know what exactly the infamous Mason Bishop considered to be cheesy pickup lines. "I'm giving you the chance. Lay them on me," she challenged as she leaned against the cool brick.

His eyes went wide. "That's how you want to spend our time?"

That just had her laughing again. "I'm sure there are better ways, but I thought I'd see if you were up for the challenge."

*Oh my God...I did not just say that!*

His gaze turned a little heated and he took a quick drink before bending down and placing the bottle on the ground. When he straightened, he mimicked her pose against the brick. "Challenge accepted."

"Bring it on."

And she only partially meant the cheesy lines.

Clearing his throat, Mason's expression went a little serious before he said, "Hey, baby. Come here often?"

She gave him a bland look. "That wasn't particularly cheesy. Boring, yes. Cheesy, no." She placed her bottle of water on the ground next to his.

Holding up a hand, he said, "Alright, alright...give me a minute." Then he paused and cleared his throat again, this time giving her a sexy grin. "I'm not a photographer, but I can picture me and you together."

Laughing softly, Scarlett nodded. "Okay, that was a good one."

"I was feeling a little off today, but you definitely turned me on." Mason waggled his eyebrows at her and she couldn't help but laugh harder. He shifted his position so he was standing straight in front of her. "Girl, you're like Netflix. Because I could watch you for hours."

Tears were starting to stream down her face and as she reached out, her hand landed on his chest. "Oh, my gosh... stop!" she said between fits of laughter. "You're clearly the king of cheesy lines!"

Placing one of his hands over hers, he pressed it firmly over his heart. "Do you have a map? I'm getting lost in your eyes."

"And we have a winner!" she cried, taking a minute to calm back down. "I...I should get back to my seat." Doing her best to casually pull her hand from his very muscular chest, Scarlett prayed her mascara wasn't running down her face. When she realized he wasn't releasing her, she sobered and looked up at him, only to find that he wasn't laughing anymore either. Suddenly they were very close and very quiet and she had no idea how they had gotten to this place so fast.

"Hey, Scarlett?" he asked, his voice low and gruff.

"Yeah?" Her own voice a little low and breathless.

"It's traditional to kiss goodnight at the end of a date."

With a small and semi-nervous laugh, she looked down and shook her head. "I thought we were done with the cheesy lines."

He tucked a finger under her chin until she looked up at him. "No line. This is me telling you what I want."

Her eyes went a little wide when she realized what he was saying. "Oh."

*Lame, Scarlett. Totally lame.*

"Is that okay?" His voice was barely a whisper and all she could do was nod.

As Mason lowered his head toward hers, she felt a moment of uncertainty. This was just supposed to be some fun and flirty banter. He wasn't supposed to want to kiss her!

But man-oh-man did she want to kiss him.

*Go big or go home, right?*

And when his lips touched hers, Scarlett felt it all the way to her toes. His strong arms slowly banded around her to pull her in as close as could be and she responded in kind as her own arms slowly wound their way over his shoulders. He was so tall and broad that she almost had to get up on her tiptoes to accomplish that move.

Soft lips, strong arms, stubbled jaw...there wasn't a thing about Mason she wasn't suddenly drawn to and as the kiss went from curious to seeking to almost carnal, Scarlett cursed the fact that they were in the middle of a concession courtyard and how she had turned down his invitation to go out later.

He let out a soft moan—or maybe it was her—but it was hard to tell because basically they were sharing breath. In her entire life, she had never been so turned on by a kiss. She wasn't a virgin and she wasn't a prude; honestly, she loved sex. It had just been a long time since she'd had any. And unfortunately, after this one kiss, the bar was going to be seriously raised before she would consider sleeping with anyone again.

Because...*wow*.

Slowly, Mason broke the kiss. What was wild was now soft and as he sipped at her lips one last time, she heard him whisper, "Damn."

Yeah. She felt the same way.

When he lifted his head, he looked down at her before one of his hands came up and caressed her cheek. She leaned into his touch and wished she had something witty or at least sophisticated to say. She knew that if she tried to open her mouth, the only things to come out would be small, one-syllable words.

And even they might be a stretch.

His hand dropped and he took a step back, his hands going to his pockets. Ducking his head, he looked...uncertain. He looked nothing at all like his usual confident self.

"I know you said you had plans later, but...if you change your mind, maybe meet me back here after the show," he said quietly.

"Mason, I..."

One strong finger covered her lips. "You don't have to say anything. I get it. Just...think about it."

And then he turned and walked away. Leaving her a little dazed, confused, and turned on.

# THREE

*Please be there. Please be there. Please be there.*

Mason slowly made his way up the aisle after the show and did his best to make small talk with his cousins and the rest of his family, but his mind was elsewhere.

Scarlett Jones.

Holy. Shit.

In a million years he never thought he'd be so completely blown away by a kiss, but...here he was. And he'd be lying if he said he'd never thought about kissing Scarlett. Hell, she was always there in his peripheral ever since middle school, but they didn't run in the same crowds and she gave a serious "back off" vibe.

Until tonight.

Yeah, holy...shit.

Impatiently, he stopped and scanned the crowd ahead of him. He was still in the aisle of the amphitheater so he couldn't see out to the concession area and it was making him crazy. All around him, people were talking about how great the show was and how much fun it was to hang out, but all Mason wanted to do was shove his way to the top and find out if she was there or not.

For the most part, he was fairly certain she wouldn't be. It didn't take a genius to see she had a serious problem with him. Well, maybe not him specifically, but people like him. And yeah, he knew her situation–she grew up poor and most people felt sorry for her because of it. But he never saw her like that. To him, she was always just Scarlett–the pretty girl with the big dark eyes, curvy body, and the shy smile he knew she made people work for.

He now knew this personally and was more than willing to work as hard as she wanted.

The fact that he came on so strong probably didn't work in his favor either. And the strangest part was that he normally didn't. Did he flirt? Yes. Did he enjoy the chase? Yes. But for the most part, whenever a woman gave him the kind of attitude Scarlett did, he wished them a good night and moved on.

But with her, he couldn't.

Hell, if she wasn't up there waiting by the wall, Mason knew he'd want to find out where she was and who she was hanging out with. He already knew it was Courtney, but that didn't help. It wasn't like he was friends with her either. So would he start asking about her around town? Yes. And it wouldn't be hard to find out. She'd lived here in Magnolia her entire life too and if there was one thing he could be certain of, it wouldn't take long for him to talk to someone who knew her.

That wasn't creepy, right?

The crowd moved slowly and he huffed loudly.

"Dude, what is your deal?" Beside him, his sister Peyton looked at him with mild interest. "Two thousand people are trying to exit through two entrances. How fast can they go?"

"Yeah, I get it, but we already hung back for a while and it's like the damn line isn't even *trying* to move!"

"What's your rush? Hot date or something?"

If he were lucky...

His sister nudged him with her elbow–her bony elbow– and looked up at him with amusement. Her black hair was pulled back in a sleek ponytail and she looked all of twelve to him–something he teased her about constantly.

"None of your business," he teased, hoping he didn't sound too annoyed.

She laughed–but not before elbowing him again. "Why are you such a jerk?"

"Why are your elbows so damn sharp?" he countered, but now they were both laughing.

"C'mon, what's going on with you?" she asked as they slowly moved along. "You've been distracted all night. If you didn't want to come to the show, why did you?"

He shrugged. "This is where everyone was going to be. I bet every place in town was empty tonight."

"I guess...but still, you disappeared for a while."

Another shrug. "Went to use the restroom and there was a line."

"Hmm..."

"Look," he began, wrapping an arm around her shoulder. "Hanging out with the folks on a Friday night is not my idea of a good time–even if it is for a concert. I just finally got settled in the new place and it was a little too soon to have to play happy family."

"I get it," she said with a sigh. "So how is it?"

"Awesome," he said with a grin, happy to see they were almost through the entrance gate to the concession area. "I'm finally all unpacked and it feels great to have a place to myself."

"You should have done it a long time ago, bro. Seriously, you never should have moved back in after graduation."

"Yeah, I know. Sam and I have had that discussion more than once."

"Trust me, we all have."

"All?"

"Well, not mom and dad, but everyone else."

It was hard to be annoyed when it was simply the truth. Everyone had seen it but him. Lesson learned.

They walked through the gate and Mason frantically began to look around even as his sister continued to chatter on about how lucky he was, how she couldn't wait to come over, blah, blah, blah.

*There she is.*

His heart kicked hard in his chest and anticipation began to hum through him.

*She's really here.*

At that moment, Scarlett looked in his direction and caught his gaze.

And then spotted Peyton beside him.

Her gaze narrowed and she immediately turned and began to walk away. Panic hit him and he gently shoved his sister away with a murmured apology as he went after Scarlett. Moving quickly through the crowd, he jumped up every once in a while when he lost sight of her. Luckily, she didn't go far and he caught up to her at one of the gates that led to the parking lot.

"Hey!" he called, reaching out and touching her arm. She spun and gave him a bored look. "What happened back there? I...I thought you were waiting for me."

The look she gave him spoke volumes and no doubt she was going to deny she was waiting at all.

"You thought wrong."

Sometimes being right sucked.

She looked just beyond him as if searching for someone and he figured she was looking for her friends. Taking a step back, he felt utterly foolish and completely out of his element while Scarlett's expression was...disappointed.

With a curt nod, Mason turned to walk away. He wasn't going to beg her to change her mind and clearly he was the only one who was affected by their kiss.

"I'm sure your friend with the dark hair will be more than happy to hang out with you," she quipped as soon as his back was turned.

Friend with the dark hair?

A slow smile crept across his face and he had to fight the urge to high-five himself.

She was jealous.

Turning back toward her, he took a tentative step forward. "You mean the petite one with blue eyes and hair in a ponytail?"

Scarlett crossed her arms over her chest and snorted with disgust. "I didn't see her eyes from that distance, but... yeah. Her. I'm surprised she wasn't running after you."

Another step.

"Well, to be honest, she has in the past and she probably will again..."

"Ugh...you are the worst, Bishop," she murmured but didn't move.

It wasn't until he was toe to toe with her that he leaned in close and said, "But considering she's my younger sister, I'd say that's normal behavior, wouldn't you?"

Those dark eyes of hers went wide, her mouth formed a perfect "O", and it took every ounce of strength to keep from kissing her.

The way he saw it, they could stand here and make

awkward conversation about her mistake, or they could simply pretend this was where they were supposed to meet up and plan on where they would go next.

"Are you hungry?" he asked. "I was thinking of grabbing a burger at the Sand Bar. What do you think?"

"I ate there last night," she replied. "And so did you." Her hands instantly flew to her mouth at her admission and Mason thought it was cute as hell.

And her blush only added to all the things he was finding attractive about her.

"True," he said casually, "but they do have the best burgers in town." Then he paused. "But I'm sure they'll be one of the most crowded now that the show is over. No doubt everyone's going to go out for drinks and a bite to eat."

She nodded but wouldn't look directly at him and Mason took it as a good sign that she hadn't turned him down.

In a perfect world, they wouldn't go out for burgers or drinks at all. He'd take her home where they could be alone and they could get to know each other, where he could kiss her without any distractions.

Now she was nibbling on her bottom lip as if contemplating something and he knew he'd be lying if he said he wasn't curious as to what she was thinking about.

"Want to go to my place?" she blurted out and Mason seriously almost choked.

"Um...what?"

Nodding quickly without making eye contact, she went on, "I'm not really hungry and, like you said, most places around town are going to be crowded so..."

As amazing as her offer sounded, he could do her one better. Closing the small distance between them, he captured both her hands in his. "Come to my place," he said thickly. "I just moved in and the thought of taking you there after the show has been on my mind ever since I went back to my seat."

Okay, he hadn't meant to admit that, but his mouth completely got ahead of him. Now he was practically holding his breath waiting to hear her response. Would she think of reasons why she couldn't or push to have him go to her place or maybe...?

"Okay," Scarlett said, finally looking at him. "Tell me your address and I'll meet you there."

He eyed her warily. She agreed way too quickly.

Then something hit him–she was probably going to ditch him. There was no way he could say with any great certainty, but right now Scarlett Jones seemed like a flight risk. He didn't doubt she wanted him just as much as he wanted her, but for some reason she wasn't fully comfortable with it.

"Where are you parked?" he asked.

"Far left side of lot three," she replied simply. "But I have to wait for Courtney. We came together."

"You drove?"

Shaking her head, she said, "No, she did."

"Any chance you can text her and tell her you're leaving with me?"

Nibbling her bottom lip again, Scarlett seemed to consider his suggestion and he had to wonder if she had been waiting for him, what had she already told her friend? He was about to ask when she pulled out her phone and quickly typed out a text. When she was done, she slipped the phone back into her purse and looked up at him. "Done."

For a moment, he was too stunned to speak. Then his

brain finally caught up and he took her by the hand. "Cool. Let's go."

* * *

IT DIDN'T SEEM at all strange that Scarlett was walking through the massive crowd while holding Mason's hand. They each waved to people they knew but they didn't stop to talk to any of them.

Hell, they barely spoke to each other.

Mason seemed determined to get to his car as fast as possible and she was completely on board with that.

When she had gone back to her seat earlier, Courtney took one look at her and knew something was up. It would have been pointless to deny it and the concert wasn't a big enough distraction to keep her friend from grilling her.

After she had briefly described her own apprehension about meeting up with him after the show–he was too rich, she was too poor, they didn't make sense, there's no purpose to even entertain such a thing–Courtney smacked her in the head and told her to stop being ridiculous.

And a few other choice names.

"Oh my God! Why are you even back here?" Courtney had cried. "You should have left with him already! You know this concert isn't going to be nearly as exciting as being alone with Mason Bishop! What is wrong with you?"

Okay, that had totally been the wrong thing to say because Scarlett had instantly gone into defensive mode and reminded her friend of all the times *she* had hooked up with guys who weren't worth it.

Then Courtney got defensive.

And all this unfolded while the band played on and the big dude beside her continued to try to dance.

"Look, I get that this sort of thing gets you all excited, but we both know that out of the two of us, you're way more comfortable flirting with guys," Scarlett explained. "This totally isn't me!"

"But it could be! I've seen you laugh and flirt and relax around guys before, but normally you're looking for some intellectual type you can have some decent conversation with." She shuddered. "Personally, I don't get it, but whatever."

"Court..."

"No, I'm being serious here. I think if Mason wasn't Mason, you wouldn't think twice about leaving with him."

"What does that mean?"

"You're insecure and you're all up in your own head right now and you need to stop it."

It was pointless to pretend she didn't know what she was referring to.

When Scarlett was silent, Courtney continued, "Aren't you the least bit curious? I mean, what if you've been wrong all this time? And FYI, I think you have."

"Hey!"

"Hey, nothing! Just go and put all your preconceived notions and snobbery aside and have some fun! Hang out and get to know him and if, at the end of the night, he's a total tool, then all you've wasted is a couple of hours of your time. You've been out with worse..."

The thing was, she was right. Scarlett had to get out of her old mindset and move on. Plus, this was just about hanging out with him for tonight. It wasn't as if she were entertaining thoughts of this going anywhere beyond that.

Maybe.

Now they were darting through the crowds and she had to laugh. It really didn't matter how fast they got to his car;

the traffic was moving slowly and it would take a while for them to make it out of the lot

She wished she had brought one of the motorcycles from her father's garage. If she had, they could have maneuvered through the line of cars and gotten out much faster.

Just the image of the two of them on a bike together made her laugh out loud. Mason looked over his shoulder at her. "What's so funny?"

Shaking her head, she explained. "I was just thinking of how much faster we'd be out of here if I brought one of my bikes."

His brows furrowed. "Bikes?"

"Yeah, I've got a couple of Harleys in the shop that I've been restoring. We could have zipped through the line and been on the road by now."

He didn't look like he believed her–or maybe he just thought she was crazy for even suggesting such a thing–and Scarlett wanted to kick herself for sharing her thoughts. A guy like Mason Bishop probably had no idea what to do with a woman who not only worked on motorcycles, but rode them too.

Hopefully he didn't come up with some lame excuse to drop her off at home as soon as they were off the amphitheater property.

Because that would seriously suck.

She had felt so brave walking out to meet him. And by brave she meant she'd left her seat five minutes before the show ended so she could beat the crowd and be sure not to miss him. Either way, there had been excitement and confidence and a whole lot of anticipation right up until she had seen him walking out with his arm around another woman. Sure, it turned out to be one of his sisters, but for a few minutes there, she had mentally called herself every name in the book for thinking Mason could seriously be interested in someone like her.

Judging by the firm grip of his hand on hers and his determined stride, she wouldn't doubt herself again.

They stopped next to a new model Jeep and for some reason, Scarlett was a little surprised. She expected him to drive some sort of sleek sports car, but she had a feeling this might be the first of many surprises where Mason was concerned. He opened the passenger side door for her and waited until she was settled before closing the door. Once he was seated beside her, she expected them to pull out of the spot and join the throng of cars inching toward the exit—after all, that's what they were rushing for, right?

Apparently not.

"Um...we're not moving," she stated once he started the engine and turned on the A/C.

"And neither are the majority of the cars," he replied, both his hands gripping the steering wheel.

For a moment, she could only stare. "So...then why rush to the car?"

Now he twisted in his seat and faced her. "Because now we're alone and it's quiet and I can turn on the A/C and we can talk. I remember you saying how uncomfortable you were earlier in the heat and thought this would be better."

She felt herself begin to relax.

And she had to admit how she misjudged him.

The cool air began to hit her heated skin and it felt wonderful. "Thank you," she said softly. "This is definitely better than standing around outside."

He gave a small nod and smiled. "So...what did you think of the rest of the show?"

"It was great and I have to admit it was cool how the guys in the band all grew up around here and shared their personal memories of our town and the coast." She shrugged. "It made it feel a little more personal and intimate, you know?"

Nodding, he said, "I agree. Although I don't remember ever seeing them hanging out here in Magnolia."

"They're all a bit older than us, Mason. By the time we were old enough to really be hanging out at the bars and clubs here, they were out touring the world."

"Hmm...I guess." He grew quiet but his gaze never left hers. "So..."

"So?"

Scarlett knew she probably had a dozen questions she wanted to ask him–things she wanted to know about him–but she had no idea where to even begin.

His laugh was low and deep and sent little shivers along her skin. Reaching for one of her hands, he held it. "So what is it that Scarlett Jones does when she's not at concerts with her friends?"

And she had to hand it to him, it was a great way to start.

"Well, on the weekends, I tend to see whatever my friends are up to. Sometimes we hit the local places for dinner or go dancing, but sometimes we head a little down the coast to Wilmington and see what's going on there."

"I'm surprised our paths haven't crossed before because that sounds a lot like how I spend the weekends."

"Really?"

He nodded.

"Well, I have a feeling we're not hitting quite the same places. A lot of the times I'm on my bike so..."

"So...what does that mean? You only go to biker bars? Because I've got to tell you, Jones, I don't see it."

Unable to help herself, she laughed out loud.

Practically snorted.

"Hate to break it to you, Bishop, you'd be surprised."

"Come on! Really?" His eyes went wide as he fully checked her out. "No. Just...no. I can't see it!"

Still laughing, she shook her head. "Okay, okay, okay... that's not where I normally go, but sometimes I do." She shrugged as her laughter faded. "Sometimes I ride up the coast for the day and find a bar or restaurant that's a little more casual and check it out. I've found some great places to eat that way–places I wouldn't normally go."

"Do you ride alone?"

"Sometimes, but I know that's not always safe. Sometimes one of my brothers are with me and sometimes I convince Courtney to put a helmet on and ride with me."

His eyes went wide again. "She rides too?"

The image of her friend riding her own hog was almost enough to make her break out in laughter again. "Oh, gosh, no. Courtney has no desire to ride on her own. When we go, she rides on the back of mine."

More like has a death grip around her, but she didn't think that would be a smart thing to point out right now.

"Wow."

"Have you ever ridden?"

He shook his head. "Can't say I have."

"It's awesome. It's the perfect way to spend an afternoon," she said almost dreamily, wishing she could show him right now.

The image almost made her laugh too because she couldn't picture the ever-put-together Mason Bishop on the back of a Harley. No doubt it would be a little too undignified for him.

"You'll have to take me out on one sometime."

*Say what now?*

"Really?" she squeaked, both excited and a little surprised by his interest. "Or are you just saying that?"

"One thing you should know about me," he began, "I try to always say what I mean. Less chances of getting into trouble that way."

"Sounds like there's a story there."

He nodded and looked down as he caressed her fingers. "Let's just say I spent too much time letting other people tell me what to do with my life. Because I wasn't clear about how I felt or how much I hated it, situations got out of control."

"Someone you were involved with?" she asked hesitantly.

"No. Family."

"Damn. That sucks."

"Let's just say I'm in the process of claiming my own damn life." Then he snorted with disgust as he looked up at her. "Lame, right?"

There was a vulnerability there and while it would have been easy to make light of it, Scarlett had a feeling he needed a little affirmation that he wasn't alone.

"Not at all," she began softly. "Some people take a little longer to know what they want out of life, while others seem to know since birth." She paused. "Then, there are those who want to try to please everyone and would be okay with it, except they get taken advantage of." Then she deliberately stayed silent until he looked up at her. "And that's not okay, Mason. It's not okay to let people do that to you. So if you're taking control of your life back, then I say good for you."

The look on his face told her he didn't quite believe her. "What about you, Scarlett? Are you in control of your own life?" he asked, his voice so quiet it was almost a whisper.

There was no way she was going to lie to him and considering what he just admitted, she owed him the truth.

"I am," she said with a gentle firmness so as not to sound smug. "I'm the only girl in the family—I've got three older brothers and my mom died when I was four, so...I learned early to stand up for myself."

"Damn, Scarlett. I'm sorry. I didn't know, I..."

Squeezing his hand, she gave him a small smile. "Why would you? It's not like we've known each other that long."

Now he frowned. "We were in school together our whole lives. Hell, we were lab partners in middle school..."

"That didn't make us friends, Mason. And it wasn't something I talked about all the time, so...it's okay."

"Still," he said solemnly. "I'm sorry. Here I am bitching about my family and..."

She cut him off. "Trust me. I still bitch about mine too. My brothers are all overprotective assholes sometimes and my dad has never quite figured out how to handle having a daughter. That's how I ended up working in his garage, learning how to work on cars. It's the real reason I love motorcycles."

"So it wasn't all bad," Mason said.

Unable to hide her smile, she said, "No. No it wasn't all bad. But they're not perfect and neither am I."

"What's your biggest fault?"

"Ooh...that's a loaded question."

Now his smile was back. "Now I'm even more curious. Come on, spill it. Tell me something about you that makes you imperfect. Because from where I'm sitting, it's not possible."

Chuckling, she said, "More cheesy lines?"

"Nah. If I were going for cheesy, I would have said something like, 'I didn't know angels flew this close to earth.'" Then he waggled his eyebrows at her like he did earlier.

And yet...she couldn't help but laugh. "You're crazy. You know that, right?"

"Crazy about you..."

"Mason..."

In a move she didn't see coming, he reached up and cupped her face and kissed her. And it was even better than the one from earlier. His hands felt wonderful against her cheeks and she simply let herself melt against him.

Or as close as she could get with the center console between them.

Scarlett reached out and clutched the front of his t-shirt just to have something of his to hold on to. Her lips opened under his and the feel of his tongue against hers had her humming with pleasure. It was a sound he mimicked moments later as they continued to taste and tease and torment each other in an act she hadn't found arousing in years.

If ever.

If all she ever got to do tonight was kiss Mason, it would totally be worth it.

And the fact that she was even thinking like that should have sent up warning signals, but it didn't. Why? Because this felt so incredibly right. He wasn't a stranger–not really– and she found she liked talking with him, laughing with him and especially kissing him.

It could only get better, right?

They kissed until they were breathless. And when the need to breathe became too great, Mason's mouth moved from hers and traveled along her cheek and then on to nibble on her ear. His hot breath felt positively panty-melting and all Scarlett wanted to do was crawl over the console to get to him.

"Mason..." she said breathlessly. "We should...I mean... can we..." He gently bit on her earlobe and it nearly had her bucking out of her seat. "This is crazy!" And at that point, she cupped his face in her hands and brought his lips back to hers.

And damn.

Scorching. All heat and need and she wasn't sure how much longer she could contain herself. Maybe it wasn't particularly a good thing–for her to be this turned on by a make-out session. And yet, here she was, ready to drag Mason into the backseat like a horny teenager on prom night.

*Yikes.*

She lost track of time and there were only two things she was aware of: first, how no one kissed like Mason Bishop, and second, his hands had stayed above her shoulders the entire time. Not once did he try to cop a feel, and she found that oddly arousing.

The man could kiss *and* had manners??

How was it possible he was still single?

Not that she cared because it was totally working to her advantage right now.

When Mason finally broke the kiss, they rested against each other's foreheads while they caught their breath.

"Damn, Scarlett. I haven't made out in my car since..."

"High school?" she teased.

Chuckling softly, he agreed. "I'm usually a little more sophisticated than this."

Her heart kicked a little hard in her chest at his admission. Good. She liked that she had him a little off his game.

God knew she was.

After a moment of companionable silence, they both straightened in their seats and froze.

The parking lot was empty.

Well, almost empty. There were a few cars scattered around but for the most part, everyone was gone.

"How...? When...?" she stammered, looking around in confusion. "Where did they all go?"

Clearing his throat, Mason pointed to the digital clock. "We've been sitting here for almost a half hour."

"What?" she cried. "That's not possible."

"And yet..." He didn't need to finish. The clock didn't lie and it would be pointless to argue about it. The fact was the lot was empty. "So...do you still want to go to my place?" he asked hesitantly.

The logical part of her brain kicked in.

"Um...maybe we should go someplace and get something to eat after all."

"Oh, okay. You hungry?"

How could she possibly answer without embarrassing herself? Turning, she looked at him and with a shy smile. "Not really, but considering what just happened here, we both know what's going to happen if we go back to your place."

"And that's bad...why?"

*Good question.*

"Other than the obvious?" she said with a nervous laugh. "I mean...it's not something I usually do." There was more she could say but Scarlett decided to leave it at that and put the decision on him as to where they went from here.

For a long minute he didn't say anything and she had a feeling it was because he couldn't say the same for himself.

And that was okay.

Sort of.

Then, Mason straightened in his seat, his expression going somewhat fierce. "Scarlett, I promise you right now that if all you want is to go someplace and talk and get to know each other better, then that's what we'll do."

And for some reason, she trusted him.

"And you'd honestly be okay? Just talking?"

He nodded solemnly. "I would. But if you also decided at some point you wanted me to kiss you again, I'd be totally on board with that too."

It took all of five seconds for her decision to be made.

"Let's go to your place."

# FOUR

Two hours later, Mason was sitting and laughing and trying to remember the last time he had enjoyed himself more.

They had arrived back at his place and Scarlett had marveled at the view of the beach and they sat out on the small deck while drinking some wine and talking about everything and nothing at all. There had yet to be an awkward pause in the conversation. Mason found she had a wicked sense of humor–which he kind of had an inkling of after their initial conversation earlier–and she was a woman of many talents.

First, there was the work she did on cars and motorcycles, which wasn't even her full-time job. Her knowledge of all things automotive was unbelievable and he was more than a little intimidated by it. During the day, she worked as a social media specialist for multiple businesses here in Magnolia Sound. And as if all that wasn't enough, she volunteered at the local animal shelter in her spare time.

They shared a love of pub food and sushi. They both enjoyed fishing and had similar taste in music and movies, too. She loved to read, but he had to admit that it wasn't a favorite pastime for him.

When they got around to talking exclusively about him, Mason felt beyond inferior. If they were to do a side-by-side comparison, he was seriously slacking off. Sure, he was working for the city on the planning board and marginally using his engineering degree, but once his day was done at five, that was it. He went out and socialized—not even giving a thought to doing much else.

Maybe he would now.

"Working with the city must be pretty exciting right now," she said, her eyes wide with curiosity. "I mean, with all the rebuilding going on, I'm sure you're very busy."

With a shrug, he reached for his glass and took a drink of his tea. "There have definitely been some challenges. I think we are a town that is all about traditions and keeping the historical look and feel we've always had."

"You say it like it's a bad thing."

Another shrug. "We've gotten some pushback from the community on some of the proposals we've come up with."

"Like what?"

"Bringing in some new restaurants—chains, mainly. It seems the good people of Magnolia like their mom-and-pop places and aren't interested in joining this century." He frowned. "And the thing is, I get it. I really do. My great-grandfather built most of this town, so he was steeped in tradition and hated any kind of change."

Scarlett nodded in understanding.

"However, he was also a brilliant businessman who knew sometimes you had to buck tradition and take risks."

"Okay, so why aren't you?"

"It's not that easy. It's not just me working there. It's a committee and we do let the community have a say in what they want. It's a lot of bureaucratic red tape and annoying as it is, that's just the way it has to be."

"Well damn."

"Tell me about it."

She was quiet for a minute, looking up at the starry sky. "If you could change anything about the town–if there were no red tape and no committee to answer to–what would you change?"

Where did he even begin?

"I'd bring in maybe only one or two new restaurants–the chain ones. Then I'd open up another public parking area with beach access," he explained. "There's some land on the edge of town that hasn't been developed and I'd love to see it turned into a park."

"You mean on the north end?"

"Yeah. There are some older businesses down that way, but I don't see them being too much of a hindrance. The bar might be a problem," he said more to himself than to her. "Not sure how it would look to have a public park–a place where kids go to play–and a run-down old bar right across the street."

Scarlett stood up abruptly and walked over to lean on the railing. Mason immediately followed. "Are you okay?"

"Yeah. Sure."

Her tone said otherwise, so he knew he had to choose his next words carefully.

"Lots of stars out tonight," he said as he slowly moved in close to her.

"Mm-hmm..."

Then inspiration hit. "Hey, girl, I think you might be a star, because I can't stop orbiting around you." Placing his hands on her hips as he stood behind her, he rested his chin on her shoulder and waited for her to respond.

Thankfully, she laughed. "You are such a dork. How did I never know this about you before? Were you like this in school?"

Now his arms slowly wrapped around her waist and he found it felt really good. Her body fit perfectly against his. She was shorter than him by at least six inches, and when he straightened behind her, he could actually rest his chin on the top of her head.

Which he now did.

"I was probably worse," he admitted. "But something about you makes these crazy statements come to mind."

Except now the only thing on his mind was how she felt.

Which was incredibly warm.

And how she smelled.

Like sunshine and vanilla.

And suddenly, it wasn't funny anymore. He didn't want to be cheesy or make her laugh. He wanted to kiss her and hear her moan with pleasure right before she cried out his name. It was all he wanted, but he made a promise to her– they wouldn't do anything she didn't want to do.

But man, oh man did he wish she wanted to do more than just talk right now.

Although, now they weren't even talking; they were just staring out at the beach. All he could hear was the sound of the waves crashing and his heartbeat drumming in his own ears. It seemed so loud to him that he had to wonder if Scarlett could hear it too.

This was all new territory for him. Normally, when he chatted up a woman, it was all superficial and mildly entertaining. Mason wouldn't describe himself as a serial dater, but he never went out with a woman more than a few times and he couldn't remember feeling the type of connection he felt right now with Scarlett. He wanted to know what was bothering her–what did he say to make her get up and go quiet? But at the same time, he wanted to take her inside and slowly lead her to his bedroom where he could make love to her all night long.

That was definitely a first.

And not just because this was the first time bringing a woman to his home.

Back in college, he brought girls back to his room all the time, so it wasn't that. This was more like...like...damn. He wanted to take his time with her–find out what she liked, what made her feel good. And then he wanted to wake up in the morning and drink coffee with her right here on the deck.

Right now, however, he wanted to know what she was thinking. Taking a small step back, Mason slowly turned her around until she was facing him. "Hey," he began softly. "What's going on?"

But she shook her head. "It's nothing. Really. I guess I was just thinking about all the changes here in town." She shrugged but wouldn't meet his gaze.

Tucking a finger under her chin, he gently guided her gaze back up to his. "Are you sure?"

Her eyes shone bright for a brief moment and then she pulled slightly away. "It's not a big deal. My mind just wandered for a minute."

"Oh. Okay."

Scarlett's back was against the railing and her breasts were practically touching his chest. If he moved in even a little bit, they would touch him and he knew it would be the sweetest kind of torture.

He was willing to find out.

Swallowing hard, he moved.

So did she.

To get closer.

There was no way he was going to push for more. For right now, this was fine. More than fine. He stayed impossibly still while he waited to see what she was going to do.

Hell, he wasn't even sure he was breathing.

Slowly, one small, delicate hand rested on his stomach. She looked up at him as if gauging his reaction. When he simply continued to watch her, she let her hand graze up toward his chest where it rested again.

He could feel himself begin to sweat.

Then he tried to make himself recite the alphabet backward so he didn't pounce.

A slow smile played at her lips when her hand moved again to caress his jaw on its way up to rake through his hair. This time his eyes closed and he couldn't help but moan as her short nails gently scratched his scalp.

"Hey, Scarlett?" he whispered, fighting the urge to lean in and taste her.

"Yeah?"

"You never answered my question earlier." He opened his eyes and looked down at her, enjoying how she seemed mesmerized by touching him.

Her hands paused. "What question?"

Dark eyes met his and it took him a minute to remember he was going somewhere with this. He was supposed to be distracting himself from kissing her–letting her set the pace and not pouncing.

Even though all he wanted was to scoop her up in his arms and do just that.

*I have self-control. I have self-control. I have self-control. Wait, do I?*

Scarlett's hands began to roam again and he swallowed

hard as his eyes drifted closed again. The moan of pleasure was out before he could stop it.

"What's your biggest fault?" he forced himself to say, but it came out sounding breathless and a little needy.

If it were possible, Scarlett pressed herself even more firmly against him as the hand in his hair seemed to tighten its grip.

"Not doing this sooner," she said, pulling his head down to capture his lips with hers.

*This girl...*

* * *

OKAY, fine...this wasn't really what she planned on doing, but a girl could only take so much. Mason was incredibly sweet and funny and he smelled so damn good. How could she possibly stop herself from kissing him again?

And...who was she kidding? She was ready for more than just kissing.

She was curious about how his hands would feel on her, how his mouth would feel on other parts of her body, and how it would feel to wrap her legs around him.

*I bet it would all feel fan-freaking-tastic.*

It was both exciting and terrifying to think about because as much as she really liked Mason, she knew this–whatever it was–was all it was going to be. Maybe they could stretch it out for the weekend, but come Monday, that was going to be it. She wasn't delusional and she wasn't going to get her hopes up that this was anything more than just two people who found themselves wildly attracted to each other. At the end of the day, she was still the girl from the wrong side of the tracks who had no desire to fit in with the country club crew.

*God, I really am a snob, only in reverse.*

Mason broke the kiss and his mouth moved down and gently bit her throat. Her pulse was beating like mad and she arched into him. Then his hands finally got in on the action and moved down to cup her ass. He squeezed ever-so-slightly and she was ready to climb him like a tree.

She had never been like this—so needy, so turned on—by anyone. Sex was good and something she enjoyed, but it never felt like this. And it certainly never felt like this before they even got naked.

Panting his name, pleading to him for more, she almost cried out "Hallelujah!" when he lifted her up and carried her back into the house. But once they were over the threshold and back in the living room, he placed her back on her feet and took a step back—his hands still firmly clasping her waist. She looked up at him quizzically.

"Mason?"

His breath was ragged and he seemed just as dazed as she was. "I'm sorry."

"Um...what?"

"I realized what I was doing. I just picked you up and carried you in here like some sort of caveman or something—after I told you we'd do whatever it was you wanted, like just talk."

Was he being for real right now? She wondered.

"But...you *were* doing what I wanted. I thought that was obvious when I grabbed you and kissed you."

He nodded. "Well...yeah. But that didn't mean you wanted to take this any further. So...I'm sorry."

If this were some sort of *thing* of his where he got the girl to beg him to take her to bed, she'd be totally on board. Yeah, she wasn't opposed to begging right now.

Taking a step forward, she reached her hand up around

his nape again and pressed up against him. "If you're looking for me to state exactly what it is that I want right now, Mason, I'll tell you. I want you to pick me up like you just did, then to carry me into your bedroom where we'll collapse down on the bed and hopefully get naked very soon."

Reaching up, he cupped her face and gave her a grin that was sexy as hell. "Scarlett Jones, you may very well be my every damn fantasy come to life."

"Good," she said confidently as she leapt up to wrap her legs around his waist.

And just as she asked, he carried her to his bedroom, his gaze never leaving hers. She caught a glimpse of a fairly masculine room that was dominated by a king size bed. Gently, he lowered her onto it and followed her down, stretching out beside her. Fighting the urge to growl with frustration that he wasn't kissing her, she rolled onto her side to face him.

"Can I ask you something?" she asked softly.

"You can ask me anything." Reaching up, he caressed her cheek and she leaned into it, loving how his hands felt on her.

"Is this your usual M.O.?"

One brow arched at her. "Excuse me?"

"This whole thing–you meet a girl, you joke, you flirt, and...you bring her home." Before he could answer, she added, "Where you have a couple of hours of wild sex and then send her on her way."

"Wow...um...I don't even know what to say to that."

"The truth would probably be best," she said, hoping she found the balance between teasing and bitchy.

His hand skimmed across her cheek, over her shoulder, down her arm until he was holding her hand in his. "I'm no angel, Scarlett," he began, "and I'm not going to pretend that I am or ever was. Have I flirted with a girl I've met in a bar or a club and left with her? Yes. Have I ever sat and had a conversation with one and found I was okay if that's all we did for the entire night? No." He squeezed her hand lightly. "And you're the first girl I've ever brought home."

She laughed softly. "That's only because you just moved in here."

But he shook his head. "Back in college, I brought girls back to my room occasionally, but...it's not the same. None of them spent the entire night." He paused and his expression seemed to grow dark. "And none of them stayed for an entire weekend."

The soft gasp that escaped her lips couldn't be helped. She licked at her bottom lip. "Is that what I'm doing?"

"If it were up to me? Yes."

She moved a little closer to him. "I didn't pack for a weekend away." Then she leaned forward and nipped at his jaw. "I don't even have my jammies with me."

Releasing her hand, Mason's hand moved to rest on her hip before reaching around and squeezing her ass. "I don't think you should worry. You won't need them."

Visions of the two of them tangled up in bed flashed through her mind and as much as she appreciated her imagination, she had a feeling the reality was going to be so much better.

"My turn," he said, interrupting her thoughts. "Can I ask you something?"

She nodded.

"Is this your usual M.O.?"

Scarlett shook her head. "Not even a little bit. And there's a part of me that can't believe I'm doing this now. I always thought there was a huge ick-factor in going home with a guy you just met..."

"We've known each other for years," he countered smoothly.

"Please," she said with a small snort. "Not really."

"We'll always have middle school science."

Now she did laugh and gave him a playful shove. "Dork."

His hand continued to knead and squeeze her ass and she had to admit, it felt really good.

"Hey, Scarlett?"

"Yeah?"

"Did you sit in a pile of sugar? Because you have a pretty sweet ass."

This time she shoved him with a little more force but he came right back at her and rolled her onto her back, stretching out on top of her, silencing her laughter with a kiss. It was deep and wet and she simply wrapped herself around him. She cursed the fact that they were still dressed, but knew it would be rectified soon.

Lifting his head, Mason smiled down at her. "I was serious before, you know. I already know I want you to stay, Scarlett. Does that freak you out?"

She shook her head. "No. The part that does freak me out is how much I want to."

"Then we're on the same page."

She nodded. "Mason?"

"Hmm?"

"Can we be done talking now?"

His smile grew. "I can't guarantee I won't say anything else. I have a feeling I'm going to have a lot to say once I start undressing you."

*Oh, my...*

"I think I can handle that," she said, sliding her hands up and over his shoulders before skimming down his back. Mason's lips claimed hers as she let herself skim up under his shirt and slowly start lifting it up. He was on the same page because he quickly sat up, pulled the shirt up and over his head before he dove in for another kiss.

After that, playtime and bantering were over. They were both on a mission to touch and tease and kiss every inch of each other. It was a little wild, a little frantic, and incredibly sexy.

She scratched her nails down his back and made him hiss.

He sucked on her nipples and then gently bit down, making her back arch off of the bed.

They rolled around, limbs tangling together, as articles of clothing went flying.

By the time they were both naked, Scarlett knew their first time wasn't going to be slow. And she was more than okay with it. With Mason's mouth doing incredibly wicked things to every spot he touched, she was slowly going insane.

"Mason?" she panted.

"Hmm?"

"Now. Please. It has to be now." Yeah, begging was totally something new to her and when Mason lifted his head and looked at her, she knew she'd willingly do it again and again just to see that heated look on his face.

And as he crawled up over her, she knew she would remember this night–this moment–for the rest of her life.

* * *

"WE SHOULD HAVE STOPPED FOR A BURGER."

"You mean...between when we...? Or after the show?"

Scarlett laughed softly as she settled in beside him and pulled the sheet up to cover herself a bit. Not that she was being modest–over the course of the last two hours, Mason had seen, tasted, and touched just about every inch of her body.

"After the show," she clarified. "I'm a little hungry."

He was quiet for a moment and she was afraid her comment made him uncomfortable–or sounded completely dumb.

She was going with dumb because...it was.

Just as she was about to comment on it, Mason stood and stretched. And just as he had seen, tasted, and touched just about every inch of her body, she had willingly returned the favor. But it still didn't prepare her for the sight of him moving around the room naked while he went in search of his boxer briefs. Once he slipped them on, he turned to her and smiled. "I'll be right back."

"Mason!" she cried, sitting up and clutching the sheet to her chest. "You're not seriously going to get us burgers, are you?"

He looked at her like she was crazy. "Um...no. I was just going to grab us something to drink and maybe a snack."

"Oh." Damn. Surely she was hitting her quota of dumb comments to make, right? And rather than risk it, Scarlett simply nodded and relaxed back against the pillows. Once he was out of the room, she let out a long breath and wondered–not for the first time tonight–just what she was doing. This wasn't who she normally was, but there was something about Mason that put her at ease and made her feel like it was okay to take the risk, the leap...the chance. Hopefully he wasn't in the other room having second thoughts.

*Oh, God...what if he is?*

She was on the verge of sitting up and searching for her clothes when Mason walked back in carrying a tray loaded with drinks and what looked like half the contents of his pantry.

"Um..."

"I wasn't sure what you liked," he said, carefully placing the tray down on the bedside table closest to her. He straightened. "I grabbed a couple of cans of soda, some bottled water, Oreos, crackers, chips and salsa, and...peanut butter."

With a smirk, she looked up at him. "Peanut butter?"

"For the crackers," he quickly explained. "You know...protein."

Okay, so clearly not having second thoughts if he was looking for them to regain some energy.

He looked adorably uncertain and Scarlett reached out, took one of his hands in hers and tugged him back onto the bed with her. "I'm going to start with water because I am thirsty, but I was wondering if you had any milk to go with the cookies."

One strong hand anchored into her hair as he gave her a fierce but quick kiss. "A girl after my own heart. I'll be right back." As he jumped back up and walked out of the room, she had to put a hand over her chest to try to calm herself. It was just a flippant phrase and yet, for some reason, the way he said it affected her way more than it should.

*Stupid heart.*

Grabbing a bottle of water, she drank half of it before Mason walked back in with two glasses of milk. He placed them on the tray and then grabbed the package of cookies and climbed onto the bed. For a few minutes, they ate in

companionable silence and it was obvious they were both
hungry.

And messy.

There were crumbs everywhere and when she tried to
clean them up, Mason simply gave the bedding a hard
shake. Laughing, she shook her head. "I can't believe you
just did that."

With a careless shrug, he reached past her and grabbed
a glass of milk. "Seemed like the easiest solution. I can
vacuum later."

"Later?"

Another shrug. "You know, any time other than now,"
he said with a small laugh. After a few minutes, they both
put their glasses aside and rested against the headboard.
Turning his head toward her, he asked, "So, um...you okay?"

"Much better now. Thanks." And when he didn't
respond, Scarlett realized he might not have been referring
to her stomach. "I mean...yeah. I'm good." Ducking her
head, she could feel herself blush.

Clearing his throat, Mason ran his hand gently up and
down her arm. It was both comforting and arousing. "Do
you need to go or...you know...would you like to stay?" His
eyes didn't meet hers as he spoke and that–more than
anything else–put her at ease. It meant he was just as off-
balance with this as she was.

"Would you like me to stay?" she asked, her own voice
quiet and a little uncertain.

Now he did look up at her. "I told you earlier, Scarlett. I
want you to stay. But if you want to leave, if you want me to
take you home, I'd do it."

There was a lot weighing on her answer. She didn't
want to appear too needy–even though that's exactly how
she felt–and she didn't want to appear overly anxious.

So...

"I believe I told you earlier that I wanted to stay, too."

His hand rested on her shoulder, his fingers caressing her nape. "I know, but that was...before. I just want you to know it would be okay if you changed your mind."

Never before had she met a man who was this considerate or one who was so willing to let her call the shots.

And it made her want him all that much more.

"I appreciate that, Mason. I really do." She paused. "The thing is...I need to go."

Disappointment washed across his face and his fingers stilled. His hand slowly moved away and he put a little distance between them. "Oh. Um...okay." He was about to get off the bed when he stopped. "I...I thought you said you wanted to stay?"

Okay, she had meant to be funny but it just turned awkward and the last thing she wanted to do was upset him. With a slow smile, she reached for his hand. "I meant I needed to use the bathroom." Jumping up to her knees, she leaned in and gave him a searing kiss—her hands gripping his hair. When she pulled back, she smiled. "But it's cute how you're so easily freaked out."

In the blink of an eye he had her on her back, bouncing on the mattress as he hovered over her and she couldn't help but laugh.

"That wasn't funny," he all but growled.

But she could see the twinkle in his eyes.

"I know. It was mean of me, but I couldn't resist."

"Oh yeah? Well...prepare for some payback," he warned and his words only made her tingle in anticipation.

"Bring it."

As it turned out, Mason's form of payback was mean in an entirely different way. His body covered hers as he kissed and touched her in a way guaranteed to arouse her. Within minutes she was panting, clawing at him, and begging for more. And just when she was certain they were on the same page, and she was on the verge of what promised to be a life-changing orgasm, he stopped.

Eyes wide, she looked up at him in shock. "What...? Why did you stop?" she cried.

Placing a gentle kiss on her nose, he said, "I remembered how you said you had to go, so...go." He was smirking by the time he was finished with that one sentence and she knew she'd found a worthy opponent.

With a playful shove, Scarlett pushed him away before straddling him. "Newsflash, Bishop," she stated, placing both hands on his chest. "I'm not going anywhere."

His arm banded around her waist as he pulled her down until they were face to face.

"Good. Because I don't plan on letting you go anytime soon," he said firmly, right before his lips claimed hers.

# FIVE

One week.

It had been one damn week and Mason was more than frustrated with the turn of events. After the hottest weekend of his life, he had driven Scarlett home and she blew him off ever since. Okay, she didn't completely blow him off, but the two texts she sent that basically said she was perpetually busy were almost the same thing. And what was worse was that he had pretty much resorted to asking around town for anyone who might know anything about her.

Pathetic.

Honestly, he had no idea what happened.

Okay, there had been an awkward moment on Saturday night with a condom mishap. But Scarlett had pulled up some app on her phone and said there was no chance of her ovulating, then they talked it out until they both calmed down. They didn't mention it again and they had sex at least two more times after it so he thought things were good.

Now she wasn't returning his calls or texts–with the

exception of those two–and as much as he wanted to say it didn't bother him, it did.

A lot.

His work was suffering because he couldn't focus and he was more than a little exhausted because he stayed up most nights obsessing about what he did wrong.

The weekend with her was perfect. For the first time in his life, he felt like he really knew a woman. They had talked for hours–almost until they were both hoarse! They had so much in common and knew so many of the same people that it was bizarre how they hadn't run into each other before the night of the concert. And when they weren't talking, they were binge-watching *Stranger Things* or eating pizza in bed.

And then there was the sex.

Even thinking about it was enough to make him hard and achy. Scarlett Jones was everything he ever dreamed of in a sexual partner and one weekend wasn't enough.

Hell, he wasn't sure if any time limit would be enough.

He wanted to talk to her.

He wanted more time with her.

Shit. He just wanted *her*.

With a heavy sigh, he forced himself to do what he needed to do. Currently, that was to get out of his car and go inside his parents' house to celebrate his sister Parker's birthday.

So not what he wanted to be doing right now.

Climbing from his car, he grabbed the gift he'd picked up on the way over and took a moment to shift gears. If he went inside looking and sounding depressed, everyone would notice. And the last thing he wanted to do was have to answer questions about his personal life.

Actually, the last thing he wanted to do was be here, period. But for his sister, he was doing it.

"Mason! There you are!" his mother called out as soon as he walked through the front door. Perfectly coiffed as usual, Georgia Bishop looked like she always did. And for tonight, he would put all negative feelings he had toward her aside.

*You're doing this for Parker. You're doing this for Parker...*

"It's wonderful to see you!" she went on, looping her arm through his. Instead of walking to the living room where everyone was, she steered him toward his father's office.

Not a good sign.

When they were alone, she released his arm and Mason braced himself for whatever it was she had to say.

"What's going on, Mom?" he asked, doing his best to hide his annoyance.

Her frown was mild and gone in the blink of an eye. "We didn't see you after the show last weekend. I thought you'd come back here for dessert with everyone."

"Yeah, well, I ran into some friends and decided to go out with them."

"Who did you go out with?" she asked mildly.

Shrugging, and more than a little uncomfortable, he said, "Just some friends from school." Looking over his shoulder, he asked, "Is it just us tonight or is the rest of the family coming over?"

"Because more than a few people mentioned seeing you leave with a woman," Georgia went on, as if he hadn't attempted to change the subject.

"Mom, there were a ton of people around. I greatly doubt anyone saw that." He wanted to groan at his own lame excuse. He had all but chased Scarlett at first and then grabbed her hand and practically dragged her to his car. If anything, he was surprised more people hadn't taken notice of them.

"Was it that Jones girl? The one who works at the...the... garage?" Her entire face screwed up with distaste as she spoke and it filled Mason with rage.

Stiffening his spine, he glared hard. "She works at the garage from time to time, but she's a social media manager for several businesses in town."

"Hmm..."

*That was it? That was her reaction?*

"Mason..."

*Here it comes.*

"Is she really the type person you want to associate with?" she asked in her usual snobbish, condescending tone. "I mean, she's a bit beneath us and honestly, I don't understand why you would want to. There are so many respectable and eligible women in this town who would love to get to know you. Why are you...slumming it with this girl?"

So many thoughts ran through his mind and as much as he didn't want to make a scene and ruin his sister's birthday, there was no way he could keep his mouth shut.

He took a step toward his mother and saw the moment she realized she had gone too far. She said his name and he held up a hand to stop her. "I will not justify this to you," he said firmly, his whole body tense. "Who I see is no one's business but my own. And I would think that after the way you pushed me until I was forced to move out, you would have learned something."

She bristled with indignation. "I did not raise you to speak to me this way. I'm sure your father..."

"Would be on Mason's side," his father said from the doorway, a disapproving look on his face. Stepping into the room, he came and stood beside his son. "I thought we discussed this, Georgia."

For a moment Mason was stunned silent. While he knew his parents had a strong marriage, it was always obvious that his mother called the shots. His father was a leader in the community and a brilliant businessman, but he tended to let his wife rule things at home.

At least...he used to.

"Now, instead of ruining our daughter's birthday and pushing our son further away, let's all go inside and cele-brate Parker. We have dinner reservations at seven and I'd appreciate it if everyone got along."

With a regal nod, his mother walked out of the room and Mason let out a long breath. He was about to mutter a curse, but his father's hand on his shoulder stopped him.

"Thank you," he said.

"For what?"

"You could have really flown off the handle and you would have been well within your rights. So thank you for being mature and respectful—even when she doesn't deserve it."

"She's going to have to stop this, Dad. I'm serious. I'm not going to allow her to keep trying to run my life or put down the people I see."

"I know and...I'm sorry. I should have stepped in sooner," he said quietly.

"You weren't much better," Mason said, his own voice low. "You pushed me to be a replica of you."

Beau Bishop looked up at his son and grinned. "And you pushed back," he stated. "Otherwise there would be two lawyers in the family now."

With a quick laugh, Mason nodded. "Yeah, well...I'm glad you knew when to let that go. Mom on the other hand..."

"She'll get there. Trust me."

"I hope so, because I don't want to keep arguing with her. It's exhausting."

They walked out to join the rest of the family and it didn't take long for Mason to relax. His sisters were both highly entertaining and pros at keeping the attention on themselves, so it was easy to get out of his own head for a little while.

After Parker opened her gifts, they drove as a family to the country club for dinner. It was something they had always done and he had to admit that he was having a good time. Maybe this wasn't such a bad idea–it gave him time away from sitting home alone with his thoughts about where things went wrong with Scarlett.

They were finishing up dessert when he looked up and saw a familiar face.

Courtney.

Without looking too obvious, he excused himself to go use the restroom and walked out to the lobby where he spotted Courtney heading toward the bar. Looking over his shoulder to make sure no one from his family was watching, he followed her. Was she here with someone? Did she work here? He stopped for a moment to get his bearings and saw her sitting at the end of the bar alone. Knowing he didn't have a lot of time, he walked over and sat beside her.

"Hey, Courtney," he said with an easy smile.

Her eyes went wide but then she quickly relaxed. "Oh, hey, Mason. How are you?"

Small talk was the last thing he wanted, but he'd do it if it meant maybe getting a little insight into what was going on with Scarlett. "I'm good," he replied. "Here for dinner with my family for my sister's birthday. What about you?"

She looked around and sighed. "I um...I'm just here to get a drink."

"You often come to the country club for that?" He looked around and it was a very subdued, older crowd–not at all the kind of place his generation came for a drink.

With a shrug, she said, "I thought I'd try something new." Looking down, she studied her hands.

"Look, I need to get back to my table, but...have you talked to Scarlett? I've been trying all week to reach her. If I did something wrong...if I did something to upset her..." Pausing, he muttered a curse, hating how desperate he sounded.

For a minute, he thought she wasn't going to answer, but then she sighed and met his gaze. "Okay," she began solemnly. "You did not hear this from me, understand?"

He nodded.

"Scarlett is pretty insecure," she explained. "She comes off as confident and she should be. But in situations with people like you..."

"People like me? What did I do?" He was beyond baffled by that statement.

Rolling her eyes, she continued. "Mason, come on. We all know you're from one of the wealthiest families in town and Scarlett...well...she had it rough growing up. Her dad did the best he could, but..."

Yeah, this wasn't news to him, which is what he said to her. "I don't get what that has to do with the here and now, Courtney."

Again, he didn't think she was going to respond, but she shook her head and continued. "Old insecurities are hard to get over. So if you're into her and you want to get her to open up to you, you're just gonna have to push past the walls she's put up. Go to her house and talk to her face-to-face."

"I'd love to except she had me drop her off at your place," he explained, his annoyance beyond obvious. "I don't even know where she lives." Not only was this conversation frustrating him, but he knew he needed to get back to his table. Standing, he muttered a thank you and turned to walk away.

"Mason," Courtney called out, and when he turned, she sighed again. "Don't make me regret this." She grabbed a cocktail napkin and quickly jotted down Scarlett's address before handing it to him.

Snatching it from her hands, he smiled broadly. "You won't."

* * *

EVERY MUSCLE in her body ached, but it was all worth it.

Standing back, Scarlett looked at her latest creation and beamed with pride. She never knew when inspiration would hit so whenever it did, she always made sure to go with it and put in the time it took to do the job right. Stretching, she smiled. Tomorrow she'd deliver it and she knew all the aches and pains would be worth it.

The knock on the door stopped her as she went to grab a bottle of water. She was sure it was Courtney.

"I knew the country club was going to be a bust," she murmured with a small laugh. Her friend was desperate for something new to do, but Scarlett had warned her that a bar in the local country club wasn't going to do it for her.

Pulling the door open, she froze.

Mason.

It took all of three seconds for her to realize what a mess she must look like and panic set in. Spinning on her heel, she walked back into her house and cursed her rotten luck. She had meant to call him back, but...she got busy. Projects like the one she just finished tended to consume her and it wasn't unusual for her to check out on the rest of the world for a while. Obviously he was tired of waiting for her so...

The sound of the door closing had her turning around and she found him standing in the entryway–unwilling to come in any further until she asked him to.

Damn him and his good manners!

Taking a steadying breath, she faced him. "What are you doing here?"

"I've been trying to talk to you all week," he explained, the look on his face a combination of confusion, annoyance, and curiosity. After seeing what a mess her place looked like, what a mess *she* looked like, he was probably wishing he'd stayed home waiting for her call.

"Yeah, well...I've been a little busy." She motioned to the mess behind her and forced herself to hold his gaze.

Her house was small–really small–and filled with a wide selection of her projects. It smelled of paint and sawdust and some pieces of furniture were covered in plastic to protect them. It was a far cry from his stylishly-decorated home on the beach. She could only imagine what he was thinking as he drove his expensive car down the winding dirt road into the wooded lot to get to her house.

Stepping into the room, Mason looked around. "Did you...did you make this?"

She nodded and stepped aside when he got close to her newest project.

"Scarlett, this is amazing," he said with a hint of wonder. "I mean...wow!"

Other than Courtney and a handful of people, she didn't share her hobby with anyone. It was something she did for herself. Okay, for herself *and* to help others. But she didn't want the attention or the praise. She preferred to simply do it and know she'd done a good thing.

"Is this the first one you've made?"

And now she was going to have to explain herself and she hated it. But first things first...

"I was just about to get something to drink when you knocked. Can I get you something?"

Shaking his head, Mason continued to walk around and look at her pieces. It was a little unnerving but Scarlett knew she couldn't avoid the conversation. She grabbed her drink and finished half the bottle before she walked back into the room with him. He looked up at her and all she wanted to do was grab him and kiss him and tell him she'd missed him this week. He probably wouldn't believe her considering how she'd all but ignored him, but it was still her first instinct.

"Remember I told you I volunteer at the animal shelter?" she began.

He nodded.

"Well, it's not the one run by the county," she went on. "Although I do go there from time to time." Other than a nod, Mason waited for her to continue. "There's a place just outside of town called Happy Tails. It's an animal rescue farm."

"I've heard of it," he said as he tucked his hands into the front pockets of his trousers. It was then she realized he was dressed up and wondered where he was before coming here.

"Anyway, I volunteer there. The owners have a couple of acres and they rescue pets from shelters and care for them and help find them their forever homes. They do it all out of the goodness of their hearts and sometimes it's not easy for them. So I..." She paused and mentally cringed at her next words. "I build these dog houses and playsets so the dogs have something to call their own. Something that's not just a sterile kennel or crate." She shrugged and studied the water in her hands. "Sometimes when a dog gets adopted, they take the little house they've claimed as theirs and...I don't know...it's like they have a little security to go with them to their new homes."

And dammit, she wasn't tearing up talking about this!

Quickly swiping at her eyes, she looked back up at him. "Growing up, all I wanted was a dog. We couldn't afford one and I swore once I moved out and lived on my own that I'd get one." More tears stung at her eyes. "But it turns out I don't have a place that's really conducive to having a dog– no fenced-in yard, no real space in here–and so I do the volunteering as a way of not only helping the dogs, but also to help me." She paused again. "Crazy, right?"

And then he moved toward her and didn't stop until his arms were around her. He placed a soft kiss on her head. "It's not crazy at all. If anything, it's the most amazing thing I've ever heard."

Scarlett snorted softly with disbelief even as she burrowed closer to him. "Please, it's really not. I'm just doing what I can to help the people who truly *are* amazing."

But he shook his head. "Nuh-uh. Don't get me wrong–I think what they do is amazing too. But the way you make something so personal–something no one else can do? Scarlett, you're not giving yourself enough credit."

"They're just dog houses and playsets, Mason. It's not

like I'm giving them their forever homes or even the space they need."

He pulled back slightly. "What do you mean?"

Now she was the one to pull away from his embrace before walking away and sitting on the plastic-covered sofa. "The couple who own the land–Christine and Ed–they need more space, more land. They want to build a kennel where they can house more animals and have more updated facilities. They get donations and I help them with their social media stuff but it's a drop in the bucket. I wish I could find land for them or help them get financing or...I don't know...anything!" She groaned. "I go there every week and I leave there wishing I could do more!"

Carefully, he stepped around the mess and came to sit beside her. Looking around the room again, he asked, "Did you make all the stuff in here?"

*Ugh...can I be any less feminine?*

"Uh...yeah. The coffee table, the console table, and those shelves," she murmured, pointing to the wall. She wanted to hide in embarrassment because these were not girly hobbies at all. Add them to working on cars and riding a motorcycle and it was no wonder most guys didn't look at her as a woman. She was one of the guys.

Except...when she turned and looked at Mason, he wasn't looking at her like she was one of the guys; he was looking at her the exact same way he did on the night of the concert.

All heat and need.

And it turned her on now just like it did then.

"So um...yeah," she repeated, hating the silence. "This is kind of my thing. I enjoy being creative and part of me wishes it wasn't with stuff like this."

Frowning, he asked, "Why?"

"Geez, Mason, look around you! This place is a freaking disaster! *I'm* a freaking disaster!" She held up her hands. "Look at me! My nails are short, my hands are splattered with paint, and these aren't the hands of some...some... prissy little debutante!"

Okay, that last part was her own insecurities coming out and she cursed herself for letting it fly.

Grabbing her hands, Mason gave a small tug. "Has it ever occurred to you that no one gives a shit about whether or not you're a...what did you call it? A prissy little debutante?"

When she tried to pull back, he only held her hands tighter.

"Here's the thing, Scarlett, all of this–the mess, the paint, the crazy talent? That's what makes you who you are and who you are is incredible! You're intimidating as hell but you know what? It just adds to the appeal of who you are!"

This time when she pulled her hands, he let go. Standing up, she paced a few feet away from him. "You don't get it and honestly, I don't expect you to."

"What is there to get? I'm here because I wanted to see you," he stated, coming to his feet. "And I wanted to see you because I like you and I want to spend time with you and get to know you more."

What was wrong with him? Didn't he see how ridiculous this whole thing was?

"Mason, look at us," she said calmly while internally panicking. Motioning to his entire body, she went on. "You're all dressed up in your fancy clothes and your polished shoes, and not one hair out of place."

"Scarlett..."

"And look at me," she continued, ignoring his attempts

to stop her. "I'm wearing three-year-old yoga pants, a wife-beater, no makeup, and my hair's a damn mess."

"The messy bun is a thing," he said teasingly, but she wasn't amused.

"I don't even think I showered today so...just stop. Please. It's..." She stopped and let out a long breath. "We had a good time last weekend and that's really all it should be. All it *can* be," she quickly corrected.

Standing there defiantly, Scarlett knew how to both look and sound intimidating. Her brothers had taught her that. Unfortunately, Mason didn't look the least bit fazed. She wanted to get snarky and tell him to leave, but...she couldn't. Damn him! Why couldn't he have just walked away like so many had before him?

The next thing she knew, he was standing directly in front of her looking just as comfortable and casual as if she hadn't just essentially told him they were through.

"Can I ask you something?" His voice was as soft as a caress.

Doing her best to look unfazed, she replied, "Sure."

"Have you had anything to eat?"

"Um...what?"

"It occurred to me as you were listing all the things you've been doing that you've probably been neglecting yourself in the process. So, have you eaten?"

Closing her eyes, she silently counted to ten before looking at him again. "What is wrong with you?" she asked, though there was very little heat behind her words and she couldn't help but laugh.

He pretended to be offended. "Darlin', I'm just making sure you take care of yourself. I was thinking we could order a pizza and talk."

Damn. She hadn't eaten anything since breakfast and pizza did sound good...

"C'mon," he prompted. "You can go take a shower and I'll order the pizza. What do you say?"

It wouldn't be the worst thing in the world to sit and talk to him. Scarlett knew she at least owed him that. And really, he was a nice guy who didn't deserve to have her acting so completely bitchy towards him. So...

"Okay," she said after a moment. "Sure. Pepperoni?"

His smile was downright dazzling. "You got it."

Knowing pizza delivery was fairly fast in Magnolia, she told Mason to make himself at home as she ran to her room to shower. It took some effort, but she fought the urge to overly primp, choosing to hit the basics–shampoo, conditioner, body wash, and a quick shave of all pertinent areas. Why? Because she was practical and no matter how much she tried to say they were just going to eat pizza and talk, there was always the possibility of more.

Hell, she wished she had told him to forget about the pizza and dragged him into the shower with her.

"Plan for another time," she murmured as she stepped out of her tiny shower and quickly dried off. Ten minutes later, she had on a clean pair of leggings, an oversized t-shirt, and somewhat dry hair and decided it was as good as it was going to get. She felt bad leaving him out there for so long and figured if he was true to his word, her appearance wouldn't be a factor.

Stepping back out into the living room, Scarlett saw he had removed the plastic from the sofa and set up some paper plates and drinks on her coffee table. When he spotted her, he looked her over from head to toe and she felt it just as strongly as if his hands had touched her.

Clearing her throat, she asked, "How long till pizza gets here?"

"Any minute," he replied. "How was the shower?"

With a soft laugh, she said, "Great. Actually, better than great. I wish I could have stayed in there longer."

It wasn't a complete lie, but she wasn't going to add how it would have been better if he had been in there with her.

"You know," he began, walking toward her, "you didn't have to rush. I would have kept the pizza warm until you were ready."

It was such an inane conversation and she hated it. Sitting down on the sofa, she motioned for him to join her. "How was your week?"

To his credit, Mason only looked mildly surprised by her question as he sat beside her. For the next few minutes, he talked about some zoning issues he struggled with at work and how he'd spent the earlier part of the night celebrating his sister's birthday.

"So you already ate dinner?"

He nodded.

"Then why did we order pizza?"

"That was for you," he said simply, his arm resting along the back of the sofa.

And in that moment, Scarlett knew what she had to do.

"I'm sorry," she said slowly. Twisting on the cushion, she faced him.

"For what?"

"For being a total bitch this week. You didn't deserve that. You're a great guy, Mason, and..."

He placed a finger over her lips to stop her flow of words. "Can I just say something first?"

She nodded.

"Was I disappointed when you didn't return my calls?

Yes. Did I spend a ridiculous amount of time obsessing about it? Also yes." He moved closer. "But I didn't take any of it as you being bitchy, Scarlett. If anything, I thought I had done something to offend you."

Her eyes went wide. "Seriously?"

"Well...yeah. What else was I supposed to think?"

"Um...that I'm a horrible person and...you know...a bitch," she said with another short laugh.

But Mason was shaking his head. "Now after coming here and seeing what you've been working on, I can understand why you were so busy." He glanced over at the dog house and Scarlett had to admit, it was one of her favorite creations. It was a replica of the barn Christine and Ed had on their property and she painted it a hunter green with crisp white trim. There were windows and a small porch area with cutouts for food and water bowls and it was tall enough to fit a full-grown Labrador Retriever.

"I'm in awe of your talent," he said, interrupting her thoughts.

"You're crazy."

"No, I'm not. The last thing I built was a birdhouse in middle school and it fell apart on the bus ride home that day!" They both laughed and she remembered that project. She was about to comment on it when there was a knock at the door. Mason instantly stood up and when she went to go grab her wallet, he stopped her. "My treat," he said, and she didn't want to argue.

Within minutes, they were back on the sofa and Scarlett was putting a slice of steaming hot pizza on her plate. "Are you sure you're not going to have any? Because there's more than enough here."

"Well...maybe," he said hesitantly, leaning forward and examining the pie.

"C'mon, there's always room for pizza," she teased.

"I guess."

"You guess?" she said with a laugh. "I've never met anyone who wasn't in the mood for pizza–no matter what else they've eaten."

He considered her for a minute and then grinned.

She was coming to recognize it and knew something utterly adorable was about to be said.

"Oh, I'm in the mood for pizza," he said, but he didn't reach for a slice. Instead, he leaned closer to her with a comically lecherous grin on his face. "A pizza you, that is!"

Unable to help herself, she tossed her plate down as she cracked up laughing. "Oh, my God! That has to be your worst one yet!"

He was laughing with her. "It's all part of my charm."

And damn if that wasn't working for him. Pizza could be reheated, but this moment couldn't be duplicated. Before she lost her nerve, she moved to straddle his lap and kissed him with everything she had. Mason's arms banded around her as he gave as good as he got.

"I swear I didn't come here for this," he said between kisses.

"I know," she said breathlessly. "But you know what those stupid lines do to me."

She was already wrapped around him as he stood. "Bedroom?"

"Down the hall on the left."

He stopped in the doorway and Scarlett was ready to whip her shirt off when she realized he wasn't moving. Slowly, he lowered her to her feet and shook his head.

"What?" she asked. "What's the matter?"

One hand reached up and gently caressed her cheek just before it also reached for her hand and led her back to the living room. For a moment, she was completely confused and once they were seated again, Mason let out a long breath. "Eat your dinner," he said. "And then we'll talk. And then..." He paused and shrugged. "Maybe then we can pick up where we left off at the end of the hall."

And right then and there, she knew—Mason Bishop was everything she ever dared to dream of.

And later that night, as they finished cold pizza in bed while laughing and watching more episodes of *Stranger Things*, all she felt was a sense of total contentment.

# SIX

"Are you sleeping at your desk?"

Mason's head shot up as he looked around in confusion. Sam was standing in the doorway to his office with a look of utter amusement on his face.

"Must have been one hell of a night to have you looking like this," he teased as he walked in and pulled up a chair. "So where'd you go? Was it that club out in Wilmington?"

Stretching in his chair, Mason yawned and did his best to wake up because...yeah, he had totally fallen asleep at his desk. Raking a hand through his hair, he forced himself to focus on his cousin. "No," he said before yawning again. "Not Wilmington." Reaching for the bottle of water he'd put on his desk earlier, he took a long drink before speaking again. "What brings you here?"

Leaning back in his chair, his cousin continued to look at him with his usual cocky grin. Normally it didn't bother him, but right now he was still a little disoriented.

"Sam?"

"You didn't answer me. Where were you last night that you're dragging ass today?"

"Here in town."

One of Sam's brows arched at Mason's snarky tone. "Dude, seriously? Last time I saw you was at that concert and you all but flew out of there. I caught a glimpse of you running through the crowd and word around town is you were chasing after a local girl. I figured you'd eventually come by and hang out and I'd get the details, but you've been suspiciously M.I.A. for over a week. So what gives?"

With a groan, Mason leaned back in his own seat and scrubbed a hand over his face. "Since when do you pay attention to local gossip anymore? I thought you were over that."

Sam shrugged. "I'm done listening to the shit about me. Shit about you, however, I'm all for hearing. Especially when you're not talking."

If there was one thing Mason knew about his cousin, it was how he was tenacious and he wasn't going to leave until he heard what he came here to find out. He took another drink of water before he opened up.

"So yeah...I met up with someone I went to school with but hadn't seen in years and...we've been spending time together."

Sam's expression went from hopeful to bored in the blink of an eye. "That's it? That's all you're going to tell me? That's the reason you were lying in a puddle of your own drool when I walked in–because you're *spending time* with someone? Mason, come on, man. There's more to the story than that!"

"If you're looking for details, you're out of luck. Not gonna happen," Mason said defensively. "Do I ask you for details about you and Shelby? No!"

And that's when he knew he tripped up.

"So this is serious?" Sam asked, straightening in his

chair, eyes wide. "Who is she? Do I know her? Does Shelby?"

With a muttered curse, Mason leaned forward, resting his arms on his desk. "Are we seriously sitting here gossiping like a bunch of teenage girls? Is that what we're reduced to?"

"Nice deflection, but...apparently," Sam replied. "I'm not looking to gossip. I'm just curious about the girl you're clearly into, since you've seen her more than once. Is it one of the girls your mother's been pushing on you? Should I be looking for an engagement announcement in the Magnolia Gazette?"

Just the thought of that made him groan as another curse flew from his lips. "It's not like that. You don't know her and she's definitely not someone my mother set me up with."

"Well now I'm even more intrigued."

Why fight it? He thought, and then the whole story came tumbling out–from seeing Scarlett at the concert, to their weekend together, and through the previous night.

"So you've spent the last two weekends with her," Sam began slowly, as if trying to wrap his brain around the whole situation. "And...what? Is this just a sex thing? Are you dating?"

*Good question.*

"Scarlett doesn't want to put a label on it," Mason said. "At least not yet. Part of me thinks she's putting up some parameters based on her own issues and I'm too damn afraid to spook her."

"That's bullshit, bro. What kind of issues does she have?"

"Let's just say she hasn't had the easiest life and she's not particularly fond of people who have."

"Damn."

"Tell me about it. I swear, I've had girls throwing them-selves at me for years because my family has money and now I find a girl I really care about and the family money is a huge turnoff for her! How's that for irony?"

"Wow. Just...wow. What are you going to do?"

"The only thing I can do is go slow and let her set the pace, right? If I push too much, she'll bail and then where will that leave me?"

"Whipped, for starters," Sam murmured.

"Hey!"

"Well, what do you expect me to say? You're letting her call all the shots no matter how bad it makes you feel. How is that fair?"

"Yeah, well...this is all new to me so..."

"Look, I get it, Mason. I know this has to be hard for you, but the sooner she sees the real you and how your family isn't calling the shots or how the money they have has nothing to do with you as a person, the better off the two of you will be."

"I don't know. My mother made a couple of snide comments on Friday night when we all went out for Park-er's birthday."

"And you're surprised, why?"

"I guess I'm not, but the last thing I want is for her to do or say something to Scarlett like that. I don't know what I'd do."

Sam looked like he was about to say something but his mouth opened and then quickly closed. After a moment of awkward silence, he asked, "So what are you going to do? Just keep having these dirty weekends?"

It took all Mason had not to go over the desk and punch his cousin for making what he and Scarlett had sound so crude. "It's not like that," he said, teeth clenched.

"When are you seeing her again?"

"Tonight. And in case you haven't checked your calendar, it's Monday."

"Yeah, yeah, yeah, I get it," Sam said, coming to his feet. "Look, whatever it is you're doing, I'm happy for you. It seems like you're into this girl and that's great. Don't let your family screw this up for you. Stand your ground and stand up for your girl."

He stood and shook Sam's hand. "Thanks."

"And don't be such a stranger. I miss hanging out with you, but now I know why."

Another yawn was out before he could stop it. "Yeah, sorry about that. I promise to give you a call later on this week."

"Maybe the four of us can go out sometime," Sam suggested. "You know, let her see how your whole family isn't crazy."

"You're crazy on a level all your own, Sam," he teased.

"And proud of it." With a wave, he walked out and Mason took a minute to stand there and think about everything they'd just talked about. Picking his phone up off the desk, he saw it was only four o'clock. Scarlett was working from home today and didn't have any plans to go to Happy Tails so maybe she'd be home...

Before he could second guess himself, he grabbed his keys and decided he deserved to cut out a bit early today. He'd make up the time later in the week. With a bit of renewed energy, he left the building and was in his car and making his way toward the edge of town where Scarlett lived. He wasn't thrilled with her living in such an isolated spot, but he wasn't going to say anything. She seemed to like it and the last thing he wanted to do was try to change her. She was perfect the way she was.

When he parked his car in front of her little bungalow, he knew he'd made the right choice. Before he was out of the car, Scarlett was opening the front door and looking out at him curiously.

Then her smile turned a little devilish and he knew they were on the same page. He wanted her. He couldn't wait any longer to see her. And by the look on her face, she was just as happy to see him.

*  *  *

BREATHLESS, sweaty, and completely sated, Scarlett rested her head on Mason's chest.

"Not that I'm complaining, but what brought this on?"

He wrapped an arm around her and placed a soft kiss on the top of her head. "I was thinking about you and couldn't wait to see you," he responded quietly. His hand skimmed up and down her back and she had to admit, this all felt good.

Better than good.

She felt a sense of contentment she had never felt before and was honestly a little scared to examine too closely. Right now they were in this honeymoon phase where everything was good and fun and–judging by this surprise visit–pleasurable. But if there was one thing she knew about herself, it was that she was a realist. Things like this weren't the norm and they certainly didn't last. So she'd take it for what it was for right now and enjoy it.

"I wasn't interrupting anything, was I?" he asked after a long moment.

"Nope. I ran some errands earlier and then did some

work online for a couple of my accounts and was just contemplating what I wanted for dinner."

"And did you come to any conclusions?"

"Food," she said and laughed. "That's about all I managed."

They were quiet again for several minutes but Scarlett didn't mind. The rhythm of his hand was soothing and almost enough to make her fall asleep.

"How about we go out to eat," he suggested, and she felt herself go completely still.

"Like...out? To a restaurant?"

"Well...yeah," he said with a small laugh. "That's where they have the food."

Shifting until there was a little space between them, she willed away a panic attack. It was one thing to be involved with Mason here in her house or in his, but it was quite another for them to go out in public.

Wait...wasn't it?

He sat up and looked at her. "Are you afraid to be seen with me or something? Because I can tell you're having some sort of internal dialogue that I can practically hear. What's going on?"

Ugh...how to explain it?

Sitting up, she figured the truth was best. "Mason, for the sake of argument, can we just agree we're from two very different worlds?"

"No, absolutely not," he said adamantly. "I'm not looking at us like that and I don't think you should either."

With a snort, she climbed from the bed and walked over to her closet and grabbed a robe–slipping it on before she spoke again. "How could I not?"

He stood and slid his pants back on. "Because I think you're making more of it than it needs to be. My family isn't the Rockefellers and I think if you took the time to get to know them—and to really know me—you'd see that!"

"You grew up in a family that never struggled, Mason! I grew up in a family where we were on public assistance and I sometimes wore my hand-me-downs from my brothers!"

"Scarlett..."

"Did you ever have to go without a meal because there was no food in the house? Have you ever come home and found out the power was shut off because the bill wasn't paid? Or slept under four blankets because there wasn't heat? Because I have!" she cried. "And I may not know your family well, but I can guarantee none of those things happened to you!"

His expression turned sad and she cursed herself for taking things out on him that weren't his fault. She shouldn't hold it against him because he grew up in better circumstances than she did.

"Can I ask you something?"

She nodded.

"What's your relationship like with your father?" he asked, his voice low and solemn.

"It's good," she replied honestly. "He did the best he could after my mom died and even though he didn't really know what to do with a daughter, I always knew he loved me."

"Did he say those words to you?"

She nodded again. "Every day."

"Mine didn't," he stated, his gaze steady on hers. "Every day I was told what was expected of me—how I was to behave, how I should speak, who I should be friends with, what kind of grades I needed to have. Every day it was an endless chore to be the son of Georgia and Beau Bishop."

Shame washed over her, but before she could speak, he continued.

"I ran for student council and played sports because of how it would look on a transcript, not because I wanted to. Every decision I made was based on those expectations and I have to tell you, it was exhausting. I was groomed to follow in my father's footsteps and up until high school graduation, I went along with it." He paused. "Until I didn't."

"What did you do?" she asked cautiously, taking a small step toward him.

"I told them I wasn't going to be a lawyer and I wanted to go into engineering. You would have thought I was telling them I wanted to be a serial killer the way my mother carried on," he said with a mirthless laugh. "They argued how they were paying for my education and needed to go where they wanted me to go and I said if that was the case, I wouldn't go to school at all."

"No!"

He nodded. "That lasted for all of three days before everyone calmed down."

"Would you have really followed through with it? Giving up college?"

"I had a plan to go to the community college and pay for it myself, but it never came to that."

"We could've been classmates if you did," she teased softly, moving closer to him.

When she was right in front of him, Mason wrapped his arms around her waist and pulled her closer. "Here's the thing, Scarlett, a better life is all relative. You have no idea how many times I wished my parents would just be proud of me for me rather than giving me some messed up list of criteria I had to meet to earn their love. If you ask me, you're the one who's richer."

Tears stung her eyes because she realized just how much she had misjudged him. Hugging him close, she rested her cheek against his chest. "I'm so sorry," she whispered. "All this time..."

"Shh...it's okay," he said just as softly. "I didn't tell you this to make you cry or to make you feel sorry for me. I wanted you to see that things aren't always what they seem. And I know it's a total cliché, but the grass isn't always greener."

Pulling back, she looked up at him. "What about your sisters?"

"What about them?"

"Were your parents hard on them too?"

He shrugged. "Not nearly as much, but they certainly weren't laid back with them either."

Because she didn't know what else to do, she hugged him. Hard. "I don't even know what to say. I made a snap judgement based on what I saw and..."

He silenced her with a finger over her lips. "It was a perfectly logical conclusion to come to, Scarlett. I'm not saying you were wrong. If our roles were reversed, I would have thought the same. You have nothing to apologize for."

They stayed close like that in companionable silence for a few minutes before Mason reminded her about his suggestion they go out for dinner.

"It would probably be very closed-minded of me to say no and suggest we order Chinese takeout, right?" she said, only partially kidding.

With a soft laugh, he kissed her cheek and stepped away to sit on the edge of the bed. "Yes, it would and you don't want people thinking you're a snob, do you?"

And yeah, she knew he was teasing, but there was a certain amount of truth there.

Sighing dramatically, she said, "Fine. We'll go to dinner. But can it be burgers at the pub? I'm in the mood for that more than anything."

By the smile on his face, she knew she'd said the right thing and when he stood and took her by the hand and led her to the bathroom so they could shower together, Scarlett also knew dinner was going to be a little on the late side.

* * *

"SO THERE I was in the middle of this massive truck engine, my brother Dean holding me by my ankles, my other brother Kyle under the truck with a flashlight, when my father comes in and all but roars at us! Kyle panics and slides out from underneath, Dean drops my legs and the hood comes down on me!" Scarlett said, laughing at the memory.

"What did you do?"

"I cursed up a blue streak and when I turned to try to move, I finally felt the damn laser pointer Dean had dropped in the first place!"

Laughing, Mason shook his head. "And how old were you?"

"Ten. I didn't know a whole lot about engines at the time, but the way Dean was instructing me made me curious."

"I can't believe he didn't try to find the damn thing himself."

Taking a sip of her sweet tea first, she said, "His arm was too big. I was pretty scrawny and I was able to fish around in places he couldn't."

"Still..."

"My dad was so pissed! He yelled at all three of us but I

started asking all kinds of questions about engines and cars and distracted him." She winked. "And once he brought in the first motorcycle to be repaired, I was hooked. He said he would gladly let me work on bikes because I wouldn't be falling into engines or having hoods fall on me anymore."

"He sounds awesome, Scarlett."

She smiled with such pleasure that Mason could almost feel the affection she felt for her father.

And it made him a little envious.

It wasn't like he hated his parents. He just wasn't overly fond of them either.

"My dad is...well...he's the greatest. But don't get me wrong, I have my issues with him, too. There were a lot of years when I resented how I ended up being a bit of a tomboy because he had no idea what to do with a daughter. Now, the older I get, I realized he did the best he could and I turned out okay."

Reaching across the table, Mason took one of her hands in his and squeezed. "You're more than okay, Scarlett. You're an incredible woman and you should be proud of that. Own it."

She blushed and it was completely adorable on her—especially because it was so out of character for her. Most of the time she came off like nothing bothered her and he knew she could be bristly and a little rough around the edges, but when this side of her came out, she was positively captivating.

After a minute, they went back to eating and Scarlett shared several more stories about life working in a garage with her dad and brothers. They were always entertaining and he couldn't help but wonder what they were going to think of him. No doubt they were going to have similar thoughts about him like Scarlett had and he feared he was going to be met with even more resistance, mainly because she was the only girl in a male-dominated household.

But he was up for the challenge.

By the time they were done eating, they agreed to skip dessert and head to his place for the night. It wasn't that he didn't like Scarlett's home. If anything, it felt more like a home than his place. But she had mentioned how clear the night sky was and how she would love to sit out and listen to the waves for a while.

Now, as they lay together on one of his loungers on his back deck, he felt completely content.

"This was a good night," she said, interrupting his thoughts.

"So far," he murmured, kissing her neck.

Humming with approval, Scarlett rested her head back to give him better access. After a few minutes she softly asked, "What are you doing this weekend?"

His mind instantly went to them spending it in bed as they had the previous two and he had to push that aside.

At least for now.

"Nothing planned yet," he murmured against her skin, unwilling to stop tasting her for long.

She squirmed against him but didn't stop him. "I was thinking you might want to go for a ride up the coast with me. On my bike."

Okay, that stopped him.

A quiet laugh was her initial response. "I can feel you tensing up behind me. It's okay if you don't want to do it. I just thought I'd throw it out there."

"It's not that I don't want to do it..."

Now she did move—twisting around to face him. "It's okay. Really. It's not for everyone."

And for some reason he took that a little too personally.

"Look, I can't say it's not for me because I've never done it. Hell, it's never even been something I thought about doing. Am I intimidated? Hell yeah! And do I want to look like some kind of pussy riding on the back of my girlfriend's bike? No!"

Rolling her eyes, Scarlett leaned in and kissed him on the cheek. "For starters, that is not what you'd look like."

"Says you." And yeah, now he was pouting and undoubtedly looking like the very thing he was trying to avoid.

"I can take you out on a short ride so you can get the feel of just being a passenger and then we'll see about loaning you one so you can check it out for yourself. Would that make you feel better? We'll even do the short ride somewhere out of town so no one you know will see you if it's that big of a deal for you."

"Now you're making me feel stupid," he muttered, frowning at her.

The smirk on her face certainly wasn't helping either. "Mason, I'm just trying to find a happy medium here. It's something I'd really like to do with you but I want you to enjoy it too. If you're going to fight me on it, then we just won't do it." She shrugged. "It's really not a big deal." Kissing him again, she turned around and resumed her earlier position.

They were quiet for a long time and Mason's mind raced through all of it. This was something that was part of who Scarlett was and if he wanted to get to know her better, it meant doing the things she enjoyed doing, right? Logically, he knew that, but the illogical part of him was annoyed with himself because there wasn't anything about his life he could counter with. He lived a fairly boring life. A safe life. And the more he thought about it, the more he realized how much he wasn't living.

And that depressed the hell out of him.

Before he realized it, Scarlett was standing up and stretching. She moved over to stand against the railing and smiled up at the stars. "I would never get tired of this view," she said quietly. "Living in such a wooded area, I don't get to see the sky quite like this." Glancing over her shoulder at him, she went on. "And the weird thing is that I never gave it much thought until a few weeks ago."

Standing, he moved in close behind her and pushed all the negative thoughts from just moments ago aside. "You're welcome to come and enjoy this view any time you want."

"Mmm..." She leaned against him as his arms wrapped around her waist. "You may regret saying that."

Unable to help himself, he smiled. "I doubt it."

"You say that now. But wait until you want to get rid of me..."

Turning her in his arms until she faced him, he looked down at her. "Who says I want to get rid of you?" His heart pounded so hard and he knew this was important. She was making light of it, but he knew there was some truth behind her words. She was worried about where they were going and this was her way of bringing it up.

But...in typical Scarlett fashion, she changed the subject. "Ever make love on the beach?"

He studied her for a moment and seriously considered pushing the subject. "Scarlett..."

In the blink of an eye her top was whipped up over her head and she was standing there in the circle of his arms under the moonlight in her shorts and a lacy white bra. She was all bronzed skin and lush curves and—not for the first time—he stared in awe at her choice of lingerie. For a woman who claimed to be a bit of a tomboy, she had the best taste in undergarments. He knew from earlier there was a matching white thong under her shorts and suddenly talking about local businesses was the last thing on his mind.

"Nice distraction tactic," he murmured, reaching up to cup her breasts.

She shrugged and gave him a sexy grin. "I do what I can."

And rather than continue with their flirty banter, he decided they could do that later.

Much, much later.

# SEVEN

"I don't understand how this happened," Mason said, raking a hand through his hair. The phone call from his great-grandfather's attorney had interrupted his day and it looked like it was also going to interrupt his life. "You said everything was fine staying the way it was."

"Mason, I'm just as surprised as you are," Richard McClellan stated. "It turns out the payroll taxes haven't been paid and neither has the property tax. I think it's safe to say it's only going to get worse. The agreement your great-grandfather had was as long as the business was running properly, and the loan being repaid, he wouldn't interfere."

"Wait...the loan's not being repaid either?"

"I'm afraid not. You really don't have a choice but to step in." He paused. "I haven't wanted to push on this, but have you thought about what you're going to do? Are you going to keep it? Or do you plan on selling? Because if you do, it's going to be hard to find a buyer willing to take on a floundering business."

Groaning, Mason stood and began to pace his small

office. His plan had been to shut the bar down, clear the property, and then sell. The location was prime. Okay, not at this moment it wasn't, but if his plan for the park he wanted to propose to the town worked, owning the adjacent lot would make it such. He hadn't been keen on sharing that information with anyone because he didn't want to reveal his hand just yet.

"I...I'm still not sure," he said vaguely. Richard was an old family friend and even though Mason knew he could trust him, for some reason he just didn't want to speak his plans out loud.

"Well, you're out of time. I would suggest going down and meeting with Tommy Flynn as soon as possible. Today, if possible. I can meet you there if you'd like."

There was no way he could put this off, no matter how much he wanted to. With a weary sigh, he agreed. "Yeah, okay. Let's...let's just get it over with. Maybe we can figure something out."

It was almost lunchtime and they agreed to meet down at The Mystic Magnolia at noon. It wasn't ideal, but he wasn't prepared to take any extra time off just quite yet. With any luck they'd talk to Mr. Flynn and figure out how to get him back on track—at least temporarily. Or...until Mason was ready to close him down permanently.

Hanging up the phone, he sank back down in his chair and wondered what he was waiting for. If the old guy was in this much financial trouble, wouldn't he be doing him a favor by shutting him down?

Feeling a little better about his decision, he quickly finished up the report he had been working on before Richard's call and sent it to his boss before gathering his things and heading out. Hopefully this wouldn't take more than an hour and he'd have time to grab a quick bite to eat before heading back to work.

The drive across town didn't take long and as he pulled into the parking lot, he couldn't hide a hint of distaste. It wasn't that he was a snob or thought he was too good for a place like this, but...the entire building looked like it needed to be power washed with bleach.

Then he laughed at himself because he'd gone to more than a handful of bars like this when he was in college and had a lot of fun. Mason was sure that The Mystic Magnolia was a great place to hang out in its heyday. But for as long as Mason knew of its existence, it wasn't a place for college kids or even those in their twenties or thirties. It was always an older crowd who frequented the place. He was sure the location didn't help, either. Just on the right side of the town limits, it was a lone-standing building with only a handful of businesses nearby. Most of the thriving bars were in the heart of downtown. It was a wonder this place lasted as long as it did.

Climbing from his Jeep, Mason looked up at the sky and frowned. "What the hell were you thinking, Pops? Why would you leave this place to me?" Unfortunately, there were no answers and he stood beside his vehicle and waited for Richard to show up. He thought about texting Scarlett just to say hello, but no sooner had he thought it than Richard was pulling in beside him.

"You ready for this?" Richard asked when he climbed from his car. He was an older gentleman and with his suit on, he looked completely out of place. Mason had to hide a grin at his thoughts. Together they looked like the least likely duo to walk into The Mystic Magnolia.

"Not really, but we might as well get it over with, right?"

They walked in and Mason had to admit, it was exactly

as he imagined–dark wood, dim lighting, stale air, and in desperate need of...hell, he didn't think there was enough to help this place other than knocking it down and starting over.

Beside him, Richard casually pointed toward the man behind the bar. "That's Mr. Flynn." The man in question was easily in his sixties with a full head of silver hair and both arms covered in tattoos. He wasn't particularly tall or intimidating, but Mason learned–especially lately–that looks could be deceiving.

They approached the bar and Tommy Flynn barely spared them a glance. There were a few other men sitting at the bar–some as old as the bartender, some didn't look to be that much older than Mason–but other than that, the place was empty.

"What brings you here today, McClellan?" Tommy's gravelly voice said as he wiped down the worn-down bar top.

"Got a few minutes so we can talk?" Richard asked, his posture stiff and uncomfortable. Mason knew how he felt because he was feeling the same way.

Flynn looked over at Mason. "Who's the kid?"

Richard grinned. "This is Zeke's great-grandson, Mason Bishop."

With a scowl, Tommy motioned for them to follow him. Mason noted the looks on the faces of all the guys at the bar and felt more than a little intimidated. With a curt nod, he followed Flynn into what he guessed to be his office.

"I don't suppose I really have to guess why you're here," he said, taking a seat behind an old metal desk.

Once they were all seated, he waited for Richard to explain the reason for their visit. "As you know, Tommy, per your agreement with Zeke..."

The older man held up a hand to stop him. "Yeah, I know. I've let a few things slip and I'm behind. It happens. I just need a little more time."

Mason was about to speak, but Richard beat him to it. "Tommy, Zeke's been gone now for almost nine months. You knew if the loan wasn't paid in full his heir would get the business. Now Mason's been kind enough to give you those additional nine months and you've used that time to get further into debt."

Tommy glared hard over at Mason. "What's this kid going to do with a bar, huh? I'll tell you what he's going to do—he's going to come in here like a vulture and pick the place apart and turn it into one of those prissy little wine bars like they have down on Main Street! He won't even care about my customers!"

Again, he was about to speak when Richard spoke up again. "It's his right to do what he wants with the place, Tom. You know that. You agreed to all of this with Zeke. You knew it was a long-shot for you to get out of the hole you were in. Sometimes you have to just...let things go."

There was an uncomfortable silence and Mason found himself almost squirming in his seat. He realized it was probably for the best if he didn't say anything just yet because it was obvious Mr. Flynn wasn't feeling too kindly toward him. So he'd sit quietly and see where this all went.

"If I can get the money to pay off the rest of the loan..." Tommy began, but Richard quickly cut him off.

"Be realistic, Tom. If you had the capability, you would have done it already."

And damn, Mason hated seeing the look on the old guy's face the moment the reality of the situation really hit.

The truth was Mason could probably work with the guy, but to what end? If there was one thing his great-grandfather had taught him, it was to know when to cut your losses. Part of his current feeling was because he knew what he wanted to do with this property and by letting Tommy Flynn stay in business, his own dream was going to be compromised. Owning this land when the property next door was going to be developed would give him some financial security. He'd lived off of his parents and had a trust from his paternal grandfather, but it would be nice if he could do this for himself. Maybe that's why Pops had left this to him–so he could break free from living under his parents' thumbs!

A sigh of relief at having finally figured out that mystery was out before he could stop and both men looked over at him–one with annoyance, the other with curiosity.

"You got something to say?" Tommy demanded, the scowl on his face deepening.

It took him a solid minute before he could make himself speak and then figured he had nothing to lose–the man already didn't like him so...

Clearing his throat, Mason straightened in his chair. "Mr. Flynn, I'm sorry things worked out the way they did. If my great-grandfather stepped in to help, it was because he believed in you. Unfortunately, it doesn't look like business has been easy for you and decisions have to be made." He paused and saw Richard relaxing a bit beside him. That told him he was saying the right things.

"I don't know anything about owning a bar, and, to be honest, I don't want to. It's not my intention to take over or change The Mystic Magnolia into something else," he continued. "This bar has been an institution in this town for a long time and I know you have some loyal clientele. But, unfortunately, they aren't paying the bills."

"You don't know a damn thing about my customers," Tommy snapped.

"Maybe not," Mason countered, "but I do know you owe a lot of money to a lot of people and you waited a little too long to let us know there was a problem. Last time Richard and I talked, I was told everything was running smoothly and the bills were being paid. I tried to stand back and see what you could do with the place while I was trying to figure out what it was I wanted to do, but no matter what either of us wants, our time is up."

"So you're not even willing to let me try to get the money," Tommy replied, teeth clenched. His face had turned red with rage and Mason knew the man would like nothing more than to lunge over the desk at him.

"As Richard pointed out," he replied, praying his voice didn't tremble, "if that had been an option, you would have taken it already." When Tommy went to speak, Mason was the one to hold up a hand to stop him. "Mr. Flynn, my great-grandfather tried to help you save the business, but it seems like it was only a band-aid–a temporary fix. You ran a successful business for decades. Maybe this is your chance to retire."

"Pfft," Tommy said before muttering a curse. "You think if I could retire I'd still be at this? I had hoped to sell this damn place so I'd have a little nest egg for retirement! Now what do I have, huh? Nothing!"

"You could always..."

"You need to go," Tommy said angrily, coming to his feet. "You've done enough." He turned to Richard. "When do I need to be out of here?"

Richard came to his feet along with Mason. "Why don't I give you a call tomorrow and we'll figure it all out? I think emotions are running a little too high right now."

"Yeah, whatever," he murmured, storming from the office.

"Well, that sucked," Mason said, turning toward the door. "What the hell was Pops thinking? I mean I get what he was trying to do for me, but why would he do that to Tommy?" When he turned to walk out the door, Richard stopped him.

"Your grandfather had a big heart and a good head for business, Mason. He gave Tommy a business plan to help him that went completely ignored. Although you and I both know that sometimes no matter what you do or how hard you try, things just don't work out." He paused. "So what are you going to do with the place?"

What was the point in staying quiet? "I want the property, Richard. I think I can make a nice profit on it once the rest of the land around here is developed. And with the transformation the town is going through since the storm, it's only a matter of time before Magnolia Sound expands. It's a small miracle this land has gone undeveloped for this long."

He nodded. "I think that's a good, solid plan."

"But..."

Letting out a long breath, Richard said, "I don't think Tommy is going to go quietly. I think he's angry and bitter about the turn of events."

Turning, Mason shut the office door before speaking again. "I'm not to blame here, Richard! I didn't do anything wrong!"

"I get that," he replied quickly. "I just want you to be prepared that there may be people who don't want to see change at this end of town—people who like that Magnolia has some green spaces that haven't been bulldozed for commercial properties."

"You can't stop progress," Mason countered, hating the bitterness in his voice. "Nothing stays the same forever."

Placing a hand on Mason's shoulder, Richard gave him a small smile. "I know and I understand what you're saying. I also want you to move forward with your eyes open. Zeke had a lot of ideas, Mason. Hell, not a day went by when he wasn't thinking out loud about business ideas and plans and ways to improve on what was already here. He watched this town grow from nothing. But you know what happened more times than not?"

He shook his head.

"He'd feel out the people, talk to them, gather information, and do what was best for the town. And believe me when I say it wasn't always what was best for him. There were times when he lost a lot of money."

"Seriously?" That didn't sound like the man Mason grew up watching.

"But there were times when he also made a lot of money." Another pause. "It would have been easy when Tommy approached him to simply let this place go. But there were a lot of people who wanted it to stay—mostly for sentimental reasons."

"That's not the way to do business, Richard."

Nodding, Richard agreed. "You're right. It's not. But whatever the reason why Tommy chose to ignore the business plan we gave him, we don't know. I hate how you got caught in the middle. It's not going to be a matter of simply closing the doors and selling the property. Just...know that."

Before he could respond, Richard opened the office door. "I need to get back to work. I'm going to grab a little lunch on the way. Hopefully you still have time to do the same too."

"Yeah," he said quietly, following him out of the office.

There were raised voices out in the bar area and there wasn't a doubt in his mind Tommy was telling his customers what had just gone down.

"Gramps," one of the guys was saying, "maybe this isn't such a bad thing. You know how you always wanted to..." He stopped when he spotted Mason and Richard walking out. Everyone glared in their direction, but not one word was spoken until they were out the door.

Which was probably for the best.

Mason wasn't quite ready to deal with an angry mob.

* * *

NORMALLY WHEN SCARLETT WAS ANGRY, she would let out a good, primal scream first and then go for a long bike ride to clear her head. Then there were times when she would bury herself in a project and build something and get the same result. But right now she wanted to go and yell and scream *and* punch someone.

Someone named Mason.

She sat in her car with a white-knuckled grip on her steering wheel and willed herself to calm down. Staring at Mason's dark house, she cursed herself for not calling first. She had no idea where he was or when he'd be home, but when he did get here, she'd be waiting. Nervous energy had her wanting to climb out of the car and pace, but she forced herself to stay put.

Twenty minutes later, Mason's Jeep pulled in beside her and she saw his smile and almost forgot to be angry with him.

Then it all came flooding back.

She climbed from her car and met him at his front door.

"Hey, beautiful," he said, leaning in and kissing her on

the cheek. "I wasn't expecting to see you here. Were you waiting long?"

"That's it?" she asked, her voice dripping with sarcasm and her arms crossed over her chest. "That's all you have to say to me?"

Pulling back, he looked at her with confusion. "Um..."

"I mean, how could you? Don't you have any conscience? And to do it without even talking to me first?" she cried, but the look on his face made her stop. "Do you even know what I'm talking about?"

He shook his head. "Not even a clue." Opening the front door, he ushered her inside and took a minute to get them both something to drink. "Okay, want to start from the beginning and tell me what this is all about?"

"My grandfather, Mason!" she snapped, angrily tossing her purse on the floor. "You put him out of business!"

With wide eyes, he slowly sat down on the sofa. "Scarlett, I have no idea what you're talking about! I didn't put anyone out of business!"

"Oh, really?" More sarcasm. "So you didn't go down to The Mystic Magnolia today and tell my grandfather, Tommy Flynn, that you were now the owner of the place and he was through?"

"It wasn't quite like that..."

"Do you realize he's poured his entire life into that place? How he has literally put every ounce of blood, sweat, and tears he has into making it a success?" she demanded loudly.

"Scarlett, it's not..."

"What do you think he's going to be able to do now? He's sixty-five years old, Mason! It's not like he can just go out and get another job!"

"I realize that," he began nervously. "But it isn't as if..."

"And you brought your lawyer with you like...like a bully! You embarrassed him in front of his customers and his family! I mean, what were you thinking?" she yelled, pacing his living room, her whole body trembling at this point. "Do you have any idea how mortified he was that his grandsons had to witness that?"

He let out a long breath and scrubbed a hand over his face before looking at her again. "Scarlett, let me just say..."

"No," she interrupted, adamant that she was not going to let him talk his way out of this. "I thought you were a good guy, Mason. A decent guy. I didn't think you would be cruel. My poor grandfather has nothing now and it's all because of you." Leaning down, she picked up her purse. "And I can't forgive you for that."

"If you would just..."

"No!" she repeated. "There's nothing you can say." She huffed with annoyance as she turned to walk away. But... she had one more thing to say. Turning back to him, she said, "This is why I should have never gotten involved with someone like you. People like you–the rich, the privileged– you get what you want by stepping all over other people. You're awful. I wish I had just walked away from you the night of the concert. This entire relationship was a mistake." She saw the anger on his face–the way he was clearly holding in whatever it was that he wanted to say.

With a sense of accomplishment, Scarlett turned and walked to the door. With her hand on the knob, she looked back at him one last time. "We're through. I never want to see you again."

What came next had her nearly jumping out of her skin. Mason's hand slammed against the door the second she turned her back on him. He towered over her and as much as she yanked on the doorknob, it wouldn't budge.

"Dammit, Mason, let me out!" she cried, still trying to pull the door open.

"You know, you've had an awful lot to say here and you haven't even tried to hear my side of things." His voice was oddly calm and that's what made her stop trying to open the door and turn to face him. He was staring down at her, his expression hard, but she wasn't intimidated.

Nope.

His jaw ticked and she straightened and met his glare. "Fine. Say what you have to say–not that it will matter–and then I can leave."

"Can you please just sit down?" he asked, but she held her ground. They stood there, close enough to touch in a battle of wills. Mason broke first and took a step away. And then another until he was on the other side of the room.

"Well?" she asked, doing her best to sound bored even though her heart was beating like mad.

"First, I had no idea Tommy Flynn was your grandfather," he began slowly.

"Right," she snorted with disbelief. "We're done here."

"No!" he yelled, surprising them both with how loud his voice was. Once Scarlett agreed not to leave, he started talking again. "I'm serious, Scarlett. When my great-grandfather died and he left me The Mystic Magnolia, I was pissed. I heard your grandfather's name but how could I possibly put two and two together? It's not like you have the same last name!"

Okay, he had a point, but still...

"I kept putting off dealing with the whole thing because my attorney assured me the business was running and all the bills were being paid and there wasn't any rush for me to make a decision on what I wanted to do."

"I think your great-grandfather was a thief," she interrupted. "There's no reason why my grandfather would have needed a loan. He's a great businessman. If you ask me, your great-grandfather probably conned my grandfather because he wanted to be part of another successful Magnolia Sound business!"

She felt proud of her little speech, but the look of pity on Mason's face had a tiny bit of doubt starting to creep into all of her bravado.

"Scarlett," he said solemnly, "I know that's what you want to believe, but it's simply not true. Your grandfather was struggling and he needed help. Pops helped him out and they had an agreement. He was also given a business plan to help him. But in the end..." his words trailed off.

"So...so..." she began nervously, her brain scrambling to make sense of the whole situation. "So your great-grandfather gave him a crappy business plan in hopes of making the business fail so he could get his hands on it!"

"He never used the plan!" he countered. "That's why the business failed! Maybe if he had listened, things would've been different!"

"Or maybe you could just leave him alone and let him keep his bar! What do you even need it for?" And dammit, she wasn't going to cry. "Don't you have enough? Your whole family...*gah*! When is it going to be enough? Do you all need to own the entire town before you'll be satisfied?"

At that point, Mason sighed and looked down, shaking his head. When his gaze met hers, all she saw was defeat. "There's nothing I'm going to be able to say, is there?" But he didn't wait for a response. "You've already made up your mind and you're not even willing to consider that maybe I'm telling the truth. Hell, you won't even listen to most of what I'm trying to tell you."

While she knew he had a point, she was too emotional–too overwhelmed–to stay and hear any more.

And he knew it too.

Turning, she reached for the doorknob again and once she pulled the door open, she paused.

"I'm sorry, Scarlett," he said quietly. "If you want to talk about this–if you change your mind and want to hear me out–I'll be here."

As much as it hurt, she looked over her shoulder at him. "I won't."

Walking out the door, unshed tears stung her eyes. She held it together until she was home, but once she was through her own front door, she cried like she hadn't cried in years.

How could she have been so wrong about him? Why didn't she stick to her guns and walk away from Mason before they ever crossed that line? Now not only was she heartbroken, but she felt like a complete fool. Luckily she never told her family about being involved with him–not that it would have changed anything. People like the Bishops didn't care about anyone but themselves. Although...maybe if her brothers had known she could have sent them over to Mason's to kick his ass.

As soon as she thought it, she knew she was wrong. She didn't want to see him physically hurt.

Much.

And the worst part of this whole thing was...she almost believed him. The little bit of his side of the story she had let him share had her wondering if her grandfather maybe wasn't being completely honest with her and the rest of the family. He was a proud man who never admitted to having any kind of weakness and there was a very real possibility that if he was struggling with the business, he wouldn't share it with anyone.

But then why would he share it with Ezekiel Coleman?

Granted, she didn't know much about the man, but... why him? And now that she was a little calmer, she realized no one would deliberately go after The Mystic Magnolia. It was a hole in the wall bar and had been for years. The location sucked and it was in desperate need of renovations–also for years. Scarlett had always wondered why he didn't do more to fix up the place, but...maybe he couldn't. Maybe the money really wasn't there.

*He was also given a business plan to help him. But in the end...*

Okay, then there was that. If someone had been willing to give him not only the money to save his business but also a plan to help him succeed, why was he still in this position? How did it even get to this point?

Her head was pounding and there were more unanswered questions than anything else. Tomorrow she was going to demand a family meeting and get to the bottom of things. It had been a while since they'd all gotten together for a meal and she knew if she was the one to put it out there, everyone would come.

It was the one blessing to being the only female in the family–everyone had a soft spot for her, especially her grandfather.

Of course there was always the possibility of her going and talking to him one-on-one, but she'd go the family meeting route first and see where that got her. For now, however, she was alone with her thoughts and she didn't want to be.

Curled up on her couch, she let herself cry–for ending a relationship she really wanted, for realizing the man she was falling in love with wasn't who she thought he was, and for her family. But more than any of it, Scarlett cried because she was so tired of making the wrong decisions and ending up alone.

An hour later, she forced herself to get up. It was still light out and even though the animal shelter was closed, Happy Tails wasn't and she often heard Christine talking about how hard the evenings were when all the dogs needed to be fed while she and Ed tried to sit down with their kids for dinner.

After quickly washing her face, Scarlett grabbed her purse and keys and walked out to her car. It was a short drive–less than ten minutes–but tonight it felt like it took forever. It wasn't until she was walking through the gate and surrounded by a pack of excited dogs that she felt herself relax.

"Scarlett!" Christine called out from her kitchen window. "We weren't expecting you tonight!"

Making her way toward the house, she shrugged. "I had a rough afternoon and thought a little dog therapy might help."

Christine gave her a sad smile. "Give me a minute, I just need to drain this pasta..."

Scarlett immediately shook her head. "You go and enjoy dinner with your family. Have these guys eaten yet?"

With a chuckle, she said, "Not yet. The day got away from me and I'm still trying to catch up."

"Then you go have a nice dinner. I've got this crew under control." And with a wave, she led the dogs over to the barn and began filling bowls with food and then turned to do another row of bowls with water. Once everyone was eating, Scarlett walked around and straightened up the doggie toys before grabbing a tote that was filled with tennis balls. Within minutes, she was playing an energetic game of fetch with twelve different dogs.

It was the perfect distraction and she felt lighter than she had all day.

But as the sun started to go down, she led everyone back to the barn and secured the gate so no one would escape before calling out a goodnight to Christine. She didn't want to engage in any kind of conversation and was relieved when her friend didn't push for it.

Once she was home, however, Scarlett really wished she had someone to talk to and weighed her options. Courtney would listen to her and undoubtedly tell her she overreacted. She could call one of her brothers. They had all been at the bar today while Mason was there. Although...it was her brother Dean who told her what happened so she didn't think she'd get anything new out of him and there was the possibility she'd have to share about her conversation with Mason.

And why she even had a conversation with Mason.

"Ugh...why can't life be simple?" she groaned, going into her kitchen and making herself a salad for dinner. Honestly, she loathed salads just on principle, but she just didn't have it in her to make anything more.

Maybe Courtney would bring something over...

Tossing the leafy greens in the trash, Scarlett grabbed her phone and sent an S.O.S. text to her friend.

**Help! Crappy day alert and need a girls' night. Bring food.**

**And wine.**

It was something they did for each other and while she had a good idea as to what Courtney's response was going to be to the whole thing, she still just needed a friend tonight. And there was no one better than Courtney.

**I have two bottles and I just called in the pizza to be delivered to your place. I'll pay you when I get there. Do we need ice cream too?**

Laughing, Scarlett studied the message and realized how lucky she was–even if the rest of her life was a mess, she still had the *best* best friend in the world.

**We always need ice cream. My freezer is stocked with it so we're good. Just drive over and maybe bring your jammies. It's going to be a long night.**

Thirty seconds later her phone dinged with an incoming text.

**Hang on, baby girl. I am on my way!!**

Feeling relieved, Scarlett put the phone down on the kitchen counter and walked into her room to put on her own jammies–which were basically a pair of boxers and an oversized t-shirt. Barefoot, she padded back into the kitchen and took out a couple of wine glasses, some paper plates, and a handful of napkins, then carried them into the living room. They would set up camp on the couch and take it from there.

And when Courtney walked in the door ten minutes later and hugged her, she let the rest of her tears fall.

# EIGHT

Maybe it was counterproductive, but for the better part of a week Mason spent way more time than he should have researching Tommy Flynn and his business. It didn't make sense. If he was continually getting behind on the bills and struggling, why not just admit defeat? Why was he putting the blame on Mason rather than accepting responsibility? And why wouldn't he be honest with his own family?

Although, if he pushed aside his own feelings of anger toward the situation, he could admit that pride probably had a lot to do with this. No man wants to admit to being a failure.

But "failure" really didn't fit Tommy either. It wasn't a title Mason would pin on him. After Hurricane Amelia hit Magnolia Sound, there were a lot of businesses that couldn't recover. There was no shame in it. And even if Mason didn't personally see any storm damage on the building, he also didn't see any new construction or repairs either.

Over and over and over he had played back the visit to The Mystic Magnolia and tried to think if he missed anything. Was there something more he should have said?

Something more he should have done? Had it been a mistake to go there with Richard? Should he have called and set up an appointment with Flynn rather than just showing up there?

It was enough to give him a damn headache. Hell, he'd had one ever since Scarlett had walked out the door. Even now as he rubbed his head and willed the pain away, he knew it was futile.

It was late on Sunday night and he was sitting alone on his back deck drinking a beer and missing Scarlett. He wanted to pick up the phone and talk to her, but he knew she needed time and, to be honest, so did he. The things she said to him hurt more than they should. Going into this relationship, he knew she was prejudiced toward him and his family, but he thought she'd moved on from it–thought he'd proved to her that she had been wrong about him. Just goes to show he didn't know her as well as he thought and maybe all of this was for the best. After all, if she thought so little of him, what was the point in trying to move forward with her?

*Because you really do care about her...*

Oh, yeah. That.

Not that it was doing him a whole hell of a lot of good right now. After a week of looking at business reports and sales reports from The Mystic Magnolia, he was no closer to figuring out where all the money went that his great-grandfather had loaned to Flynn and why the old guy was so hell-bent on holding on to a place that clearly wasn't making money. Sure there was always the sentimentality of it–he'd built the place and owned it for close to thirty years. But, as a businessman, couldn't he see it was time to throw in the towel? There was no shame in it, not really. Wouldn't it be better to walk away and not have to deal with all the stress and aggravation a floundering business was bound to cause him?

And the other thought that ran through his mind more than it should, why didn't he just close the business and sell the property? Surely Mason wasn't the only one to realize that was where the real money was. He was sure that any commercial developer–or a residential one–would love to have property here in Magnolia. It was a thriving beach community. Or...it would be again. Hopefully sooner rather than later. With so many homes and businesses that sustained damage after the storm, it might not seem like a good investment to buy property here just yet, but once everything was back on track it would be. And at that end of town there were endless possibilities of places that were needed to make it more desirable–more homes, more family-friendly businesses, a park...

Groaning, he took a pull of his beer, stared out at the ocean and wished Scarlett was there with him. He looked forward to their weekends and sitting out on the deck talking late into the night. What he wouldn't give to be able to talk to her about this. Not only because she was intelligent, but because she would challenge him and suggest things he might never think of. And if she weren't Tommy Flynn's granddaughter, she might even come up with something better than Mason ever could have imagined. He missed talking to her and hearing her laugh. He missed seeing her smile and hearing about her day. He missed sleeping beside her and holding her all night long.

Letting out a long breath, he forced himself to accept the fact that it didn't matter how much he missed her. They were through. The only positive thing he could find in the whole damn situation is that they had gone for years without running into each other before and hopefully that's the way it would be now.

Only...he wanted to see her–wanted to make sure she was okay. If her grandfather came clean and told the family why he had to let the business go, maybe...

Shaking his head, he stood and walked back into the house. It didn't matter. Even if Tommy explained everything to his family it wouldn't change anything. If Scarlett knew the truth and came to him to apologize, he'd accept it, but they couldn't go back. It wouldn't be right and in the back of his mind he knew he'd always be wondering if she were being honest with him about her feelings or if she were still holding onto her resentment.

It would be a shitty way to live.

Closing the French doors behind him, Mason shut off the lights and made sure the front door was locked before he went into his bedroom and stripped down to his boxers. He went through the motions of brushing his teeth, tossing his laundry in the hamper, and basically puttering around hoping to pass the time. Ultimately, he knew his only option was to go to sleep. Once he was in bed, however, he knew he wasn't tired but he also knew he couldn't stand sitting alone obsessing about what a mess his life was at the moment.

It was too late to call anyone, too late to text anyone, his only option was to watch a little TV and hope he could clear his mind enough to go to sleep. With a weary sigh, he reached for the remote and did his best to get comfortable against the stack of pillows. He positioned himself in the middle of the bed because...well...he really hated sleeping alone now. It was crazy how a few short weeks had done this to him, but...there it was.

Netflix was already queued up and he knew instantly he was going to go to *Stranger Things*. It certainly wouldn't help him not to think about Scarlett, but maybe he was looking at it all wrong. Maybe it wasn't about not thinking about her. Maybe it was about finding a way to feel closer to her.

And that was what finally helped him fall asleep.

* * *

"SOMETHING SMELLS GOOD. What's the occasion?"

Scarlett smiled as her father leaned in and kissed her on the cheek. "No occasion. It's just been too long since we had a nice family dinner together."

It wasn't a total lie…

"Don't we usually do this sort of thing on a Sunday?" Dominic Jones asked. He was covered in engine grease and a little stinky, but his big blue eyes showed how much he loved and appreciated what she was doing.

"It's not as easy getting everyone together as it used to be," she explained. "I figured a Monday night wouldn't be too much of a hardship on anyone. Now go wash up so I can get this lasagna in the oven."

He was about to walk out of the kitchen when he turned back to his only daughter and smiled. "Your mom always made a lasagna when everyone came over for dinner."

Scarlett heard the emotion in his voice and although she didn't personally remember this was her mother's thing, her father and brothers talked about it enough that she knew it. "I thought everyone would like it," she said softly. "Now go wash up. The guys will be here any minute."

Once he was out of the room, she quickly finished assembling the lasagna–two pans worth–and placed them in the oven. She had just finished wiping down the counter when her brother Dean came through the front door. He was six years older than Scarlett–the oldest of her brothers– and he was the most levelheaded out of the bunch. Most of the time she considered him to be like her second father because he was always looking out for everyone.

"Hey, squirt," he said, walking into the kitchen and giving her a bear hug. He stopped and sniffed the air. "Lasagna?"

Pulling back, she smiled. "Yup. Used mom's recipe and everything."

He leaned against the counter once she moved away. Crossing his arms, he narrowed his gaze at her. "What's going on?"

She busied herself setting the table. "What do you mean?"

"Why the sudden need for a family dinner? And why go through all the trouble with lasagna? We usually just grill some burgers."

Shrugging, she placed the last plate on the table. "I thought this would be nice. We haven't had Gramps over in a while and I thought he'd like this."

At first, all Dean did was nod but Scarlett wasn't fooled. He always knew when she was lying or when something was afoot. It was just a matter of time before he put it all together.

"This is about the bar," he stated. It wasn't a question.

Okay, maybe it was better to talk to him alone before everyone got there. "Kind of," she admitted.

"Scarlett, don't do this. It's a sensitive subject."

"We have to find a way to help him, Dean!" she cried. "We can't let some greedy little rich kid put Gramps out of business!"

And yeah, that was still how she felt about Mason. A

week later and just the thought of him had her feeling full of rage. It was awful. But if she held on to her anger, it was easier. She didn't want to feel sympathy for him and couldn't allow herself to think that he had been telling her the truth.

Or think about how much she missed him.

"Okay, dramatic much?" he teased, pushing away from the cabinets and helping himself to a bottle of water from the fridge. "Gramps isn't talking too much about it. I don't know what you think he's going to say tonight, but I wouldn't get my hopes up if I were you."

In general, her grandfather was a man of few words but she was hoping to sweet-talk him into sharing with her what exactly was going on and how they all could help.

"I just think we can all pull together and help him pay off this loan," she explained. "I know I've got some money saved and I'm sure you and the guys do. We could make it a family business."

Dean choked on the water and began to cough furiously. When he finally calmed down, he looked at her as if she were crazy. "Do you even hear yourself?"

"Well..."

"Scarlett, the last thing I want to do is invest in a bar. I've got a job already and if I'm going to invest, it's going to be in the garage with Dad."

"I get it, but..."

"And you know Dad puts every extra dime he has either in the shop for improvements or into his retirement fund. You can't ask him to take away from that."

"Okay, but..."

"And don't even get me started on Hunter and Kyle," Dean went on. "They both have enough on their plates. Hunter's salary with the fire department isn't much. And even though he and Melissa broke up, he's still got a baby to take care of and support!"

Right. Her brother and his ex had a nine-month old baby. No one in the family ever got along with Melissa and they all thought it was mistake for them to be having a baby from the get-go, but...here they were. So it would be really inappropriate for her to approach him about helping Gramps with the bar right now.

Oblivious to her inner dialogue, Dean continued. "Kyle's finally settled on a career in construction working with Jake Summerford over at Coleman Construction."

"What?" she cried. "So he's working for the enemy? For the family who is essentially stealing the bar away from Gramps?"

Chuckling, Dean shook his head. "I thought it was the greedy rich kid doing that." He reached over and ruffled her hair the way he used to when she was a little girl. "Face it, Scar, there isn't a whole lot we can do. Gramps got himself into this and he must know what he's doing."

"But that's just it!" she countered. "I don't think he does! I think whatever deal he made with Ezekiel Coleman wasn't on the up and up! We need to see whatever contract there was because I'm telling you, it can't be right! There's no way Gramps would have accepted the kind of terms where he would lose the business! It's just not possible!"

The smile he gave her was filled with pity and she hated it. At times like this she had to fight the urge to punch him and run to her room. But she was an adult now and that wasn't an option.

She took a few minutes to get her emotions under control. "There has to be something we can do," she said dejectedly. "I can't bear the thought of him losing his livelihood."

Before her brother could respond, the man in question walked in followed by her other two brothers. Dean gave her a reassuring smile and a shrug before walking over to greet everyone. Within minutes, the house was filled with loud voices and laughter and Scarlett did her best to go with the flow and not get anyone riled up before dinner.

Her father was sitting in the living room listening to Hunter talk about some big fire in the next town over when her grandfather came strolling into the kitchen. He took a whiff of the air and smiled. "Pretty as an angel and you cook like a dream. You're going to make some lucky man very happy one day," he said in a way only a grandfather could get away with. He came in close and hugged her. "How are you doing, little miss?"

It was a nickname he'd given her years ago and it always made her smile. "I'm doing okay," she said and realized a little too late just how sad she sounded when she said it.

He leveled her with a look. "Want to try that again?"

She waved him off and turned to check on dinner. "I'm fine, Gramps. How about you? I hope you brought your appetite!" Everything was cooking as it should and when she turned around to face him again, he was still staring at her. "What?"

Most people were intimidated by Tommy Flynn–especially when he stared them down–but he never tried that tactic with his grandkids. The only way she could describe his look was mildly concerned. "I think something's going on. You call this family dinner, make the one dish you know has the most sentimental meaning to us all, and you look sad and like you haven't slept in a few nights. So tell me again, how are you doing?"

And for some reason, everything came tumbling out.

Well, almost everything.

"I was dating a guy I really liked and saw maybe having a future with," she said, hating the tremble in her voice. "But it turns out he wasn't who I thought he was. Actually, he was exactly who I thought he was before we started dating. I just thought he had changed or that I was wrong about him." With a groan, she sat down at the kitchen table and shook her head. "I can't believe I was so wrong. Or...so right. Depending how you look at it."

Pulling up a chair beside her, he took one of her hands in his. "So what did this boy do, huh?"

Ugh...her and her big mouth.

"Let's just say he comes from a privileged family and it turns out he's just like them."

"That's not really an answer, little miss."

"Gramps..."

"Did he hurt you?" he asked gently.

"Physically? No. But...I'm hurt because of what he's doing. He's trying to hurt someone who means a lot to me." Pausing, she groaned. "And the thing is, I knew from the get-go we were all wrong for each other. I mean, he's from this big-time prominent family here in town and totally out of my league. I should have just kept my distance."

"That's how it works sometimes. Just because..."

"I've known him almost my entire life! It's not like we were friends or even ran in the same circles, but we knew each other enough so it wasn't weird when we started hanging out together," she went on, talking more to herself than anything. "And here's the thing–I really liked him! Trusted him! I opened up to him more than I ever have with anyone else and I thought he'd done the same with me." She paused and shook her head again. "But it was all a lie. This is how the big shots in this town stay on top, I guess. I just hate how I was so wrong about him. I know it's business and

I don't know all the particulars, but I didn't think Mason would ever..." She gasped and quickly pulled her hand from his as she jumped to her feet. "Um...why don't you tell the boys dinner's just about ready? I'm going to pull the lasagna from the oven."

"Scarlett," he began and she could hear him walking over to her. "I think we should talk."

It's what she wanted more than anything. Tossing the oven mitt aside, she was about to speak when Kyle walked into the kitchen.

"For the love of it, Scarlett, when is this dinner going to be ready? I've been on the go all afternoon and skipped lunch!"

Giving her grandfather a small smile, he nodded in understanding. Turning to Kyle, she said, "I was just telling Gramps everything is ready. I'm pulling the pans out now."

"Yes!" Kyle cried out happily. "Guys! C'mon! Dinner's ready!"

There was no time for any one-on-one talks because there were easily three different conversations going on at any given time. It was loud and boisterous and honestly, it was exactly what she loved most about occasions like this. She could have cursed herself for revealing too much to her grandfather, but maybe it wasn't going to be a bad thing. If it opened the door to the conversation she wanted to have, then that was a good thing, right?

Still, she wished her father and brothers were as concerned as she was.

By the time dinner was done, Scarlett was feeling more than a little dejected. No one brought up the situation and now she felt foolish about bringing it up. So where did that leave her? Where did it leave Gramps?

"I think you boys should clean up since Scarlett cooked for us," Gramps said as he stood and stretched.

"Good plan," Dominic said. "You boys haven't been on dish duty in a long time."

"Nuh-uh," Gramps said. "I meant all of you. I'm taking my best girl here out to sit on the porch swing for a little visit. You call us when coffee's ready and you have dessert out."

Four pairs of wide eyes stared at him and Scarlett had to stifle a chuckle. Luckily, no one argued and a minute later, she was stepping out onto the porch with her grandfather right behind her. They sat down on the old porch swing and her nerves started to kick in. She had a feeling their conversation wasn't so much going to be about what he was going to do about the bar as it was going to be about her and Mason.

Damn her and her big mouth.

"Do you remember how many afternoons we spent out here on this swing?" he asked once they were seated.

"Too many to count," Scarlett replied, resting her head on his shoulder.

"The summer your mom died, we sat out here every afternoon," he said solemnly. "I would hold your hand and tell you about heaven. We would talk about all the beautiful flowers your mom was planting with the angels and how she would be surrounded by butterflies. Do you remember?"

Tears stung her eyes because she remembered it like it was yesterday. Unable to speak, she simply nodded.

"As you got older, the conversations would change. We talked about school, how your brothers annoyed you," he added with amusement. "You would tell me about your friends or about all the dogs you were going to adopt when you were older."

Another nod.

"We never talked about boys." It was the truth. "At the time, I was happy about it, but I'd be lying if I said I wasn't curious about this relationship you're in with Mason Bishop."

To her credit, she didn't move, gasp, or try to deny it.

"I'm gonna say something," he went on. "And I'm only going to say this once." He paused. "I'm disappointed in you."

Straightening, Scarlett looked at him in disbelief. "What?"

He nodded. "You heard me." His expression was mild–like he didn't just nearly break her heart.

"How can you say that?"

Without looking at her, Tommy gave the swing a little push with his leg. "I don't believe you were raised to be someone who should feel inferior to anyone," he said. "The fact that you feel this way about Mason and his family really disappoints me."

"But...you know as well as I do that everyone in this town looks up to them!" she argued. "They're like...in a class all their own and no one can compete with them!"

Shaking his head, he looked over at her. "That's where you're wrong. There are lots of hard-working people in this town with just as much money as the Bishops. And for the most part, they're all nice people too. Now, I will admit his mother is a little too uppity for my taste, but she's basically harmless. On the flip side, she's done a lot for this town." He shrugged. "Same with old Zeke."

Okay, here was her opening...

Twisting in the seat to face him, she asked, "Gramps, how can you say that? Isn't it because of Zeke that you're losing the bar?"

His expression hardened in the blink of an eye. "That's none of your business, Scarlett, and I'm not going to discuss it with you."

"But..."

"It has nothing to do with you!" he snapped and his tone surprised her. She was about to mention how it had a little something to do with her—especially because it was the main reason she ended things with Mason—but decided to keep that to herself. "You don't know anything about my deal with Zeke."

"I would if you would explain it to me!" she cried, shocked at her own need to talk back to him. She was so nervous at her own outburst that she felt sick to her stomach and started to shake.

And she willed her dinner to stay put.

"Scarlett..."

"From where we're all standing, it seems like you got screwed! How do you expect us to just stand back and let that happen?"

"The way I see it, it has nothing to do with any of you. I made the deal and I'll handle the consequences," he said, seeming to relax a little. "I don't need anyone fighting my battles for me, little miss. And you shouldn't let what's going on with me interfere with your life."

"Gramps..."

"Coffee's ready," Kyle said, sticking his head out the door. Scarlett wanted to scream at him to go away but her grandfather was already up and heading for the front door.

When they joined the rest of the family back in the kitchen, she smelled the coffee and the apple pie one of her brothers had heated up and her stomach seemed to roll. Neither smell ever bothered her but lately, everything seemed to make her queasy. Most of the time she could breathe through it, but as soon as she sat down and had a mug of coffee in her hands, she said, "Nope" and ran for the bathroom.

By the time she rejoined her family, she could safely say there wasn't one bit of her lunch or dinner left inside her. She cautiously moved through the kitchen and was relieved when her father placed a cup of tea in her hands.

"You okay?" he asked.

With a weak nod, she took a sip of the tea. "So weird. I guess I overate."

"Isn't there a stomach bug going around?" Hunter asked. "A couple of guys on the squad were down with it last week or something. Maybe it's that."

"Hopefully it's only a twenty-four-hour thing," she murmured, but she had a strong feeling it was anything but.

"Why don't you sleep here tonight," her father suggested, and she was so worn out that she agreed. And with nothing more than a small wave, she got up and went to her old room where she curled up in bed and promptly fell asleep.

* * *

"WHILE WE THINK a new park would be a great thing for the town, Mason, now just isn't the time for a project like that. Not with all the rebuilding that still needs to be done," George Ellis, his boss, explained. "I love what you're thinking but..."

"Yeah, I get it," he replied dejectedly. "That part of town needs help, George. It's always been a bit of an eyesore, but with a little attention, I think we could draw more businesses down that way." He began to fidget with the files on his desk when George stopped him.

"Okay, now...let's think about that for a minute. So your plan isn't just about a park," he stated. "You're talking about a revitalization of the north part of town."

It wasn't something Mason had thought about initially, but after actually going there last week and looking around, the idea had taken root. "There are already several small businesses down that way that are struggling–mainly because the majority of the area is a little...undesirable."

George nodded.

"I think if we start with something small–like the park– it will show the town is taking an interest in the area. Maybe we can offer some incentives to new businesses willing to move that way."

"I'm not sure we're ready for that, but I like where you're going." He paused. "There's...what...a garage, an auto parts store, a bar, and...what else?"

"Not much else, I'm afraid. There's a gas station with a convenience store but I think that's it. If we could find a way to get another couple of eateries down there, clean up the common areas and maybe even freshen up what's there already, I think it would make a world of difference. We can make it a community outreach thing–get the people out to volunteer to help with painting, power washing, and even the landscaping. We've put so much focus here on the main strip in town that we're forgetting it's not the only part of Magnolia that needs help."

George studied him hard for a moment. "I'm going to need to think on this. If you can get the community on board on the cleanup and see what kind of interest we can spark, then we'll form a committee to start planning. How does that sound?" He stood and held out a hand to Mason.

Standing, Mason shook it and smiled. "Sounds like a great way to start. And don't worry, George, I think you're going to be surprised at what we can accomplish. The north end of town deserves our attention just as much as the central part right here."

His boss was almost out the door when he turned around. "You know, Mason, I'm really impressed with you."

"Thank you, sir. I appreciate the compliment."

But George still didn't leave. "I want you to know it's nice to see someone young like you taking an interest in something like this." He chuckled softly and shook his head. "When you were hired, I have to admit I figured you'd choose projects that were a little more...shall we say...easy."

Unable to hide his frown, he asked, "Meaning?"

"Well, I've been friends with your parents for a long time and most of the projects and causes they get behind benefit them in one shape or form." He paused. "No offense."

"None taken," he replied stiffly, mainly because he knew exactly what George meant. His parents and most of their friends put on a good show about taking care of the community, but a lot of it was on a very superficial level. They had never been ones to get their hands dirty. He, on the other hand, was more than willing to.

And not just to prove he was nothing like them.

"I particularly like your addition of making a section of the park a dog park," George said, a little off-topic. "My wife and I have several dogs and we often wondered what it would be like to take them someplace where they could play with other dogs." Another pause. "I really like the way you're thinking outside of the Magnolia Sound box, Mason. And I look forward to seeing you do great things."

"Thanks, George."

Once his boss was gone, Mason sank down in his chair and wondered where he could possibly begin. He could put out the word on social media about a community clean up day, but he figured he should probably speak to the business owners first. Hell, he should probably put a small committee together of his own first to help coordinate everything that was going to need to be done.

Feeling energized, he sent out an email to several people in his department to gauge their interest in helping out. Once that was done, he made a plan to reach out to his family–primarily his sisters and cousins–to see if they wanted to join in and get involved. Sam had a landscaping business so maybe he wouldn't mind bringing some of his equipment down to help clear some of the overgrown property. His cousin Mallory's fiancé was in construction and maybe he could give a hand along the same lines with equipment and maybe even consulting on any building repairs that might need to be done on the existing businesses–or even just offer advice on what could be done to freshen up the exteriors.

As for his sisters...neither were skilled in the heavy labor part, but he knew that between the two of them, they knew a ton of people and could help get the word out.

So could a social media manager and maybe that was the kind of thing he could use to get Scarlett to talk to him. Hell, he just wanted to see her and make sure she was okay. He could handle her not wanting to date him any more–sort of–but he knew he wouldn't be able to move on until they at least saw each other one more time and tried to talk.

Even if it wasn't about them.

With a sigh, he leaned back in his chair and raked his hands through his hair. It wasn't a perfect plan by any means, but...it's all he had right now. And he'd reach out to her professionally–through her website and not via text–so maybe that would work in his favor. He was just about to do that when a knock on his office door had him looking up.

And there stood Tommy Flynn–looking all kinds of intimidating.

Mason started to sweat.

"I want to talk to you, Bishop," he said sternly.

And with little more than a nod, Mason watched as the older man stepped into his office and closed the door behind him.

# NINE

Several thoughts ran through Mason's mind at once.

First, he should call George back into his office. Second, why didn't someone at the front desk alert him that Flynn was here? And lastly, why did the old guy have to close the door?

Doing his best to appear calm, he smiled. "Won't you have a seat, Mr. Flynn?" With nothing more than a curt nod, he did and Mason quickly followed suit. Should he call Richard and ask him to drive over? He had no idea! But, once again, he opted to force himself to look calm. "What can I do for you today?"

The older man stared at him for so long that Mason started to squirm. And then he finally spoke. "I came here today to discuss something very specific with you," he began. "But after hearing your conversation with your supervisor, I've had to reconsider."

"Oh?"

More awkward silence.

Leaning forward slightly in his chair, his gaze narrowed at Mason. "Here's the thing. I heard what you said about the north end of town. Was that true or were you blowing smoke up the old guy's ass?"

"Wait, were you eavesdropping on our conversation?" he asked incredulously.

Tommy simply shrugged. "Let's just say I was waiting my turn to see you and neither of you talk all that quietly."

With his curiosity piqued, Mason had to ask, "What did you originally want to talk to me about?"

"We'll get to that, but first I want to know if you were being honest about the north end. And with the door closed, no one will hear you if you admit to lying."

Frowning, Mason didn't appreciate the accusation, but he also wasn't looking to fight with the guy. "I wasn't lying," he said confidently. "I had a plan for what I wanted to do with some of the property in that area and after visiting with you, I realized there was so much more that needed to be done."

All Tommy did was nod and Mason realized Mr. Flynn wasn't going to communicate in a way he understood and he had no choice but to wait.

After a minute, Tommy relaxed a bit and even offered a small smile. "Your great-grandfather was a good man," he started. "He used to come into the bar once a week since the first week we opened." With a small chuckle, he went on. "Zeke used to enjoy a good whiskey and some of my wife's homemade clam chowder."

Mason arched a brow at that.

"Yeah, back in the beginning, we were more of a tavern where you could eat. My wife passed after we had only been in business for two years." He paused and shook his head, studying his hands which were folded in his lap. "I lost my wife and daughter young, to two different ailments. My wife to an aneurysm and my daughter to cancer."

Unsure of what to say, he murmured "I'm sorry" and waited for whatever else he was going to share.

"The plan was always to make it more of an eatery than a bar," he continued. "But once she was gone...I honestly didn't know how to do it. For a lot of years, business was good. My place was where the locals could come and relax without dealing with the tourist crowd. I enjoyed offering that to them. But people move away or long to try something new..." He shrugged. "Zeke bailed me out back in 2000 with a small loan to do some updates around the place. It was more like he sent tradesmen out to the bar to do the work and he would pay them." He looked up at Mason. "They were all guys who worked construction with Zeke–a plumber, an electrician, a carpenter, that sort of thing."

Mason nodded and knew it was the kind of thing his great-grandfather had done for many people. It was the first time, however, that he was hearing about it firsthand like this.

After letting out a long breath, he met Mason's gaze. "Five years ago, I got into a bit of trouble. Gambling." After another brief pause, he went on. "I started going on weekend trips with friends to the local casinos..."

"I didn't know there were any local."

"Well, by local I mean here in the state."

"Ah...okay. And..."

"And I got myself into a lot of debt and couldn't seem to quit. Even though we weren't close friends, Zeke noticed something was going on–I was around less and less and looked stressed. So he came in one night, sat me down and asked me flat out what was going on. By that point I was drowning in debt and at my breaking point. I was too embarrassed to tell my family, but Zeke had a way of getting you to talk. I spilled my guts to him that night and he told me he'd help me, but I had to help myself first."

"What do you mean?"

"I had to get help–go to Gamblers Anonymous and quit going to the casinos. He told me if I did that, he'd loan me the money to get the bar back on track."

Now he knew he could finally get some answers! "Mr. Flynn, I don't understand how it went from him loaning you money to get you out of debt to him owning the bar and leaving it to me. It doesn't make sense."

"Well..." he began, rubbing the back of his neck, "I was a little arrogant and said some stupid things."

"Like...?"

"Like...how I needed our agreement to be something that would force me to stay on the straight and narrow. I had it put in our contract that if I ever gambled again, I would lose the bar to him."

"But...that's crazy! I can't believe my great-grandfather would have agreed to something like that!"

"He didn't want to, but I pushed," he said with a mirthless laugh. "Man, did I push." He shook his head. "Needless to say, within a year I was back at the blackjack tables and Zeke found out. I had resigned myself to losing the bar."

"So what happened?"

With a crooked smile he replied, "He gave me another chance."

Mason sagged back against his chair, unable to believe what he was hearing. "How?"

"He let me resume making payments on the loan and once it was paid off, the bar would go back in my name."

"But...?"

"But it had to be before he died, otherwise..."

"It would go to one of his heirs," Mason finished for him. "Well...shit."

"Exactly."

They sat in silence for several minutes before Mason could even begin to speak. "You realize this isn't my fault, right? I honestly didn't know about this agreement you had with him."

"I know."

"Then why were you so pissed at me when I came to the bar?" he demanded. "If you knew this was coming and you knew I had nothing to do with it, why go off on me?"

"Honestly? Because I'm mad at myself. Things never should have gotten to this point. I should have paid Zeke what he was owed and I should have honored my word and never gambled again. It's not you I'm mad at," he said solemnly. "I'm mad at myself."

Mason wanted to add that he was mad at him too but thought it would be counterproductive.

"Where does that leave us, Mr. Flynn?"

He was quiet for so long that Mason started to get uncomfortable again. "The property would be very useful to you if this revitalization of the north end happens," he said, holding Mason's gaze.

Why deny it? With a nod he agreed. "Yes, it would."

"So my earlier question still stands—were you telling the truth about your plans for that part of town? Are you seriously going to see about getting some new businesses down that way and helping the existing ones?"

"I am," he replied firmly. "I'm a man of my word, Mr. Flynn."

"That's good to know."

"Can I ask you something?"

"Certainly."

"What are your plans now?"

"You mean since losing the bar to you?" There was no malice in his tone, but the statement still made Mason feel bad.

"Um...yes."

"I'm not sure," he replied. "But I'd be interested in perhaps working with you on the revitalization of the north end."

That surprised Mason more than anything else that had been said about this entire situation. "Seriously?"

Nodding, Flynn added, "I'm not stupid, Mason. I knew it was only a matter of time before this day came. And honestly, I held on to the bar more because it was something my wife wanted. It was a connection to her. Unfortunately, I never could turn it into the kind of place she always envisioned."

"Other than an eatery, what did she want?" he asked, mildly curious as ideas began to come to mind.

"She saw it more of a family place–you know, where you could sit in some booths with the kids, but where you could also have a bar for those who just wanted to come in for a drink." He shrugged. "I'm certainly no chef. I'm more comfortable behind the bar. Now we do just the basics for food–burgers, a few sandwiches, and fries–and even I know they're not very good. The only guys who eat there are older guys who can't cook for themselves or my grandsons. And they only come around so they can eat for free," he said with a wink.

It was on the tip of his tongue to ask if Scarlett ever ate there, but...he knew that would be a little suspicious and it was probably for the best that no one in her family ever knew they had dated.

"What if you could turn it into the kind of place your

wife wanted," Mason said carefully, still unsure of why he was even bringing it up.

"Son, that would mean ripping the place down to the studs, rebuilding, rebranding, and bringing in someone who understands restaurants to handle the kitchen. I could still manage the place, but I'm getting old and the restaurant business is a young man's game."

Now the wheels in his mind were really spinning. "If there were someone who could do that–could run the kitchen while you were...say...the general manager, would that be something you'd be interested in?"

Tommy's eyes narrowed at him. "Why are we even talking about this? Seems to me it would be a lot more lucrative for you to let me walk away and sell the property to someone else."

"Let's just say I was maybe thinking a little too inside the box up until now," Mason said, a small grin crossing his face.

"And why the sudden change of heart?"

He shrugged. "I spent some time recently with someone who made me realize I shouldn't let other people dictate my life to me. Taking the inheritance, selling the property... that's the exact sort of thing my family would expect from me. Actually, as soon as the will was read, my parents immediately started making arrangements for me to speak to a realtor so I could list the property."

"And why didn't you?"

"For starters, I wanted to do it in my own time," he explained. "And then...then I got the idea for the park and how it would work to my advantage to wait to sell."

"So...this person who told you not to let other people dictate your life...what do they think you should do?"

Now it was Mason's turn to let out a mirthless laugh.

"That is a long story and one I don't really want to get into. Suffice it to say they weren't in agreement with my original plans."

"Then by changing your mind, isn't that just someone else dictating to you?"

For a moment that gave him pause. Was it? Was he only rethinking his plans because of Scarlett? He instantly pushed the thought aside. His ideas about the north end of town started after going there and seeing it for himself. Maybe she'd appreciate what he was doing or maybe she wouldn't. At this rate, it didn't matter. They were done. She'd made her feelings very clear.

With a sad smile, he said, "No. Not really. And it doesn't really matter anymore."

Tommy gave him a sympathetic look. "That's too bad. I'm sorry."

"It happens, right?" He was going for a light tone, but emotion had him by the throat. It took him a minute before he could talk again. "Sorry."

"So this is...uh...new, huh?"

Ugh. Did he really want to talk relationships right now? And with Scarlett's grandfather who had no idea it was his granddaughter they were talking about?

"Yes," he replied and then quickly changed the subject. "Look, I can't guarantee anything right now. If you were interested in keeping the bar and doing the updates and renovations, I do know someone with knowledge of the restaurant business. And as for the conversation you overheard, it was the first one I had on the subject. But as soon as I know something, Mr. Flynn, I'd be more than happy to sit down and talk with you about it."

Standing, Tommy smiled down at him. "Your great-grandfather would be very proud, Mason. He loved this town more than anyone else and I know he'd be thrilled to see what you're trying to do."

Mason came to his feet. "Thank you. I appreciate that."

"I think we'll be seeing a lot more of each other. I'd like it if you could maybe come down to the bar for lunch one day next week so we can talk some more about where we realistically see things going."

"I'd like that very much, sir."

They shook hands. "And call me Tommy. That's what all my friends do." And with a nod, he turned and walked out of the office.

* * *

"YOU LOOK LIKE HAMMERED SHIT."

Groaning, Scarlett curled back up on her sofa and ignored her best friend's poor excuse of a greeting. "It's good to see you too."

Sitting on the coffee table, Courtney studied her. "Scar, this can't still be from nerves. You yelled at your grandfather. So what? The sky didn't fall and Tommy wouldn't hold a grudge–especially not against you."

"There's a stomach bug going around. Hunter told me."

Pulling back slightly, Courtney looked around nervously. "Maybe I should go..."

"Too late," Scarlett murmured. "You've already breathed the air. Deal with it."

"But I don't want to be sick!" she whined as she fought a smile. "Can you eat anything? Want me to make you some soup or something?"

"No, it's okay. My brother brought some over earlier."

Courtney straightened and immediately began fidgeting

with her hair. "Oh...um...really? Which, uh...which brother?"

Frowning at how weird her friend was acting, Scarlett said, "Dean. Why?"

Looking a little wide-eyed, Courtney replied, "No reason. Just curious." She jumped to her feet. "But um...you should probably rest."

"Just knock it off, will you?" Scarlett said wearily.

Sitting back down on the coffee table, Courtney studied her. "Okay, I'm totally not trying to be a drama queen or to freak you out, but...have you thought about this...you know...not being a stomach virus?"

Scarlett wasn't going to pretend that she didn't know what she was talking about. "I have."

"And?"

"And...I'm trying not to think about it. It would...oh, God...it would be so incredibly awkward! How would I even tell Mason?"

They were both quiet for a moment. "Well, for starters, we'd order an everything pizza to eat while we discuss how you'll do it. Then, we'd have to eat at least a gallon of cookies and cream ice cream while I convince you that you can say and do all the things we discussed."

"You do realize that just the thought of food right now makes me want to vomit, right?"

Waving her off, Courtney continued. "We'd sit on the couch with our hands on our bellies because we ate too much–even though we'd secretly be thinking how we should have made brownies to go with the ice cream."

"In other words, our usual."

Laughing, Courtney agreed. "Sure. Our usual, just on steroids. We could totally do that." She went quiet for a moment before letting out a long breath. "You know you need to get a legit answer to that, right?"

Unfortunately, she did.

"I know."

Another long sigh. "Okay, how about I run to the drug store and get a test? I'll be right here with you and...you know...at least you'll know, right?"

A wave of nausea washed over her at the thought of that, but if anything, Scarlett was a realist. Squeezing her eyes shut, she said, "Just go and do it before I chicken out!"

Courtney was up and running out the door and promising to be back in a jiffy. It didn't matter how fast she returned. Scarlett knew she wasn't mentally prepared for any of it. The night the condom broke she and Mason had talked about all the what ifs until she thought she'd lose her mind. But the reality of it? Um...yeah. It was nothing like she imagined. They had talked about it like they would be calm and practical, but there was nothing calm or practical about the way she was feeling right now. And what was worse, she had no idea if Mason would either.

Probably not.

Not after the way she lashed out at him when she last saw him.

Damn her and her big mouth.

With her eyes still closed, she willed herself to try to relax until Courtney got back. She was almost asleep when she heard the front door open and her friend coming toward her. Forcing herself to sit up, she sighed.

Without a word, Courtney held out the bag and Scarlett took and walked to her bathroom like someone would walk to their execution.

And ten minutes later, she repeated the walk–but this time Courtney was right there beside her holding her hand.

"I don't want to look," Scarlett whined and hated how she sounded. "Can't we just say it's the stomach bug and move on?"

Hugging her close, Courtney rested her head on Scarlett's shoulder. "We could, but I have a feeling we'd just be doing this again next week."

"Dammit." She paused. "Can you look?"

"Dude, you peed on that stick. I'm not touching it."

Rolling her eyes, Scarlett straightened and knew what she had to do. "It's like ripping off a Band-Aid, right?"

"Yup."

Looking over her shoulder, she saw her BFF looking just as nervous as she did, and for some reason, it made her feel better. Letting out a long breath, she took a step toward her vanity and looked down.

Pregnant.

Without conscious thought, her hand went to her stomach as she stared down at the words on the stick until they blurred. Courtney came to stand beside her and they stayed like that for several minutes. Tears stung Scarlett's eyes and she finally looked away. "Okay...now what?"

Wrapping one arm around her shoulders, Courtney led them from the bathroom. "First, we leave the bathroom. Then...we maybe go up to the urgent care and see if they can give you something for the nausea until you can get in to see your doctor."

Scarlett nodded. "Okay."

"Then...we figure out how to get you to eat without vomiting so we can stay up all night and talk about how you're going to tell Mason he's going to be a daddy."

And just like that, she knew she was going to be sick again. Pushing away from Courtney, she made the short run back to the bathroom.

Once she was done, she did her best to freshen up. On the other side of the door, she could hear Courtney cleaning the place up. She was a bit of a neat freak and as much as she would normally be teasing her for it, right now she appreciated it. For almost a week she had been too tired and too sick to do just about anything. Her laundry was piled high and so was the kitchen sink with dirty dishes. It was starting to make her crazy but any time she got up to try to do anything, she would start to feel dizzy and queasy and needed to lie down.

Opting to skip looking in the mirror for fear of scaring herself, Scarlett ran a brush through her hair and walked back out into the living room where she found Courtney wiping down the coffee table. In the short time she'd been in her bedroom, Courtney wiped down everything, picked up the trash and sprayed the place with disinfectant.

And the smell was nauseating.

"Uh-oh...you're looking a little green again," she said, gently grasping her shoulders. "Do you need to run to the bathroom or is it safe to get you into the car?"

It took a few minutes before she could answer with any certainty. "The car. Let's get this over with. I need some of that anti-nausea stuff so I can function like a normal person."

Together they walked out to the car and fifteen minutes later they were sitting in the waiting room of the local urgent care.

It took an hour, but after a test to confirm her pregnancy and an IV to help her dehydration, they were in Courtney's car and on their way back to Scarlett's.

"I'll drop you off at your place and then go pick up the prescription for you."

"Thanks," she replied distractedly.

"Want me to pick up something for dinner on the way back?"

She shrugged. "Only if you're hungry. I still feel too iffy."

Courtney sighed. "I get it, Scar, but you are going to have to try to eat. That's really important."

Now wasn't the time to point out how much she'd love to eat, and how her body was rejecting it all. "I could go for some egg drop soup," she said wearily. "If you don't mind Chinese takeout."

As if sensing she wasn't really in the mood to talk, the rest of the drive was made in silence. Back at the house, Scarlett went in alone and struggled with whether or not she should call Mason right now and just get it over with, or if she needed some time to come to grips with everything herself.

"Come to grips first," she murmured, sitting down on the sofa. "Look at what happened the last time you spoke to him without thinking things through first."

Yeah. That was going to be a big hurdle for her to overcome.

With her head thrown back against the cushions, she closed her eyes and wondered–not for the first time–what she was going to do.

In a perfect world, she and Mason would still be together. He would have been the one walking into the bathroom with her, holding her hand and telling her everything was going to be okay.

Not that Courtney didn't do a stellar job, but...still.

They would be the ones sitting down to eat Chinese food and talking about how it was all going to be all right– how they were unconventional and how it wasn't weird since they'd known each other since grade school. Then he'd pull her in close, kiss her on the top of her head, and talk about what awesome parents they were going to be right before he told her he loved her.

Tears stung her eyes and her heart ached at how much she wanted that scenario to be a reality.

*Who says it won't?*

Sadly, Scarlett was a realist and there wasn't anything that had ever happened in her life to make her believe she could have something so amazing happen to her. Things like that...they just didn't. She was the girl who lost her mother too soon. The girl who became a tomboy because she was raised by a group of men. The girl who was a closet girly-girl because she was too scared to show another side of herself.

And the girl who let the boy get away...

With a groan, she forced herself to get up off the couch and get drinks and plates and silverware for dinner. It was mindless work, but it was a distraction from her sad thoughts.

Once she was done, she wandered around the house, starting up her laundry and continuing the cleanup Courtney began earlier. The sound of her phone ringing startled her and she was surprised to see her brother Dean's name on the screen. She'd already talked to him today—and every day since she got sick. What could he possibly want now?

"Hey," she said, a little breathless. "What's up?"

"Have you seen Courtney?"

That was...not what she was expecting. "Yeah, why?"

"I just ran into her at the drug store and she was acting weird."

"O-kay..."

"And I know I heard them call your name at the pharmacy counter, not hers, and when I asked her about it, she told me I was crazy and then practically sprinted out the door! What's going on, Scarlett?"

Well...crap. "She was just picking up some anti-nausea stuff for me, that's all. No big deal. No need to freak out. I mean, you don't ever pay any attention to Courtney and how she acts or reacts or...anything! Seriously, why the third degree?"

"Why are you rambling?" he asked, with a slightly annoyed tone.

"I'm not rambling. You're rambling!" she countered and wanted to kick herself. "And I don't appreciate you grilling my friends. For crying out loud, why would you freak out Courtney like that?"

"Who said she was freaked out?" he demanded and yeah, now he sounded totally annoyed. "What is going on with you, Scarlett?"

"I already told you. Nothing! Geez, relax, bro!"

"That's it. I'm coming over..."

"No!" she cried. "You...you can't!"

"Why?"

She groaned. "Look, we're having a girls' night, okay? I'm tired of throwing up. I'm starting to feel better and she's helping me out by picking up the prescription I got from my doctor so just...don't come over, okay?"

His sigh was audible. "I worry about you, squirt. When I stopped by earlier you didn't mention going to the doctor."

"Yeah, well...Court talked me into it."

"When I tried telling you to do that, you yelled at me."

"Yeah, well...Courtney told me to stop being a baby."

He chuckled softly. "Well...good for her then and...tell her I'm sorry for freaking her out."

"I'm sure she'll get over it."

"I don't think I've ever seen her eyes go quite so wide," he said, still laughing slightly. "Maybe I should apologize in person..."

"Stop trying to find excuses to come over," she whined, totally onto him. "I'll tell her you're sorry. I'm fine, we're all fine, and you just go back to doing...whatever it is that you do, okay?"

"Fine. Whatever." He tried to sound grumpy, but it totally wasn't his thing. If anything, Dean was serious, responsible, and levelheaded. He never got angry or in a bad mood. It was adorable when he tried.

"I'm sure I'll talk to you tomorrow so...have a good night," she said.

"Night, squirt."

# TEN

For the better part of a week, Mason put in long hours trying to implement his plans for the cleanup down on the north end of town. His sisters managed to get a team of about fifty volunteers. Then Sam donated two days' worth of equipment use and crews followed by Jake Summerford doing the same with his equipment and crews. And as if that wasn't enough, the local businesses who were located in the north part of town arranged for their own team of people to help out. If his calculations were correct, there would be over a hundred people donating their time and energy to paving the way to a revitalization in that part of town. It felt good to know things were coming together.

His parents offered their help and as much as Mason wanted to scoff at the offer, he knew they could be beneficial in raising money for the cause. When his mother had questioned his need to put work into "*that* part of town," he simply said that Magnolia Sound was home and it included all of it, not just the already-pretty parts.

It was shocking how she didn't argue.

What wasn't surprising was how she immediately

segued into asking if he was still hanging around "that Jones girl." He'd done his best to change the subject and after several minutes of snipping back and forth, he did something he was discovering to be most effective–he firmly told her it was none of her business.

Then he'd hung up, so...

The sound of his office phone ringing snapped him out of his musings. "Mason Bishop."

"Mason, it's Tommy! How's it goin'?"

It was still a little mind-boggling that Tommy Flynn now considered him a friend when he had initially done his best to intimidate him, but...Mason really liked the old guy. Not only did he know a lot of the town's history, but he single-handedly opened the dialogue between Mason and all the businesses in the north end. And while one of those businesses included Scarlett's father and brother's shop, he'd done his best to keep everything on a professional level and not ask how she was doing.

And it was still slowly killing him.

Three weeks.

It had been three weeks since he'd seen or talked to her and he couldn't seem to move on. He'd lost count of how many times he picked up the phone to call her and then stopped himself.

*You're awful. I wish I had just walked away from you the night of the concert. This entire relationship was a mistake.*

Yeah, those words came to mind every damn time and it didn't matter that it was just in his head. He felt the sting of them as if she were standing right there in front of him and saying them to his face all over again.

So he'd reached out to her in a more professional manner and contacted her through her website to see if she'd be interested in helping with the campaign to clean up the north end. And other than a generic auto-generated response thanking him for his inquiry, he hadn't heard from her.

He wasn't sure if it was a good thing or a bad thing.

"Mason? You there?"

Oh, right. Tommy. "Yeah, um...sorry. I'm a little distracted at the moment."

"So this is a bad time, huh?"

"What? Oh, no. Really. It's okay. What's going on?"

"I was wondering if you could come down to the bar for lunch. I swear we'll make you something good," he said with a hint of humor. "I found some of the original plans my wife had made for this place all those years ago and...I thought maybe...you know...you might want to see them and see if they're something we can use."

"Yeah, sure," he agreed. "I'd like that. How does twelve-thirty sound?"

"Perfect! See ya then!"

Pushing back from his desk, Mason leaned back in his chair and–not for the first time–wondered what he was doing. This project was going to be an amazing thing for the town–especially with how much they were going to accomplish in volunteer power alone. That wasn't his real issue, however. By keeping The Mystic Magnolia, he was tying himself to Scarlett–even though that wasn't part of the plan or even a reason why he was doing it. By owning the bar and maybe transforming it into a more family-friendly place, Mason would be making money in the long-term rather than in one lump sum. It had the potential to be a good investment if he got the right people on board to help him out.

His sister Peyton was already planning on helping out with a new menu and working with Tommy on a new kitchen design and staff. He loved how this project wasn't just going to benefit him–it was giving his sister a chance to grow in her restauranteur skills. She had inherited a local café from their great-grandfather, but she had yet to take over because she lacked the confidence. This gig working with Tommy would hopefully give her the boost she needed.

For the first time in his entire life, he felt productive–like he was doing something that had a purpose. Bringing the community together on a project that would help so many, and would generate more revenue to the town when new businesses came in, was exactly the sort of thing his great-grandfather did. For most of his life, Mason never thought about things like that. He had simply enjoyed the benefits of being part of the founding family of Magnolia Sound. He liked living off of the name. But now...now he was the one carrying on the family tradition and values that were started so long ago. And it felt good. It felt right. He was making Magnolia Sound the kind of place that years from now, his kids would grow up in and love just like he did.

The same way his great-grandfather had.

As that thought sank in, he realized he no longer harbored any anger toward his inheritance. He understood it now. And even if this wasn't exactly what anyone thought he would do with it, Mason knew it was the right thing.

For him and the town.

* * *

"HEY! Look who has color back in her face!" Yup, that was Courtney's greeting today. "Although, that lovely shade of green you were sporting was starting to grow on me."

"Ha, ha. You're hysterical," Scarlett deadpanned from her perch on her sofa. Today was the first day she was back to working full-time on her social media stuff and she was feeling good about how she wasn't too far behind. Looking up at her friend, she frowned. "Why don't you have food with you? I thought we were doing lunch."

"We are. But I took an extended break and I thought we could go out someplace. You've been cooped up in this house for too long. Besides, the fresh air will do you good!"

"I'm going to Happy Tails this afternoon so I'll be getting plenty of fresh air," she explained. "I was hoping to just...talk. I'm still kind of a mess with this whole thing and I'd like to avoid running into anyone we know."

Sitting beside her, Courtney let out a sigh. "You're going to have to see Mason eventually, Scar. It's only right."

"Yeah, I know, but...not yet."

Twisting a little so she could face her, Courtney's expression was extremely serious. "I know we've talked like every day since you found out and we've covered how you feel about having a baby and how you've finally cut back to vomiting only twice a day, but...I think we need to talk about how you feel about Mason. Every time I bring it up..."

"Court, we've been over this. I said some awful things to him and..."

"Yeah, yeah, yeah. You were a super-bitch. I got that. But if we forgot about that–if we pushed your rage-filled words aside–how do you feel about him? We all know you only said those things because you were upset. But if that day never happened and you found out you were preg-nant..." She let her words die off.

Now it was Scarlet's turn to sigh. "Okay, if that day never happened, Mason and I would–hopefully–still be dating."

"And?"

"And..." Another sigh. "I'd be head over heels in love with him. I already was," she said miserably. "I threw away a great relationship because I'm a hothead who doesn't think before she speaks!" Tears swam in her eyes and as much as she used to hate when that happened, she was sort of getting used to it.

Damn pregnancy hormones.

"Scarlett, we all know that about you and we all still love you. I'm sure if you just talked to Mason, you guys could work it out!"

"Oh, please! Would you be realistic?" she cried. "All of my stupid words aside, do you really think the Bishop family is going to like the idea of me having Mason's baby? I mean...come on! Get real!"

"Oh my God!" Courtney yelled with frustration. "You have got to let that shit go! You're like some annoying extended disco version of a song! Move on the next verse, for crying out loud! Get over this obsession you have about not being good enough!"

But before Scarlett could comment, her friend was yelling again.

"And you know what? It doesn't matter if the Bishops like the idea or not! The fact is, you *are* having Mason's baby! So stop making excuses and looking for trouble, all right?"

And yeah, Scarlett knew she had to do that. The problem was it was easier to use it as an excuse than to make the tough step and actually put herself in the vulnerable position of telling Mason she was pregnant.

And risk having him say he didn't want anything to do with her.

"Can we please change the subject?" Scarlett asked,

rubbing her temples. "And where are we going for lunch because I'm actually hungry."

Wordlessly, Courtney got up and walked to the front door. She opened it and reached out for something and then came back in. "This was Plan B. I had a feeling taking you out in public might be an issue so I came prepared." She held up a cooler bag. "I stopped at the deli and grabbed a couple of sandwiches and chips."

It was scary how well her friend knew her. "Wow, um... that was very..."

"I know," Courtney interrupted. "I can be very insightful. You should totally pay more attention." They worked together to set up the food on the coffee table and took a few minutes to dig into their lunch.

Once Scarlett felt safe that her lunch was going to stay put, she placed her sandwich down and faced her friend. "Okay, I know we need to talk about me, but not yet. I feel like that's all we've been doing. What's going on with you?"

With a dramatic eye roll, Courtney relaxed back against the cushions. "I'm bored, Scarlett! I'm bored and you being sick and all...you know...pregnant, isn't helping!"

Unable to help herself, she laughed. "Sorry to be such a drain on your social life."

"Yeah, well...you should be. I swear, I'm losing my mind. All I want is to be in a relationship and I can't seem to find anyone who interests me!"

"There's got to be someone, Court. I find it hard to believe there's no one out there for you."

"It's just...any guy I'm interested in is either already in a relationship or...off limits," she said. Her cautious tone instantly piqued Scarlett's interest.

"Aren't those the same thing?"

"I guess..."

"I thought you were going to try that dating app thing."

"I was, but then I realized they're just not my thing, I guess."

Scarlett wasn't buying it but she didn't want to push right now.

"So I got an inquiry on my website from Mason," she said quickly, feeling like this was another topic she needed to deal with.

"*What?* And you're just telling me now? What did he say? Do you think he's making up a job just to get you to call him?"

"Calm down," Scarlett replied. "It seemed like a legit job. Apparently there's some big stuff going on with the north end and he's heading it up. I guess he's looking for someone to help with getting the word out."

"I don't know why," Courtney said with a small frown. "The whole town's talking about it. It's been in the paper and it seems like everywhere you go, there are flyers and stuff. I'm telling you, if half the stuff gets done that they're talking about, it will make the north end the place to be."

"Seriously? I thought they were just doing a cleanup?"

"That's just the beginning! I heard there's going to be a couple of new restaurants, a dog park, and a gym. I'm surprised you don't know this. Your dad's garage and Tommy's bar are right in the middle of it. Haven't you talked to them?"

"I haven't really talked to anyone since the night I got sick. I mean, they've all texted to make sure I was okay, but other than that, Dean's the only one I talked to. He stops by all the damn time now to check on me."

"You know you're going to have to tell your family too, Scarlett. There's going to come a point where you can't hide it."

"I know, I know. When did life get so damn complicated?"

"Do you want an exact time or just a generalization?"

"Not funny, Court."

They resumed eating while tossing around ideas about the best way for Scarlett to tell Mason she was pregnant. She'd put it off long enough. Unfortunately, in every scenario, she envisioned him turning her away because of the things she'd said to him. It didn't matter how much Courtney tried to convince her otherwise. Scarlett refused to believe her behavior could be forgiven.

Or that Mason could really be *that* great of a guy to be *that* understanding.

Her luck couldn't be that good, could it?

After Courtney went back to work, Scarlett finished getting caught up on two accounts and then stared at Mason's inquiry. Maybe that was how she could ease into seeing him—they could meet someplace and talk about business and then she could gauge where he stood on talking about...not business.

"It shouldn't be this hard," she murmured as she clicked to compose a new email. Finding the right balance between professional and personal, she quickly typed out her message and then sat back to read it a dozen times before hitting send.

Mason, thank you for reaching out regarding social media packages for your new endeavor. If you would like to get together and discuss your options, just let me know what your schedule looks like. Maybe we could meet for lunch one day this week?

And before she could chicken out, she hit send and

quickly closed her laptop. Knowing if she stayed home, she'd obsessively watch her inbox for his response, Scarlett decided to head over to Happy Tails a little earlier than planned.

Sliding on a pair of sneakers, she looked around to make sure she had everything she needed–including her anti-nausea prescription just in case she started to feel iffy while playing with the dogs.

Within minutes, she was in her car and wishing she could have taken her bike. It was a beautiful, sunny day and under other circumstances, she'd consider this perfect bike weather. As she drove through town, she smiled. Having taken the first step in reaching out to Mason, she felt like a giant weight had been lifted off her shoulders. And as she hit the north end of town, she couldn't help but wonder how much change was coming its way. She drove by her father's garage and saw how there were more cars than they could handle parked in the side lot. Part of her felt guilty because she hadn't been in to help out in a while–not that anyone called her on it or expected it.

"Note to self, call Dad."

She slowed down as she drove by The Mystic Magnolia and then slammed on the brakes when she spotted Mason's fancy Jeep in the parking lot. There was no way she could just drive by and pretend she didn't see it. Her curiosity was too strong, so she had to pull in and see for herself what was going on.

Her hands were shaking and her legs felt a little weak, but as she climbed from the car Scarlett gave herself a quick pep talk.

"Gramps is here and won't let anything bad happen," she murmured. "And if everyone is speaking the truth, Mason's being here isn't a bad thing. Deep breaths. You can do this." She stopped at the front door of the bar and prayed she wouldn't throw up.

Again.

Pulling the door open, she stepped inside and froze.

Music was playing. People were laughing. And she could smell something other than stale beer and greasy food.

"Clearly I've stepped into some sort of alternate universe," she said quietly as she slowly stepped farther into the room.

Her grandfather spotted her first.

"Hey there, little miss! You feeling better?"

Unfortunately, her eyes instantly strayed to Mason who was looking at her with concern. "Um...yeah, Gramps. Much. Thanks."

Shaking his head, he said, "So weird how it was only you who got sick. I thought for sure we were all going to get it." With a small chuckle, he added, "Last time I saw someone turn so green so fast was when your mother was pregnant with you!"

And right then, she could actually feel herself turning green.

He looked at her expectantly. "Well? Are you going to stand in the doorway all day or are you going to come in and greet me properly?"

With no other choice, Scarlett walked over to the bar and smiled when her grandfather walked around and hugged her tight. But when he turned her around to face Mason, she wasn't sure what she was supposed to do.

"Scarlett, you know Mason Bishop, right? You two went to school together. I think you even graduated the same year," he said conversationally, completely unaware of how her heart was about to pound its way right out of her chest.

For a moment, she was confused. She'd told her grandfather all about her relationship with Mason, but maybe he was trying not to let on that he knew. "Um...yeah. Hey," she said quietly, finally forcing herself to look away.

"Did you get my email?" Mason asked, his voice so deep and smooth that it almost made her sigh at how much she missed it.

"Email?" Gramps chimed in. "What email?"

With a grin, Mason turned to her grandfather. "I heard Scarlett is the go-to person in town for social media marketing. I thought she might be able to help us get the word out on the revitalization of the area and maybe even help us come up with a campaign to attract new businesses."

She glanced over at Gramps and could tell he was impressed. "I knew you were smart, Bishop. And by hiring my Scarlett, you proved it even more." With his arm around her, Gramps hugged her close.

"Tommy? You got a minute?" Someone called from the kitchen and he excused himself and walked away, leaving Mason and Scarlett alone.

Knowing she needed to say something before the silence got awkward, Scarlett looked up at him. "So, um... how've you been?"

He shrugged. "Okay. Busy, actually. This whole project sort of took on a life of its own and I've been struggling to keep up."

"That's a good thing, though, right? I mean, I hear the response from everyone has been positive." She offered a small smile and when he smiled back at her, she went a little weak in the knees.

"It has," he agreed and then looked around the room and motioned to a booth in the corner. "Why don't we sit down?" They walked across the room and sat. "You didn't answer me before—did you get my email?"

"Oh, yeah. I did," she said quickly, shifting on the cracked vinyl trying to get comfortable. "Right before I left my house a little while ago, I messaged you back about setting up a time to meet up and talk about what you were looking for."

"Great! Any chance you have time now or were you on your way someplace?"

Talking to him now would have been convenient, but... she really didn't want to take the chance that their conversation would move into personal territory here in the bar. Quietly, she cleared her throat and suggested, "I'm on my way to Happy Tails right now. I haven't been there in over a week so I'd really like to go and give them a couple of hours of my time. But if you're free later on, maybe we can get together and talk?"

Mason relaxed back against his seat, one arm resting along the back of the booth, a serene smile on his face. "I'd like that. How about The Sand Bar? I know how you like their burgers."

Just the thought of them made her stomach lurch and she could feel herself pale. "Um..."

"Oh, right. Tommy said you've been sick. Are you feeling any better?"

She let out a mirthless laugh as she shook her head. "It changes from minute to minute."

He looked at her oddly but didn't question her statement. "So..."

"How about some takeout Chinese at my place?" Then she paused to make sure her stomach didn't reject the idea. Finally, she gave him a lopsided grin. "Yeah, that should work if you're okay with it."

Blinking at her for a long moment–as if he couldn't believe what she was suggesting–he nodded. "Uh...sure. Seven o'clock work for you?"

As much as she knew they needed to do this–needed to talk–there was still a part of her that wanted to flee and say never mind! Instead, she forced herself to nod in agreement.

"Scarlett?" her grandfather called out. "You want something to eat?"

"No thanks, Gramps!" Then she let out another low laugh.

"What?" Mason asked. "What's so funny?"

Still chuckling softly, she said, "He knows I won't eat anything from here. We joke about it all the time and yet he's always asking me if I want anything."

"Well...it's not so bad..."

"Oh gosh, did you eat here?"

He nodded.

"A burger?"

"No, a turkey club." He shrugged. "It was...well...it was..."

"It was awful," she whispered, leaning across the table slightly. "It's okay, you can say it. He knows his food isn't particularly palatable."

"We're hoping to change that," Mason replied, sounding confident. "It's what we were talking about when you walked in. Right now my sister Peyton is in the kitchen looking over his setup and she's going to work on a plan to revamp the menu."

Her eyes went wide. "Seriously?"

Nodding again, he said, "Seriously."

"Why? Why would you do that? I thought..."

He held up a hand to stop her. "Yeah, I know what you thought." There was no malice in his tone, only a hint of sadness. "We'll talk about it later." Looking at his watch, he frowned. "I should have left here an hour ago. I need to get back to the office and make some calls." Sliding from the booth, he smiled and held out a hand to help her out. Once she was standing in front of him, he seemed a little hesitant to let her go. After a minute, he asked, "So, you're sure seven is okay for you?"

"Definitely. I'll be back from Happy Tails by then."

He turned to walk away and then looked back at her. "Your usual order?"

Scarlett felt herself blush. "Um...yeah. Add a pint of egg drop soup if you don't mind." Her hand went to her stomach without her even realizing it. Mason's gaze narrowed again but he simply said he'd see her later and walked back to the kitchen to presumably talk to his sister and Gramps.

Unsure of what she was supposed to do, Scarlett had no choice but to follow so she could at least say goodbye to her grandfather. She hadn't gone more than five steps when he came out of the kitchen with a smile on his face. When he was standing in front of her, his smile grew.

"Don't think for a minute that I believe you stopped in here to see me," he said lightly, but in a hushed tone.

Why deny it? "Okay, fine. I was on my way to help out Ed and Christine and saw his car here. What's going on, Gramps?"

He waved her off. "Just working through some stuff. But I've got to tell you, Mason's a really nice guy. I think you misjudged him."

And yeah, she rolled her eyes. "Gramps..."

"What? I'm serious! I figured he'd be some smart-mouthed punk who I was going to have to put in his place, but..." He shrugged. "He won me over. Why?

Because he's a smart businessman and he reminds me of Zeke."

"You mean the guy who swindled you out of your livelihood?" she asked, unable to hide her sarcasm.

His expression fell. "Scarlett, is that really what you think?"

And something in his tone made her realize just how wrong she possibly was.

And just how much she may have cost herself.

"Well...it just seems like..."

Tommy wrapped an arm around her and led her back to the same booth she had just vacated with Mason. When they were both seated, he reached across the table and took her hands in his. "Zeke was the fairest man I've ever met. He did nothing but try to help me, Scarlett. I was the one who messed up. Me. No one else. No one swindled me. No one took advantage of me. If anything, you could say that I was the one who took advantage–mainly because I thought he would keep giving me chance after chance after chance..."

"Gramps..."

He squeezed her hands tight. "No, you listen to me–I said a lot of things in the heat of anger, but the only one I was mad at was myself." He turned and looked over toward the kitchen. "That man in there is doing something he doesn't have to do. He could have had me out of here months ago and had this place bulldozed to the ground so he could sell the property. And he would have been one hundred percent right to do that. But look at him back there–walking around my filthy kitchen with his sister trying to find ways to make this crazy ol' place work. He could have a big, fat check in his hand by now if he really wanted it."

Sighing, she looked at him sadly. "He really is a great guy..."

"Then maybe cut him some slack, okay?"

"I'm going to see him tonight for dinner to talk about this campaign..."

Tommy squeezed her hands one more time. "Sure. You keep telling yourself that," he said with a wink.

# ELEVEN

Confidence was never a problem.

Then he started spending time with Scarlett Jones.

Mason sat in his car and stared at the long driveway that led up to Scarlett's house and wondered–not for the first time–if he were crazy to be doing this.

They were done–as she had so clearly told him not so long ago. So why was he here? Why was he sitting here parked on the side of the road contemplating driving up to her house, bringing her dinner, and pretending he actually gave a damn about the social media campaign she could come up with?

Okay, the last one was a lie because he really was curious, but tonight being here in her house and talking to her with no distractions was going to be the worst form of torture for him. And he had no idea how he was going to get through it.

Had he ever stepped away from a challenge?

Maybe a time or two.

Was he ready to step away from this one?

Not on his life.

As he put the car in drive and made his way closer to Scarlett's house, he called himself every kind of fool. She had the potential to break his heart like no one ever had. Again. But it didn't matter. The bottom line was that he'd be willing to do it all again because she meant that much to him. She'd captured his heart, his mind, and all his attention the night at the concert whether she knew it or not.

And she still had them.

But he really hoped she didn't stomp all over them again.

"Man up, Bishop," he murmured, parking the car. Grabbing the bag of food, he climbed from the car and walked up to her front door. It felt a little weird to be knocking, but... here he was. Hand raised, he was just about to knock when the door opened and...his heart kicked hard in his chest.

It didn't matter that he had seen her only hours ago. When he looked at Scarlett, he saw everything he ever wanted in a woman.

"Hey," she said, her smile a little nervous. Opening the door for him to come in, Mason noticed she gave him way more space than he needed.

He didn't take it as a good sign.

Refusing to dwell on it, Mason walked in and began unpacking the food at her kitchen table. "How were the dogs today?" he asked.

Scarlett walked over and together they worked to finish setting the table. "A litter of puppies was dropped off this afternoon and we were scrambling for supplies for them." Sighing, she placed a pitcher of sweet tea on the table. Straightening, she looked at him. "It breaks my heart how people do that–how they can just walk away without even trying to take care of them."

"You don't know that for sure..."

"They were left in a box on Christine's porch," she said sadly. "They didn't even knock to let her know they were there. It's not the first time it's happened, and I'm sure it won't be the last. It just sucks."

Nodding, he walked over and pulled her chair out for her. She looked at him oddly before a small smile played at her lips.

Lips he wanted desperately to kiss.

"Thank you," she said.

Sitting beside her, he watched as she placed the smallest amount of food on her plate and then filled a bowl with the egg drop soup. She clearly wasn't fully over whatever ailment she had since she was eating so cautiously. He was about to ask her about it but figured it probably wasn't the best dinner conversation.

"What kind of puppies were they?" he asked, scooping some shrimp and broccoli onto his plate.

"I'm pregnant," Scarlett blurted out quickly, her eyes a little wide and wild.

The spoon clattered to the floor as he stared at her for what felt like a solid minute. He couldn't even be sure he blinked or breathed. "Um...what?" His heart was hammering hard in his chest and he couldn't feel his hands.

She nodded and then looked away. "Uh...yeah. So..."

A million thoughts raced through his mind and it was hard to form even one coherent word. He tried. Multiple times. But his throat was dry and his tongue felt like it was the size of his fist. Out of all the things he imagined he'd talk to Scarlett about tonight, this totally wasn't on the list. Hell, he hadn't even thought of it being a possibility in weeks. In his mind, it was a crisis-averted type of situation.

*And now my chest hurts...*

Reaching for the pitcher of tea, he poured himself a

glass–spilling a good portion of it–and quickly drank it down.

"Mason...say something," Scarlett prompted, jumping up to grab a towel to clean up his mess. "I know this is a shock..."

He took several long breaths and carefully placed the glass back down on the table. Staring up at her, he could see the panic on her face and knew this couldn't have been easy for her.

"When did you find out?" he finally forced himself to ask.

"Last week," she said, and he heard the hesitation–and possibly regret.

With a curt nod, he stood and began to pace. His first thought was how he was glad he hadn't eaten anything yet because he certainly felt like he was going to be sick. Then he looked at Scarlett and...

He couldn't help it–the look of utter panic on her face had him walking over and wrapping her in his arms. Holding her tight, he kissed the top of her head. "Are you okay?" he asked after a moment of letting himself simply enjoy the feel of her there–where she belonged.

Her body trembled slightly as she burrowed in close to him. "I'm getting there," she said quietly. So many questions raced through his head, but he knew they both needed this moment to come to grips with everything together.

After several minutes, Mason guided Scarlett back to her chair and they both sat down. He immediately missed the feel of her and reached for her hand. Letting out a long breath, he offered her a small smile. "Okay, so...now what?"

She was about to answer when her phone rang. He was hoping she would ignore it–and it looked like she was going to–when his phone began to ring too.

"That's a little freaky," Scarlett commented, standing to reach for her phone.

Pulling his phone from his pocket, Mason looked down and saw Peyton's name on the screen and was about to ignore it, but Scarlett had walked out of the room to take her call and he figured he could make this quick.

"Hey, Peyton. What's up?"

"There's a fire at the bar!" she cried. "Come quick! We're waiting on the fire department!"

Jumping up, he said, "I'm on my way" just as Scarlett ran back into the room looking a little wide-eyed. Reaching for her hand, he said, "Let's go!"

It wasn't until they were in his car and he was speeding out of the driveway when Scarlett asked how he knew what was going on.

"My sister called," he said, both hands gripping the steering wheel. "She's been helping Tommy with the kitchen and we had an inspector come in to talk about what was needed."

"Oh, God," she groaned. "How outdated was everything?"

"It wasn't that bad," he replied, "although...you wouldn't know it from looking at the stuff. He gets inspected every year and has kept up with any repairs he's told to, but..." He shrugged. "Who called you?"

"My brother, Dean. He was leaving the garage when he heard an explosion."

"An explosion?" he cried. Why the hell hadn't Peyton mentioned an explosion? "Did he say what happened?"

She shook her head. "It sounded like pure chaos! It's going to be crazy when we get there. I just know it!" She paused. "What if people got hurt? What if my grandfather is hurt?"

Mason could hear the near hysteria in her voice and reached over and grabbed for her hand. "We have to think positive, Scarlett." As much as he tried to sound calm, the truth was that he was a bit of a mess himself. His sister could be hurt and he was the reason she was there. Tommy could be hurt, customers...and he owned it all. This could all possibly be his fault.

They drove the rest of the way in silence and when they got close to the scene, it was already littered with fire trucks, ambulances, and dozens of spectators. Mason pulled over to the side of the road and threw the car in park. Scarlett was out and running toward the building which was seriously engulfed in flames. He chased after her, banging people out of the way as he went.

Now wasn't the time to remember how he had chased her through a crowd once before...

There were barricades already up and someone grabbed her before she could break past them. When he caught up to her, he heard Scarlett cursing at whoever was holding her. It took Mason no time to realize it was one of her brothers. The resemblance was that strong.

"But he's still in there!" she screamed, wriggling in her brother's arms. "We have to get to him!"

Mason's eyes instantly began scanning the scene looking for his sister. He was growing more and more frantic by the minute. Even though she called him and didn't mention being hurt, he needed to see her to be sure. He was about to turn away when...

"Ow! What the hell, Scarlett?" her brother yelled. Mason turned and saw her take off again, but this time he was closer and reached out and grabbed her before she could go more than a handful of feet.

"Put me down, Mason!" she cried out. Her back was

against his chest and she was doing her best to elbow him in the stomach and kick him at the same time.

She succeeded more times than he cared to admit.

"That's enough!" he snapped, his arms holding her like a vise. "You can't go in there!"

"He's still inside! Someone has to get to him!"

"There are firefighters all over the place," he argued heatedly. "They are going to get Tommy out! You going in there isn't going to help anything!"

The curses that flew out of her mouth were enough to make most people blush. Her brother stormed over and looked ready to kill him for manhandling his sister, but Scarlett merely kicked at him too.

"I'm...just..." Kick. "Going to..." Elbow jab. "Help him!" Headbutt to the chin.

Mason's arms loosened as he saw stars from her last blow, but as soon as both her feet were on the ground, he reached out and spun her around–done with being assaulted.

Grasping both her shoulders hard, he gave a quick shake. "That is enough, dammit! You are not going in there!"

"How dare you...?"

"Not only are you endangering your grandfather by running in there–because you'll be distracting the firefighters from doing their job–but you'll risk hurting yourself, Scarlett!" Another shake. "You're pregnant, for crying out loud! I'm not going to allow you to risk yourself and our baby over this!"

Her eyes went wide at his words and Mason suddenly felt several people close in around them.

"*What?!*"

Uh-oh...

\* \* \*

SHE STILLED INSTANTLY and stared at Mason in shock.

In every scenario she played out in her head about telling her family she was pregnant, not once were they standing in front of a burning building while Mason blurted it out there for all the world to hear!

Her eyes never left his, but she knew Dean and her father were behind her and she spotted Peyton standing there looking shocked too.

*Dammit.*

Mason was instantly pushed aside as her brother and then her father stepped in front of her. "Is this true, Scarlett?" her father asked. "You're pregnant?"

"Um..."

"Is that why you were sick?" Dean asked, his brows furrowed as he stared down at her.

Looking between the two of them, she felt herself starting to panic because she wasn't ready to talk to them about it yet. Hell, she hardly had time to talk to Mason about it! "Can we please focus on the real issue here? Gramps is trapped inside the bar!" she cried out, pointing toward the building. "Doesn't anyone care that they haven't brought him out yet?"

As if on cue, there was a flurry of activity by the building as the paramedics met a team of firefighters who were carrying her grandfather out of the building. Scarlett went to run toward him, but three pairs of hands held her back. Tears and smoke stung her eyes and when she was pulled in close to someone, she instinctively knew it was Mason.

"I've got her," he said to her family, and she was mildly

surprised when no one argued. He held her close and she just wanted to collapse to the ground. This was all too much–everything. It was hard to focus on which situation was causing the most stress, but right now all she needed was to know her grandfather was okay. Straightening, she shifted in Mason's arms and looked toward where the paramedics had taken Gramps. Looking up at Mason, she said, "Please."

With a curt nod, they began making their way toward the ambulance with her father, Dean, and Peyton hot on their heels.

Tommy was on a stretcher with an oxygen mask on his face, but he was awake and coughing. Scarlett almost sagged with relief. They loaded him into the ambulance and she couldn't find her voice to ask if he was going to be okay. Watching the doors close and the paramedics run around climbing in, she could do nothing but watch them drive away.

"We need to go!" she demanded, looking up at Mason. "C'mon! We'll follow them!" He looked toward the building and could tell he was torn.

"Dad," Dean said authoritatively, "take Scarlett and go to the hospital to make sure Gramps is okay." He looked over at Peyton. "You should probably go get checked out too."

Shaking her head, Peyton hooked an arm through Mason's. "I will in a little bit. I need to make sure everyone else is okay."

Scarlett didn't know Mason's sister at all, but in that moment, she had a lot of respect for her. Looking up at Mason, she said, "I have to do this. I need to make sure he's okay."

He was so tense and so serious and for a minute she

thought he was going to tell her no. Instead, he leaned in and gave her a fierce kiss. "Go. I'll catch up with you later."

Relief washed over her and she cupped his face and kissed him again. "Thank you." And then she looked over at her father and nodded. "Let's go."

Making their way quickly through the crowd and then across the street, neither spoke as they climbed into her father's truck and began maneuvering through the traffic along the main road. It wasn't until they were driving the speed limit that Scarlett realized she was going to have to be the one to break the silence. Dominic Jones was a man of few words as it was, and when it had to do with anything emotional, he said even less.

"Do we know what started the fire?" she asked, figuring this was the safest way to begin.

He shook his head. "We heard the explosion and Dean called out for me to call 9-1-1. He took off and ran over, but everyone was running out of the building and after that..." He shrugged, his eyes never leaving the road.

"Dad?"

No response.

Reaching across the console, she placed a hand on his arm. "Dad?"

"I know I tend to stay out of your business," he began quietly, "but it bothers me sometimes, Scarlett. It's not like I don't want to talk to you. It's just...I don't know what to say." He paused. "I know I'm a bit of a disappointment to you..."

"What?" she asked, her own voice barely a whisper. "How can you even say that? You've never been a disappointment to me!"

Now he did look over at her. "Scarlett Marie...you and I both know I did you a disservice while you were growing up. I had no idea what to do with a girl and apparently, I still don't. You're involved with the Bishop boy and you never said a word–not to me and most likely not to your brothers. And you're pregnant." He stopped and shook his head. "And you didn't tell any of us. I think that speaks volumes."

Ugh...how did she even begin to explain this?

"To be honest, I was in a bit of denial. About all of it. My relationship with Mason...well...it took me by surprise. And then when everything came out about him owning the bar?" She let out a mirthless laugh. "Let's just say I didn't handle it well."

"What do you mean?" he asked, glancing at her before focusing on the road again. They were still ten minutes away from the hospital.

She explained her attitude toward Mason and his family and then how she went off on him after finding out about his inheritance. "I said some horrible stuff to him and ended our relationship. Then I found out I was pregnant."

Dominic was quiet until they pulled into the hospital parking lot. Scarlett thought she'd go mad. But she knew her father and knew he needed time to absorb everything she just shared with him. Once the truck was parked, he turned to face her.

"You need to know the problems your grandfather had with the bar have nothing to do with Mason..."

"Yeah, I'm finding that out..."

He held up a hand to stop her. "But...I want you to know that just because you're pregnant, it doesn't mean you have to have anything to do with Mason Bishop if you don't want to. We are all here for you–me, your brothers, Tommy–all of us. There isn't a thing you'll have to worry about. This baby will be loved and well cared for. Don't put yourself in a relationship if it's not what you want."

Wow. That was...both incredibly sweet and more than a little surprising. In her entire life, her father had never spoken that many words to her at one time. Unable to help herself, she lunged across the console and hugged him.

"Thanks, Dad," she whispered, fighting back more tears.

Damn pregnancy hormones.

When she pulled back, Dominic used the pads of his thumbs to wipe away her tears. "I might not always know what to say, but I'm always here for you. No matter what."

She nodded because she was too choked up to talk.

"C'mon. Let's go check on your grandfather."

Together they made their way to the emergency room. Her grandfather was being treated for multiple second-degree burns and smoke inhalation along with cuts and bruises. They weren't allowed to see him and with no other choice, they set up camp in the waiting room.

First, her brother Kyle showed up. He hadn't been on the scene, but had heard enough and came down to see how everyone was doing. Hunter showed up later after the fire was out and he was off duty. When Scarlett spotted him, she thought for sure Mason and Peyton wouldn't be far behind.

"Any news?" he asked as he came and sat with them.

Dominic gave the latest update, but no one had been allowed back to see Tommy yet. "What about the fire, Hunter? What happened?"

"Grease fire," he said solemnly. "Luckily Gramps had an Ansul system in place—which should have kept the fire to a minimum—but it just moved too quickly to contain. That's what he was trying to do, at least, according to Peyton

Bishop. She was in the kitchen with Gramps when it happened. The system kicked in–which is there to suppress restaurant kitchen fires–and I think he may have panicked. He shoved Peyton out and had everyone running for the exit but after that, all we can speculate is the flames moved too far too fast for the system to stop."

Both her father and Kyle cursed but Scarlett was still scanning the entrance for any signs of Mason and his sister.

"Was anyone else hurt?" Kyle asked.

"They treated Peyton and a few others for smoke inhalation, but luckily no one was hurt. Just Gramps."

Her father took one of her hands in his and gave it a gentle squeeze. "Where is Peyton now?"

"She stayed behind with Mason to talk to the fire inspectors and to make sure the site was secured. Mason was on the phone almost the entire time with the insurance company," Hunter explained.

"How do you know?"

"Because once the fire was under control, I walked over to make sure he and Peyton were okay."

"Where's Dean?" Kyle asked.

"He was walking around with Mason and making sure everything was secure." He looked over at Scarlett. "Courtney showed up looking for you, but Dean told her you'd left. Did she come by here?"

"No," she replied, rubbing her head.

"Are you all right?" they all asked her at the same time and she had to stifle a laugh. She had a feeling her entire pregnancy was going to be handled like this.

"I'm just tired," she said, hoping to put them all at ease. "I was hoping we'd get to see Gramps by now, but..." She stopped and yawned. "Damn. Sorry."

"Maybe you should go home," her father suggested. "I

promise to call you once we see him and speak to the doctors. You really need your rest, Scarlett."

As much as she wanted to argue or at least be annoyed, she couldn't. She was tired, hungry, and had a bit of a headache. Going home wasn't the worst suggestion in the world. Still...

"I didn't have dinner. Dean called just as I was sitting down so...maybe I just need a little something to eat."

Kyle instantly stood up. "I'll go to the cafeteria and grab you a sandwich or something. Okay?"

Suppressing a grin, she nodded. "Thanks, Kyle."

"I'll go with you," her father said. "I need to stretch my legs."

Once they were both gone and it was down to her and Hunter, Scarlett knew it was only a matter of time before he was going to bombard her with questions.

"So...you're pregnant," he said, moving to sit closer to her.

Chuckling, she turned her head and looked at him. "Yup."

"It was the first thing Dean said to me when I saw him," he explained, shaking his head. He studied her for a moment. "You doing okay?"

She shrugged. "I'm still getting used to the whole thing."

"It is pretty terrifying in the beginning–especially when it's not planned." He paused. "Wait...it wasn't planned, was it?"

She laughed again. "No, definitely not planned. Not completely a surprise though, either."

Shifting beside her, Hunter turned to face her, his arm draped along the back of the chairs. "When Melissa found out she was pregnant, we weren't exactly surprised either.

Shit happens sometimes. But those first few days after she did? Man, I think I aged like a hundred years."

Scarlett rested her head on his arm. She remembered when he had come home and told them all the news. He and Melissa had dated since junior year of high school and while it was always tumultuous, Scarlett remembered thinking how maybe now they were finally maturing and ready to settle into a normal relationship.

"I read every damn book on pregnancy and childbirth and then moved on to all the parenting ones. I spent every night reading everything I could find so I would be ready."

Patting his arm, she said, "You're a great father, Hunter."

"Yeah, well...parenting is scary, Scarlett. And it's hard."

"I know."

He looked down, not meeting her gaze. "And it's even harder when you're doing it alone."

Wait...was he saying...? "What's going on, Hunter?"

Shrugging, he tried to move away but Scarlett wouldn't let him. "We're co-parenting, but...Melissa's around less and less." He paused. "And I can't say I'm sad about it."

Sitting up straight, she studied her brother. "Seriously?"

Finally he looked up at her and nodded. "I knew—even way back when we found out she was pregnant—I knew it wasn't what she wanted. Motherhood, marriage, none of it. I kept thinking she'd change her mind once the baby was born and that day in the hospital, when they placed Eli in her arms, I knew I was kidding myself."

"Oh, Hunter...I'm so sorry."

Another shrug. "Look, I'm not saying any of this to make you feel bad for me. I'm saying this because... well..." He let out a long breath, raking his free hand through his hair. "Don't go into this with Mason if you're not both one hundred percent committed. I mean, I'm not saying don't have the baby. I'm just saying...know where you both stand so you won't be disappointed down the road."

"There are no guarantees in relationships, Hunter. I'm not that naïve."

"Yeah, I know there aren't, but...relationships are hard enough on their own. Take a new relationship and throw in the added stress of an unplanned pregnancy and it gets so much harder." He squeezed her shoulder. "I don't want to see you get hurt. That's all."

Moving in close, she hugged him. "I'm so sorry you're dealing with all of this."

"Me too," he said quietly. Hugging her a little tighter, he added, "If you ever need anything–like someone to kick Mason's ass–you let me know."

Laughing, she pushed her brother away. "No need for an ass kicking. Everything's fine."

"My offer stands." He looked like he was about to say more, but his attention focused just beyond her shoulder and his expression turned a little tense.

Turning, Scarlett saw Mason walking through the ER doors looking tired, anxious and ten kinds of yummy. When he spotted her, he visibly relaxed.

"Well, shit," Hunter murmured.

"What? What's the matter?"

"I was hoping to kick someone's ass tonight. Guess it's not going to be Bishop's."

Shaking her head and laughing, she asked, "Why do you say that?"

"The way he just looked at you? That's the look of a guy who isn't looking to bail." Standing, he kissed Scarlett on the head and moved to shake Mason's hand when he approached. "Hey. How are things over by the bar? Everything secured?"

Scarlett knew Mason was explaining everything, but all she could do was drink in the sight of him. She'd missed him these last few weeks-even when she was still mad at him-and just knowing he was here for her made her feel like everything was going to be okay.

He looked at her and smiled. "How's Tommy?"

"They still haven't let us see him, which concerns me. The last time we got an update, the doctor told us he had some burns and cuts and bruises and they were treating him for smoke inhalation. I wouldn't think they would keep us away for this long."

Mason looked around. "Where's your dad?"

"He and Kyle went to get me something to eat," she told him. "I have a bit of a headache and I'm hungry, so..."

"Do you mind if I stay?" he asked cautiously. "I mean, I know I'm not family and they're not going to let me in to see Tommy, but...I'd like to know he's okay."

And if she wasn't already in love with him, that one statement would have sealed the deal. "I'd like that. But... are you hungry? You didn't get to eat either. Our Chinese food is still sitting out on my kitchen table."

Hunter looked between the two of them. "Tell you what, why don't the two of you go home and eat-maybe not the Chinese food because it's probably gross by now-but something fresh. I'm here and so are Dad and Kyle and you know Dean's probably on his way too. We'll call you as soon as we see Gramps."

She nibbled on her bottom lip. "I don't know, Hunter. They just went to grab me a sandwich..."

"I'll eat it," he said, grinning. "I'm always hungry."

"But..."

Looking at Mason, Hunter continued, "Get her home and make sure she eats something. She's going to argue with you and try to convince you to bring her back, but don't let her until tomorrow."

"I'm right here, jackass," she griped, but her brother wasn't the least bit fazed.

"Just go. We've got everything under control here."

Just then, her stomach growled loudly and for the first time in what felt like forever, her hunger wasn't immediately followed by a wave of nausea.

Better take advantage of it...

"Fine," she said dramatically. Then she leaned forward menacingly, poking Hunter in the chest. "But you better call the second you know something!" Then she punched him for good measure before facing Mason–who was watching with amusement. "Okay, now we can go."

# TWELVE

It was almost midnight when they walked through the front door of Mason's place. It had been his intention to bring her back to her house, but as they drove away from the hospital, she talked about how much she needed to relax and wished she could just breathe in some fresh air. That's when he knew this was where they needed to go. So after a brief stop at the drive-thru to grab some burgers, here they were.

Scarlett instantly walked through the living room, opened the sliding glass doors and stepped out onto the deck. There was a chill in the air and he wasn't really looking forward to eating outside, but if that's what she wanted, then that's what they'd do. He followed and put their food out on the small bistro table before guiding her over to sit down. They ate in silence for several minutes before Scarlett spoke.

"I'm sure this isn't the best meal for me to be having, but after being sick for the last two weeks I'm sure it's okay."

He hated the thought of her being sick.

Hated even more that she went through it alone.

"So you're feeling better?"

She shrugged. "It comes and goes, but I got a prescription for some anti-nausea meds and I have an appointment with my OB-GYN next week so hopefully she can shed some light on what else I can do to get through this part."

Frowning, he asked, "Isn't morning sickness a normal part of pregnancy?"

"It is, but this wasn't only a morning thing. It was an all-day-every-day thing. Trust me. It's a horrible way to live."

Tossing his burger down, he shook his head. "Geez, Scarlett, why didn't you call me?"

The last reaction he expected from her was laughter, but...that's exactly what he got. She finished up her french fries and grinned at him. "Mason, there isn't anything you could have done for me. Knowing about the pregnancy doesn't give you some magical powers to make me feel any less gross."

"Yeah, but..."

"Ask Courtney. It was not pretty."

"You don't look...you know..."

"Give it time," she said, reaching for her drink. "We've got like eight more months to get through. I'm sure you'll see it for yourself."

And for some reason, this ridiculous banter made him feel better. The fact that she was talking about him being around through the pregnancy gave him hope.

Picking up his burger, he quickly finished it along with his fries and relaxed back in his seat. "You know your place is going to reek in the morning from the food being out all night."

She agreed. "I know, but I was too tired to deal with it tonight. The fresh air is really helping. Between the smell of smoke from the fire and then the hospital smell..." She shuddered. "This was way better for me, so...thank you." The smile she gave him was everything and Mason had to fight the urge to pick her up and carry her to bed.

Which reminded him...

"Uh...I'm glad the fresh air is helping but...it's late." He waited to see if she would comment, but she didn't. Leaning back in her seat with her head tilted back, Scarlett looked completely relaxed and at ease. "I thought we would have heard something about Tommy by now."

"Me too."

Seriously? She had nothing else to say? Wasn't it weird that she was here this late? How she wasn't making any move for him to take her home? Did she want to spend the night? Were they back together? Just like that? Without even talking about it?

"Um, Scarlett, I know we got interrupted earlier, but there are a lot of things we need to..."

Now she did straighten and met his gaze. "I know, Mason," she said softly. "But for tonight, I'd really just like to...not talk about all of it. I'm so tired and now I'm so full and I'm worried about my grandfather and..." She shrugged. "I really don't want to be alone."

Part of his hope faded. It wasn't like she was here because she wanted to be with him. She was here because she didn't want to be alone.

Rising from his seat, he stretched and cleared the table. Inside, he grabbed his phone and typed out a text to Peyton to make sure she was doing okay. And once she replied that she was, he wasn't sure what to do with himself.

The sound of Scarlett's phone had him wandering back to the deck where he heard her talking.

"How is he?" She paused to listen. "How long are they going to keep him?" Another pause. "Wow...okay..." And yet another pause.

Mason prayed the news wasn't all bad. He saw the way Tommy looked when he came out and there was no doubt his age would factor into the length of his recovery, but he sincerely hoped he was going to be all right.

"Okay," Scarlett was saying. "Thanks." Sighing, she listened for another minute. "Yeah, I'll come by tomorrow after lunch then. Thanks, Dad. Goodnight." Turning her phone off, she placed it on the table and looked up at him.

"How's he doing?"

"He's got second-degree burns on both his arms and his neck along with a concussion from wherever he must have fallen in the kitchen from the explosion." She paused and he could see her fighting back tears. "He's sedated and on oxygen and he's going to be hospitalized for at least a week."

"But..."

She swiped a hand over her cheek, wiping away some stray tears. "But they expect him to make a full recovery."

"That's great news, Scarlett," he said, walking over and crouching down beside her. "He's going to be okay."

She nodded as more tears fell. "I know, I know...I just hate how this happened to him."

There wasn't much he could say to that. Instead, he straightened, took her hands in his and led her back into the house. "Come on, you need to get some sleep."

Scarlett went willingly but when she was next to the bed, Mason wasn't sure what he was supposed to do. It would be easy to just move in close, kiss her, and crawl under the blankets with her, but...he couldn't. *They* couldn't.

Could they?

Completely oblivious to his internal thoughts, Scarlett kicked off her sandals, slid her shorts off and walked in nothing more than her panties and tank top into his bathroom. Mason stood rooted to the spot wondering just what the hell was happening. He was about to strip down and climb into bed when his conscience hit him.

Hard.

With a sigh, he walked out of the bedroom and closed the door behind him. He locked the doors and then went about setting up a spot on the sectional for him to sleep. It wasn't ideal, but it was only one night so...he'd live. He had everything set up and pulled his shirt off when he heard Scarlett clear her throat from the bedroom doorway. Turning, he looked at her.

"What are you doing?" she asked, leaning against the doorframe, looking confused.

"Uh...going to sleep," he said slowly.

"Out here? Why?"

Slowly, Mason moved away from the sofa and walked toward her. "Um...I didn't think it was right...I mean...I wasn't just going to assume..."

"Mason?"

"Hmm?"

She pushed away from the door with a bit of a sigh. "Look, I know this is weird and not the way things would have gone if circumstances were different tonight, but..."

He didn't let her finish. "I don't want to be the guy you settle for because you don't want to be alone."

"Mason..."

"No, I'm serious. I understand why we didn't get to talk and why the time wasn't right to hash things out, but I'm not okay with just passing the time with you! You mean more to me than that!" When he saw her start to argue, he cut her off. "And it's not because you're pregnant. This is the way I feel about you, period!"

He was a little breathless and afraid he'd said too much. He knew he had no choice but to let her speak now.

"Are you done?" she asked, almost sounding bored.

Letting out a long breath, he nodded.

Then, to his surprise, she moved in close and took both his hands in hers. "You're not some guy I'm settling for, Mason Bishop, so let's get that out of the way first. I'm here because I want to be here," she explained. "I'm here because I suck at this sort of thing–at saying how I feel and what I want." She paused. "But mostly, I'm here because I missed you."

And damn if those words didn't nearly bring him to his knees. Gently pulling one hand from hers, he reached up and caressed her cheek. "I missed you too."

She yawned loudly right before she gave him a sleepy smile. "Okay, then. Can we please go to bed now? Together?"

Like he was going to say no...

This wasn't about sex–he knew Scarlett needed her rest–but once they were under the blankets together and she was snuggled up against his side, Mason knew he'd do whatever it took to make sure they talked everything out and were back on track. Kissing the top of her head, he knew he wasn't going to lose her again, no matter what.

* * *

THERE WAS a smile on Scarlett's face even before she opened her eyes. Mason's arms were around her and she slept better than she had in weeks. Her cheek was against his chest and even though they had done nothing more than sleep last night, she couldn't resist placing a soft kiss on his skin.

"Good morning," he said sleepily, hugging her a little closer. "Did you sleep okay?"

Nodding, she said, "I don't think I moved all night."

"And how do you feel this morning?"

It took her a minute to realize what he was asking, and she actually had to take a minute and do a bit of a silent exam. Do I have to pee? No. Headache? Gone. Do I need to throw up? Um...as if on cue, her stomach rolled a little but she willed it to relax. Going still, she waited to see what would happen.

"Scarlett?"

"Just...give me a minute..." And yeah, everything was staying put for now. "Okay, whew! This is the first morning in weeks I haven't..."

Spoke too soon.

She was out of the bed and running for the bathroom and feeling all kinds of mortified. Slamming the door shut behind her, she made it to the bowl just in time. As much as she was getting used to this being the way she started her days, she would have loved to skip it just this once.

A few minutes passed before Mason softly knocked on the door. "You okay?"

There was a snarky comeback on the tip of her tongue, but she kept it to herself. "Uh...yeah. Just...give me a minute."

"There's a new toothbrush under the sink and mouthwash if you want it."

It would be foolish to take offense, so she simply thanked him and forced herself to get up off the floor.

It took ten minutes for her to feel well enough to leave the bathroom. Without any remorse, she grabbed the robe Mason had hanging on the back of the door and slid it on. She padded out into the bedroom but...he wasn't there. She looked longingly at the bed and felt a pang of regret that they weren't both still lying there tangled up together. Reaching out, she ran her hand along the cool fabric of the comforter when she heard someone banging on the front door. The bedroom door was closed, so she pressed her ear against the wood to listen for who was being so damn loud this early in the morning.

"Mom?" Mason said incredulously. "What are you doing here?"

"How could you not call me and tell me your sister was almost killed last night thanks to you?"

"What?!"

That was Scarlett's reaction too. Was this woman for real?

"Like it's not bad enough you find the need to hold on to that awful bar, but then you have to drag your sister into it and force her to work there?"

"No one forced Peyton to do anything, Mom!" Mason snapped and Scarlett could hear the frustration in his voice. "And we both know if I called Peyton right now, she'd tell you that!"

"Whatever! The fact still remains that because of this ridiculous project of yours, your sister could have been hurt!"

"A week ago, you were on board with the north end project and praising my work!"

"That was before I realized how dangerous it was and had to hear how my daughter nearly got trapped in that filthy place!"

Reaching out, Scarlett's hand was on the doorknob ready to yank the door open and give this woman a piece of her mind, but she waited.

And it was harder than she thought.

"Okay, enough with the theatrics!" Mason yelled. "You do not get to barge in here and start yelling at me about things you know nothing about! What happened yesterday was an accident and–in case you didn't realize it–Tommy Flynn is in the hospital after suffering second-degree burns, a concussion, and smoke inhalation! He made sure Peyton and everyone who was in there got out rather than trying to save himself!" He let out a string of curses and Scarlett imagined him pacing back and forth. "Peyton was looked at by the paramedics and didn't require a visit to the ER! She was frightened, but so were all the people who were there!"

"You should be looking out for your sister rather than endangering her!" Georgia Bishop cried and Scarlett had to roll her eyes at the woman's dramatic tendencies. "Where were you when this was going on? Why was Peyton there and you weren't?"

Uh-oh...she didn't like the direction this conversation just went in.

"I didn't need to be there, Mom," Mason stated, trying to calm them both down. "I didn't know Peyton was still there. She told me she was leaving just a few minutes after me when I saw her earlier in the day."

"Why did you leave her there?"

*Oh for crying out loud...*

"Mom, I had to get back to work and then I had...I had a date last night," he said.

"Oh...that's right," Georgia said with a lot of distaste. "You went out with Scarlett Jones again. I heard she's claiming to be pregnant with your child. Well if she thinks..."

"*Enough!*" he bellowed and Scarlett actually jumped. "You don't get to have an opinion on this! You don't get to tell me what you think or how you feel because I don't care!

And you most certainly don't get to stand here in my home and say anything bad about the woman I love!"

*Say what now?*

"Now I suggest that you leave," he went on. "And I would think twice if I were you about what you say about Scarlett or about anything else where I'm concerned because if I hear that you so much as *tried* to say something slanderous about her, I swear to you we will never speak again!"

"Mason!" Georgia cried. "You're not being rational!"

"Say one more thing against Scarlett and watch how irrational I can be," he challenged.

In the bedroom, Scarlett held her breath and waited to see what was going to happen. It took a solid three minutes before she heard the front door open and then close, and another minute or two before she heard a car pull away. Her heart was beating wildly and she had no idea what she was supposed to do. Did she just walk out into the living room and pretend she hadn't heard the argument? The way his mother spoke about her? Or the fact that Mason had said he loved her? For all she knew, he had said it just to shut his mother up, but...now she really wanted to know if he meant it.

Now would be a really inappropriate time to ask that, right?

There was no way she could hide out in here all day, so with a steadying breath, she opened the door and the sight before her made her want to cry. Mason was standing with his hands braced on the granite kitchen island and his head was bowed. He looked completely defeated.

Wordlessly, she walked up behind him and placed her hands on his shoulders, unsure of what to do or say.

"I'm so sorry," he said, his voice low and gruff.

Her eyes went a little wide. "What are you apologizing for?"

"That you had to hear any of that." When Scarlett started to deny it, he straightened and looked at her with disbelief. "This is my life, Scarlett," he went on. "This is what I've been dealing with. The night we met? When we were talking about why I had to reclaim my life? That's why. She's why!"

"Mason..."

"I can't believe she came here and would say all that! I don't know why she's so damn hateful!" Now he was pacing and Scarlett had no choice but to stand back and let him. "I honestly don't know what else to do or say to make her understand! She takes everything and blows it out of proportion! And when I get my hands on my sister..."

"Okay, okay, okay," she interrupted. "There's no reason to get upset with your sister. She was traumatized by what happened yesterday. It's only normal she'd talk to her mother about it."

"Don't defend her," he snapped, but Scarlett knew he wasn't really mad at her.

"Look, if you know your mother has a tendency to over-react and embellish the truth, then you know she took what-ever it was that Peyton told her and completely blew it out of proportion." She paused and saw he was looking a lot more relaxed. "You should probably call your sister and talk to her before you let this fester."

Groaning, he raked both hands through his hair. "This really wasn't how I envisioned our morning going." Then he gave her a lopsided grin and her heart squeezed.

"Yeah, this totally wasn't my dream morning either. Running from bed to vomit and then...well...this..."

He groaned again. "How much did you hear?"

Ugh...did she really want to answer that?

"Scarlett?"

"All of it?" she said weakly.

He muttered a curse before growling with frustration. "Well that's just great!" he snarled. "Leave it to her to ruin something else for me!"

"Um...what?" Now she was a little confused. Georgia had no idea Scarlett was there so how could she be ruining anything?

He was back to pacing again. "I mean, she shows up here uninvited and the first time you hear that I love you, it's while I'm screaming it at my mother in the middle of an argument! How freaking fair is that?"

It would be easy to let him keep spiraling here, but she knew she needed to do something to calm him down and get him out of this funk. Stepping in front of him, Scarlett reached up and cupped his face in her hands and forced him to look at her. "Say it."

He frowned. "Say what?"

Rolling her eyes dramatically, she gave him a sassy grin. "Say it now when you're not yelling at anyone."

He blinked several times before he finally understood what she was saying. "You're pretty bossy. You know that, right?"

"Damn straight I am. C'mon, Bishop. Say it." It was crazy how her heart was so jittery and that she was trembling as she waited. A trickle of fear and doubt crept in as she worried he might not be able to tell her he loved her because he hadn't meant it. Now queasiness began to kick in and she prayed she wasn't going to vomit right here in the middle of his living room.

Reaching up, Mason covered her hands with his and slowly dragged them away from his face until they were resting over his heart. "Scarlett Jones, I thought you were pretty and a bit of a badass when we were lab partners in middle school. And you were all that and more when I saw you at the concert. One look at you and my entire life turned upside down even as it fell completely into place." He paused and smiled at her. "That's what you do for me. And I know we still have so much to talk about, but you need to know that I'm so in love with you. Every day we were apart was torture for me."

"For me too," she admitted.

He looked ready to say something–or at least like he was ready to lean in and kiss her–when he suddenly pulled back.

"Mason? What's the matter?"

"We need to do this right," he said after a long pause.

A nervous laugh was out before she could stop it. "I think we're a little beyond that, don't you agree?" She put one hand on her stomach for emphasis.

Shaking his head, he laughed with her. "That's not what I meant. Well...sort of." Stepping away, he walked to the kitchen and poured her a glass of orange juice. "There are some things we need to clear up first–I need you to understand the situation with my inheritance and how I ended up with The Mystic Magnolia."

Before he could say anything else, she was in front of him, placing a finger over his lips. "It doesn't matter," she said emphatically. "It wasn't my place to get involved." Then she groaned and moved away. "In case you haven't noticed, I tend to speak first and think later."

"Well..."

She shot him a look before continuing. "The whole situation seemed a little unreal to me–a little too coincidental." Then she sighed and almost hated the words she was about to say, even though she couldn't stop them. "And even right now all I'm thinking is how you still got your way! The bar is gone! Now you can bulldoze it to the ground and sell the property and make lots of money and be done with it!"

His expression turned fierce and then sad. "Is that seriously what you think?"

"I...I...don't know. I honestly don't know anymore, Mason! I can't help where my mind automatically goes! For years this is how I saw the world–how I saw people like you! And I..." She paused and fought the urge to walk away and cry. "I'm afraid to let myself believe...that maybe..."

He didn't let her finish. Walking to her, Mason wrapped her in his arms and held her as the tears began to fall.

"Dammit, I am so over all this crying!" she said weakly, even though she stomped her foot to make her point. "It's the worst."

Chuckling softly, he kissed the top of her head. "I think it's cute."

She groaned and wanted to be mad at him for making fun of her, but she couldn't. Pulling back slightly, she looked up at him. "What is wrong with you?"

Brows furrowed, he asked, "What do you mean?"

"I mean I am a horrible person and yet...you just keep putting up with me! Why?"

He looked at her like she were crazy. "Do you say some really mean things? Yes. Do they bother me? Sometimes. But here's the thing, Scarlett, I also know you and who you really are. And part of who you are is this mean girl who speaks her mind, but would also give someone the shirt off of her back. You're someone who likes to look like a badass, but you volunteer at animal shelters and build little houses for dogs who are waiting for their forever homes. You are fiercely loyal to your friends and family and would do anything for them." Then he reached up and cupped her face. "All those things–the good and the bad–make you this incredible woman. And I happen to be crazy about you."

Well damn.

"But..."

One strong finger went over her lips. "Stop arguing," he said softly, resting his forehead against hers. They stayed like that for several minutes. "Can I make you some breakfast?"

"I normally just have some tea and toast," she replied, burrowing close to him.

"I can do that."

It was her usual, but...she wanted something different right now. "Do you have any eggs?"

He nodded. "Want me to scramble some?"

It was a possibility. "Do you have the makings for pancakes?"

Laughing softly, he nodded again. "I do. And syrup so... you want pancakes?"

Did she?

Mason's hand stroked slowly up and down her back and it felt so good, so hypnotic...so damn sexy.

Shifting in his arms, Scarlett placed a small kiss on his chest. She wished he hadn't put on shorts and a t-shirt, but it would have been awkward if he hadn't–considering he'd been standing here just a few minutes ago, arguing with his mother.

Her hands skimmed down his chest and slowly snaked under his shirt. His skin felt so warm and wonderful.

"Scarlett..."

But she wasn't really paying attention. She was sure he was trying to stop her, trying to be a gentleman, but that was the last thing she wanted right now. For right now, she wanted them to be the way they were a month ago. She wanted to pretend that all the bad, all the negative stuff, never happened. It was foolish of her to think that way, but in this moment, all she wanted was the right to touch him and be touched by him.

"You really should have some breakfast," he said weakly, but her hands were busy exploring and his breath hitched slightly.

She loved when that happened.

"I will," she said. "Later." Her hands moved up until his shirt was almost off. Mason whipped it over his head right before scooping her up in his arms and carrying her back to the bedroom.

Placing her gently on the center of the bed, he studied her for a long moment before lying down beside her. "How am I supposed to take care of you if you won't let me?" he asked, even as his hands skimmed her legs that were now exposed. "Nice robe, by the way."

Smiling impishly, Scarlett pulled open the tie and quickly shimmied out of it. "I figured I'd try to be proper." Then she laughed. "Of course, it was before your mother arrived."

"Ugh...don't remind me..."

Reaching up, she caressed his cheek, his jaw. "How about I remind you of this?" Then she guided him close until their lips touched and kissed him. It went from a sweet touch to full-on heat and need in the blink of an eye.

*I've missed this...*

After that, there was no need to remind anyone of anything. What little clothes they were wearing were quickly stripped and thrown aside and when Mason's body covered hers, Scarlett was beyond ready. Beyond turned on.

He paused and looked down at her. "I promised myself we weren't going to do this. Not yet," he said, his voice low and gruff and oh-so serious.

Again, it was on the tip of her tongue to make a sassy comment, but...she knew what he meant. "Yeah. Me too."

Just then, he moved—just a little—and Scarlett knew there was no way they could stop now.

"I'm okay with breaking this one promise," she said, her back arching so she could press against him. "How about you?"

His smile was slow and sexy and it made all her girly parts sigh with happiness. "Just this once," he said, right before capturing her lips with his.

# THIRTEEN

The days that followed were insanely busy, but Mason and Scarlett spent all of them together. It was a little surreal to her because they were on the same page on just about everything. He had taken time off of work to deal with the insurance companies regarding the bar and he also wanted to make sure he was in constant contact with her grandfather to see how he wanted to proceed. Every time she watched the two of them together, Scarlett's heart felt ready to burst with love.

It didn't take long for her grandfather to decide it would be best if Mason simply demolished what was left of the building and used the property for something that would benefit the community. The conversation had been beyond emotional–for all of them–but in the end, they all agreed to honor his request.

The more Scarlett thought about it, however, the more she realized that Mason never really commented on what exactly his plans were. She wanted to push, but she had things of her own to deal with.

Mainly, figuring out what to do about his family.

Yeah, she never brought it up with him, but the argument she'd overheard between him and his mother was never far from her mind.

One day led into another and soon they were taking her grandfather home from the hospital. Her brother Kyle was going to stay with him for a few days to make sure he was truly doing okay and that gave her a little peace of mind. Volunteers were busy working on the north end of town and Scarlett had been putting together a proposal to send out to several businesses to help spread the word about the work. At the end of every day, she and Mason either crawled into her bed or his and she was starting to feel a little better physically. While she knew it couldn't possibly be because she had Mason beside her, there was a little part of her that hoped it was.

Now, as they sat in an exam room in her OB-GYN's office, she wondered how Mason was feeling.

"You okay?" she asked, noticing him studying the posters on the wall.

"I know we learned all of this in health class, but...holy shit there's a lot to know," he said, with a small, nervous laugh. "I mean, look at all this."

"Believe me, I have. The day I found out I was pregnant, I started reading all kinds of stuff online. I fear I have too much information now."

Looking over his shoulder, he smiled at her. "You're going to kick ass at being pregnant."

That made her laugh out loud. "I don't know about that. I kind of got off to a very wimpy and weepy start."

"Totally normal."

She arched a brow at him. "Have you been reading up on pregnancy, Bishop?"

"Let's just say I've been Googling a few things."

"Why does that sound just a little dirty?" she teased and was about to say more when Dr. Jackson walked in.

For the next twenty-minutes, Scarlett fought off mortification as Mason stood by her shoulder while she was examined. They had argued about it before they even left the house, and he was adamant about wanting to experience everything with her.

Every. Single. Thing.

"Okay, let's see if we can hear a heartbeat," Dr. Jackson said, smiling as she poured some gel on Scarlett's belly.

"We can hear one already?" Mason asked.

She nodded. "If your calculations are correct, Scarlett's eight weeks pregnant so it's the perfect time to detect a heartbeat."

The gel was cold and the wand rubbing over her stomach tickled slightly, but Scarlett reached for Mason's hand more for moral support than anything else. And as she looked up at him from her spot on the exam table, she could tell he was holding his breath, just like she was.

A minute later, Dr. Jackson's smile grew. "There it is," she said softly. "That's your baby's heartbeat!"

It was the most amazing thing Scarlett had ever heard in her entire life. Mason squeezed her hand as he leaned in and kissed her. "We did that," he said with a hint of awe, and all she could do was nod.

They listened for a few more minutes before Dr. Jackson explained what appointments she needed to schedule next and the things she needed to be doing to help with her morning sickness. By the time they left, Scarlett felt like she was floating on a cloud. Out in the parking lot, she noticed the goofy grin on Mason's face.

"Should we go grab something to eat?" she asked, her own smile firmly in place.

"I wish I could, but I really need to go into work for a couple of hours today. How about tonight? And someplace other than the Sand Bar," he quickly added before she could even suggest it. Now that her nausea was more under control, she was starting to have cravings. For burgers. All the time.

With a dramatic sigh, she said, "Fine. Whatever. Take me out for real food, I guess."

Kissing her soundly, Mason dropped her off at her place and promised to call her later. Scarlett watched as he drove away and contemplated what she was going to do next. She had work to do—that was a given—but she had too much on her mind to sit down and focus. So she did the only thing she could...

She got in her car and decided to go share her news.

* * *

THIRTY MINUTES LATER, Scarlett let out a long breath and placed her hand over her nervous stomach.

"Don't throw up," she murmured right before she climbed the steps and knocked on the door. She didn't have to wait long for it to open.

And come face to face with the disapproving glare of Georgia Bishop.

*Don't throw up...*

"Can I help you?" Georgia said, her expression pinched.

Scarlett knew several things about herself: first, she had a terrible poker face. If she was thinking or feeling something, it showed. Second, if someone didn't like her, it didn't really bother her so...screw them. And lastly, she was raised to be polite to her elders.

Plastering a serene smile on her face, she said, "Good afternoon, Mrs. Bishop. I'm Scarlett Jones and..."

"I know who you are," she replied, her pert nose wrinkling ever-so-slightly.

Doing her best to ignore every instinct that was telling her to just say what she had to say and then leave, Scarlett kept her smile in place. "Yes, well...I was wondering if you had a few minutes to talk." And for the life of her, she truly believed the older woman was going to tell her no and ask her to leave. But to her surprise, Georgia opened the door and stepped aside for Scarlett to walk in.

Once through the door, a little of her confidence faded. The house was like something out of a decorating magazine and she was afraid to touch anything. Georgia led the way to the kitchen and offered her a seat at the table. Everything was white and shiny and expensive-looking and she said a quick prayer of thanks that she hadn't worked in the garage for a while now.

If she expected the woman to show some manners by offering her something to drink, she was sadly mistaken. Taking the seat opposite her, Georgia Bishop simply stared at her expectantly.

And that's what did it—that one little act of defiance from that woman. Everyone in the South offered a guest something to drink! Every. One. So if that's the way it had to be, then so be it.

Her smile went from serene to cocky as she shifted to get more comfortable in her seat. "I thought I'd come here today so we could get to know each other," Scarlett began. "It bothers me how you and Mason aren't speaking and I honestly thought I might be able to help with the situation. But now, I don't think it's the right thing to do."

One perfectly blonde brow arched at her, but other than that, Georgia's expression didn't change.

"You see, I was raised to respect my parents. When I met Mason, one of the things I most admired about him were his manners." She paused just as Georgia was starting to look smug. "Clearly he learned them from his father." Rising, she added, "Be sure to thank Mr. Bishop for me. He raised a great son."

She'd gone no more than three feet when Mason's mother stood. "Who do you think you are coming in here and speaking to me that way? I knew you were nothing more than..."

Scarlett whipped around and faced her. "I'm nothing more than the woman your son loves! The woman who loves him back!" She took a menacing step forward. "And the woman who is going to have his baby."

Georgia's eyes went wide and it was good to see she clearly hadn't had Botox.

"We had that confirmed this morning," Scarlett went on, grinning with triumph. "Heard the little heartbeat and everything. So here's the way I see it–you can apologize to Mason for being an overbearing pain in his ass and apologize to me, too, because you've been incredibly rude and judgmental where I'm concerned–or you can miss out. I know my grandparents loved being involved in my life. Some of my greatest memories of when I was growing up involve them."

Georgia's mouth opened and closed multiple times, but no words came out.

"I'm not looking for us to be friends, but I just thought my child might want to know his or her grandparents." She paused and cursed how choked up she was getting. "My mom died when I was four so...you'll be the only grandmother he or she has and...I thought that was important. So..."

In that moment, Georgia's entire demeanor changed. "I didn't realize you were so young when she died," she said quietly. "It must have been very difficult for you."

Nodding, Scarlett agreed. "It never gets easier. I love my dad and my brothers, but...there's definitely something to be said about a girl needing her mom." Swallowing hard, she knew she'd said all she came to say. "Anyway, I just really wanted a chance to talk to you face to face. You judged me without even taking the time to know me. But I love your son and I see what this rift between the two of you is doing to him and it bothers me."

Looking a little meeker than she did moments ago, Georgia replied, "It bothers me too. I...I didn't realize just how harsh I was being."

"I think you did," Scarlett said, not caring how unsympathetic she sounded. She had a feeling Georgia was used to playing for sympathy and that wasn't going to fly here. "I think you like pushing your children into falling in line with what you want. The only problem with that logic is how all you're accomplishing is pushing them away. Is that really what you want?"

"Well...I..."

"I mean, Mason is an incredible man," she went on. "And Peyton is a pretty amazing woman. I haven't met Parker yet but I'm pretty sure I'm going to think the same about her. Why would you want your own kids not to want anything to do with you?"

"That's not how it is! My daughters..."

"If you do to them even half of what you do to Mason, trust me, they'll walk away too! Take some advice, and learn from your mistakes!" Letting out a long breath, Scarlett took a step back. "Now if you'll excuse me, I have puppies I need to find homes for. Have a good day, Mrs. Bishop."

Again, she hadn't gone more than three feet when Georgia asked, "Are you...are you talking about the puppies over at Happy Tails?"

Unable to help herself, Scarlett's eyes went a little wide. "I am. How do you know about them?"

"I've seen the posts on social media about them and..." She smiled and let out a soft laugh. "They're all just so cute. I can't believe anyone would abandon them."

"It happens all the time. I'm so thankful for Ed and Christine and the service they provide but it's really turned into a full-time job for them. They need a lot of help and they get a ton of volunteers, but what they really need is more land and more funds. I do what I can with my time–helping feed and bathe and play with the dogs–and I do handle most of their social media stuff for them, but some days it doesn't even feel like a drop in the bucket."

"What type of funding do they need? Where do they get their supplies from? Do they get any help from the county?"

And that's when an idea came to mind that might just accomplish more than Scarlett could have done on her own. "Why don't you come with me?"

"Excuse me?"

She nodded. "Come with me. Meet Christine and the staff and see for yourself what their setup is like."

"Oh, I'm not...I'm sure I wouldn't know what to do. And look at me. Am I dressed to walk around a...a dog farm?" she laughed nervously.

"Well, I'm sure you have something a little more casual to change into and a pair of tennis shoes, don't you?"

Georgia nodded.

"So go change and I'll take you over with me. It'll be fun!"

"Fun?" Georgia repeated with another laugh. "Ask anyone in my family and they'll tell you I don't know how to have fun."

"Well, now's your chance to prove them wrong!"

* * *

Meet me at Happy Tails. There's something here you have to see.

MASON STARED at his phone and smiled. Actually, he hadn't stopped smiling all day. Every time he thought about hearing the baby's heartbeat he would stop and wonder how he got to be so lucky. Was everything perfect right now? Hell no! Their lives were crazy and hectic and complicated, but at the end of the day, he got to go home to his girl and that made it all okay.

This weekend, he planned on asking Scarlett to marry him. It was fast, he knew that, and people didn't need to get married because they were having a baby, but...it's what he wanted for the two of them. And, he felt it was something Scarlett wanted too.

At least, he hoped he was reading her right.

As for meeting her at Happy Tails, that was a little puzzling. They hadn't talked about it earlier and while he did go there a couple of times with her, it was primarily her thing. What could he possibly need to see?

A knock on his office door pulled him from his musings and he looked up to see Richard McClellan standing there. Mason stood and shook his hand. "Hey, Richard. What can I do for you?"

"I drew up those papers you asked me to." Reaching into his briefcase, he pulled out a folder and handed them to Mason.

"Thanks. That was fast."

"Well, I figured there might be a bit of a rush in order," he replied, taking a seat. "I stopped and saw Tommy on my way here. He's damn near giddy. I don't think I've ever seen him smile so much."

Yeah, Mason felt pretty good about that. Tommy was healing well and it was a big relief to everyone. Then he and Scarlett told him about the baby and he was over the moon at the thought of becoming a great-grandfather again. But the biggest contributor to his good mood was...

"I have to admit, Mason, I didn't think you'd really do it," Richard stated, but there was a very pleased smile on his face.

"I don't think anyone expected me to," Mason said, scanning the documents. "Not even my great-grandfather."

"I wouldn't be so sure about that."

Placing the file down on the desk, he frowned. "What do you mean?"

"First, I just want to go over a few things on the papers," Richard explained. "You're splitting ownership of the property The Mystic Magnolia stood on 50/50, correct?"

Mason nodded.

"And the café you are building in its place will have you being even partners with Tommy, even though you are the one investing the money and not him, correct?"

Mason nodded again, wondering why Richard was stating everything like this.

"And lastly, you're paying off all the outstanding debt Tommy accrued, giving him a clean slate moving forward, correct?"

"Richard, what's going on? We discussed all of this already and it's all here in the paperwork, isn't it?"

He held up a hand. "Just...humor me for another minute, okay?"

What choice did he have?

They discussed everything that was on the document and Mason signed it, then handed it back to Richard.

"When your great-grandfather came to me to write up his will and he told me his plans for all of you, most of it made sense. Jake got the construction business because he was already running it. Mallory got the décor shop because it was one of her favorite places. Your sister got the restaurant because she always wanted to own one."

Again, Mason nodded, still unsure where all of this was going.

"Then he told me he was leaving The Mystic Magnolia to you and it just didn't fit." He paused. "We actually argued over it. I told him it was wrong—it made no sense. Then he explained himself."

"I think I know what you're going to say, Richard," Mason interrupted. "Pops left it to me so I could sell it have some financial security of my own to break away from my folks."

Richard looked at him oddly. "Um...no."

"What?"

Reaching into his briefcase, Richard pulled out another envelope and handed it to Mason. "This is what Zeke was thinking." He stood. "Give me a call tomorrow and we'll talk some more." He stood and was about to walk away.

"Wait!" Mason said, coming to his feet. "What is this?"

"That," he said with a very pleased smile, "is the rest of your inheritance." He paused. "Have a good night, Mason."

Curiosity got the better of him and rather than ask

Richard more questions, he sat back down in his chair and carefully opened the envelope.

---

*Mason,*

*I sure hope you actually get to read this. It would tick me off if I spend all this time writing and this paper does nothing but sit in Richard's office collecting dust. For argument's sake, let's say you're reading it.*

*Actually, I'm sure you're reading it. Why? Because I have faith in you. Your folks did a great disservice to you by trying to force you to live their way, but I always knew, deep down, that you were going to be different—that you were going to take a stand and be your own person. And if you're reading this, then you're well on your way.*

*What am I talking about? I'm talking about Tommy Flynn and The Mystic Magnolia. It had to make your mama crazy when she heard I left it to you, huh? And I'm sure you wondered why too. But if you're reading this, you didn't take the easy way out. You saw something in Tommy Flynn like I did. He's a man who lost a lot in his life—and I know we all have—but...Tommy never quite got over it. I did as much as I could for him and I hate not knowing exactly how it all went down, but the fact that Richard gave you this letter tells me you wanted to help ol' Tommy too.*

*Some would say in doing so, I sort of robbed you of an inheritance. And to a certain degree, it's true. But what nobody knows—other than Richard—is that I had something else planned for you. Everyone knows I owned a lot of property in this town. I bought it when it was dirt cheap and there's a lot I never had the opportunity to develop. I saw so much of myself in you, Mason, and I only wish we had spent more time together to really explore that.*

*There are two parcels of land I always wished I could do more with. There's never enough time, you know? Anyway, there's seven acres out on the north end of town—right on the town limits—and I want you to have it. Do with it whatever you want—do something for the town or something for yourself. I trust you. But there's another piece of land right on the Sound. It's beautiful. My father always said he was going to build my mother a new house—a bigger house than the one we had. He never had the chance and honestly, she was happy right where she was. It's two acres and it's only a half-mile away from my house. I hope you'll keep it and build a home for yourself—something your folks have no say in. Maybe someplace you can raise a family and teach them about all those who came before them and created Magnolia Sound.*

*Be well, son. Be happy.*

*But most of all, be proud of yourself. You're a hell of a fine man.*

*Love, Pops*

---

It wasn't until the wet spot appeared on the paper did Mason realize he was crying.

Well damn, he thought. All this time he thought Pops didn't really know him and it turned out, he was rooting for him all along.

He was probably the only one in his family who was.

Now he knew why Richard wanted him to call tomorrow. Gathering up the letter, the folder, and a few other things, Mason headed out of the office. This was a lot of information to digest and he knew the only person he wanted to share it with was Scarlett. In his car, he quickly made his way across town and he wondered what he was going to do with everything he just received. He was already investing in a restaurant with Tommy, and now he had the opportunity to build a house of his own right on the water, and to create something with the property on the north end. If Pops only knew of the plans for that part of town, he'd be thrilled.

Pulling into the small parking area for Happy Tails' guests, Mason spotted Scarlett's car and smiled. They were going to celebrate tonight for sure. As he made his way through the gate toward the barn, he thought about the kind of house they could build and couldn't wait to hear her plans for her dream house because–thanks to Pops–they could make them a reality.

"Hey!" Scarlett called out, a Golden Retriever puppy wriggling in her arms. "You're early!"

"I was anxious to see you," he said, walking to her and kissing her soundly. When they broke apart, he rubbed the puppy's head. "Is this who you wanted me to see?"

"What?" she asked, laughing. "No. Not this guy, although isn't he precious?"

It would be way too much to take on pregnancy, a marriage proposal, a new business, building a new home, and adopting a dog. He had his limits, but...if Scarlett asked, Mason knew he'd find a way to make it happen. "So, what's going on?"

The sound of laughter floated from the barn and

whoever was in there was having a great time. He couldn't help but smile. Scarlett looked over her shoulder and motioned for him to follow her. "This is what I wanted you to see."

He walked beside her as the puppy continued to try to get down. He was about to offer to take the dog from her arms when he caught sight of who was laughing.

"*Mom?!* What are you doing?"

Still laughing while sitting in a pile of hay, his mother looked up at him with pure delight. "Oh, Mason, look at all these sweet dogs!" She was surrounded by probably eight puppies who looked exactly like the one in Scarlett's arms.

"What is happening right now?" he murmured, leaning toward Scarlett.

Placing the puppy down to go play with his siblings, Scarlett stood and pulled him a few feet away from the melee. "Okay, don't be angry, but...I went to talk to your mother today."

"Why?" he asked with more annoyance than he probably should have.

"Mason, she's your mother and we're having a baby together and all this fighting isn't good for anyone. Plus, I was a little miffed at the way she spoke about me."

"Yeah, well...that's her for you."

"Oh, I got that. Believe me," Scarlett said with a small laugh.

"So how did it go? I mean, obviously it must have gone well if you got her here."

"Um...honestly? It was awful. I've never had my patience tested quite like that before."

"God, Scarlett," he said, pulling her into his embrace. "I'm sorry." Then he cursed under his breath. "Then why is she here?"

Pulling back, she smiled up at him and told him about the rest of her visit. "We talked a lot on the way over here..."

"It's a ten-minute drive," he commented. "How much could you have said?"

"We didn't jump out of the car the minute we got here," she replied sarcastically. "And once we got her out of the car and got the stick out of her ass, she really seemed to mellow."

The imagery alone made him laugh. Looking over his shoulder, he saw his mother still sitting on the ground playing with the dogs while talking to Christine. "This is all just a little bizarre to me. Are you sure you didn't drug her or hit her on the head?"

"I was tempted to, believe me, but...I don't know. I think she just forgot how to put her guard down and live like a normal person."

"What does that even mean?"

"It means she lives her life for appearances! She usually only does things to make herself look good–and by look good I mean for vanity's sake. Coming out here, she realized how ridiculous she'd look in one of her Chanel suits or Vera Wang dresses. Sometimes it's good to get dirty, you know?"

He hugged her close and leaned down to whisper in her ear, "Personally, I enjoy getting dirty with you."

She giggled and he loved the sound of it. "Stop it!" she hissed. "Someone will hear you."

He doubted that, so he quickly asked, "Hey, Scarlett?"

Groaning, she rested her head on his chest and started to laugh. "Please don't..."

"Hey baby, I must be a light switch, cuz every time I see you, you turn me on!" They were both laughing and holding each other tight and it was little things like this that made his day. When they finally stopped, he looked over at his mother again who was watching them both and smiling.

It was a little unnerving.

Turning, he figured he should talk to her. With one arm wrapped around Scarlett's waist, he asked, "So what are you doing here, Mom? This hardly seems like something you'd be interested in."

Scarlett pinched him and he had to stifle a curse.

Standing, Georgia wiped the hay from her shorts as she walked over to them. "I'm actually very fond of animals, Mason," she said pleasantly. "I just never realized there was such a need so close to home."

It was on the tip of his tongue to make a snarky comment, but he refrained.

"I'm coming back tomorrow to talk to Christine and her husband about their immediate needs and we're going to work on a plan to raise some money and perhaps find them a larger piece of land."

Mason thought about what he'd just been given, but he wasn't ready to share it with his mother. He wanted to talk to Scarlett when they were alone. Which reminded him...

"Are you almost finished for the day?" he asked Scarlett. "I made dinner plans for us."

Beside him, she blushed. "I think I'm done." She glanced around before looking at his mother. "Ready for me to take you home?"

"Actually, I texted Beau and asked him to meet me out here. I'd like him to get a look at things as well. Plus," she went on, smiling, "Christine invited us to stay for dinner."

Mason knew his eyes were practically bugging out and he didn't have to look at Scarlett to know hers were as well.

"Seriously, what is happening here?" he said quietly.

"Just smile and wave," she whispered beside him and

within minutes they were both at their cars. "Your house or mine?"

"Do you have everything you need at my place to go out tonight or do you need to stop and get stuff?" In all honesty, they could go to either, but he wanted to sleep at his place tonight and to be there when he told her about everything he found out today.

"You go and I'll be a few minutes behind you. I need to grab a few things." She kissed him and Mason stood back and watched her drive away.

# FOURTEEN

The French doors were open and there was a cool breeze blowing in the room. Scarlett was exactly where she wanted to be–in Mason's arms.

"You okay?" he asked quietly.

They had gone to dinner and he told her about the inheritance he just learned of today. Then they drove around trying to figure out where the properties were but it was dark and they really couldn't see anything.

"I'm perfect," she replied, snuggling closer to him.

"Yeah, you are."

"This was an amazing day. Like everything about it was just...incredible. I feel like I've stepped into some kind of dream and I'm afraid I'm going to wake up and it's all going to be gone."

"I swear I'm still in awe over hearing the baby's heart-beat. I didn't even know it was a possibility this early on in the pregnancy."

She nodded. "I'm not going to lie–I was nervous."

"How come?"

"What if they couldn't find a heartbeat? What if the test

results weren't accurate? I mean, I've finally gotten used to the idea and...I'm already in love with this baby." And she seriously was. She was still scared as hell about the thought of being a mother, but that was normal.

"Me too," he agreed, playing with her hair. "I wish I could have been there when you went off on my mother and told her about the baby."

"Yeah, I guess I should have run that by you first, but...I felt like it had to happen this way. I know she's your mom and all, but I couldn't imagine treating my child the way she treats you. And I think by doing it this way, we're going to have a fairly solid relationship."

"How do you figure?"

"She knows I'm on to her," she said simply. "I'm a bit of a bull in a china shop compared to her and by laying my cards out on the table from the get-go, she knows where I stand."

"I thought I was seeing things when I walked into the barn."

"Your face was pretty comical."

"Yeah, well...a little bit of heads-up would have been nice."

"Nah, I was living for seeing that expression!"

"You are never boring, Scarlett."

"Do you want boring?"

He shook his head. "For a long time, I thought that was what I was going to get–that it was all I deserved."

"Well that's just sad."

"And then I went to grab a beer at a concert and I haven't been bored since."

"Such flattery," she preened, kissing his chest. They lay there in companionable silence for several long minutes until he spoke.

"It wasn't just today that was wild. This whole last week has been pretty crazy," Mason said, his tone a bit more serious than it was a minute ago.

"That it has."

"I feel like we've spent so much time focusing on Tommy, the bar, the campaign for the businesses in the north end...I don't know...it's like we've glossed over...us."

Pushing up a little, Scarlett looked at him in confusion. "What do you mean?"

He shrugged. "I mean, we're here and we're together and it's exactly what I want."

"But..."

"But..." he continued. "I guess I'm wondering if we'd be here if you hadn't found out you were pregnant."

Okay, wow.

Not that she hadn't thought it herself, but it was a little scary that Mason was thinking it too.

And how they hadn't really talked about it until now.

It had been easy to just slip back into relationship mode and to fill any awkward time when they should have been talking with making love or just talking about the things going on around them. But it looked like they were finally going to have to address the elephant in the room.

"I'd like to think we would," he said, interrupting her thoughts. His hand was stroking her arm as he went on. "I don't want there to be any doubts, Scarlett. I know why I'm here and I'm in it for the long-haul. Forever. But...in all the times we've talked, I feel like...it's been a little one-sided. I pour out my heart and you don't. Not really. You haven't said where you see us. We talk about the baby and about being together, but what does together look like to you? Are we living together like roommates? Are we co-parenting? I mean, these are things we really need to be talking about."

It shamed her that he was right. "It's hard for me, Mason," she admitted lowly. "I didn't grow up in a house where we did a whole lot of sharing our feelings. I mean, I knew we all loved each other, but we didn't...talk about it. And before you, I never dated a guy who wanted to talk about his feelings." She paused. "But I'm trying, I really am."

In the moonlight, she saw him nod and she wasn't sure what to do or say to put his mind at ease.

"I love you, Mason. I love the way you make me laugh. I love all of our crazy conversations. I love that you're the one I'm going through all these changes with." Pausing, she smiled and caressed his cheek. "I love that you're going to be the father of this baby. But more than anything, I love you." She almost couldn't finish speaking because she felt overwhelmed with emotion.

"Scarlett..."

"Just like I was scared today while Dr. Jackson tried to find the baby's heartbeat, I'm scared to let myself think too much about what the future holds for us. If you want to know where I see us–it's together. Not co-parenting, not roommates, but partners. I look at you, Mason, and I see everything I ever wanted but didn't know I could have, too."

Tears streamed down her cheeks, slowly wetting his shoulder.

"Sorry," she whispered, wiping at her face.

"Baby," he cooed softly, "please don't cry."

"I swear it's almost as bad as the vomiting," she said, hoping to joke herself out of the tears. "These pregnancy hormones are going to be the death of me."

"Nah. They're not so bad."

"We still have months to go, Bishop. By the time our

due date comes, you're going to be thankful I can go back to normal."

She wasn't going to mention the postpartum hormones would kick in at that point...

"There's nothing wrong with you right now, Scarlett, and you need to stop freaking out about crying."

"Easy for you to say," she murmured.

"If I cried, would that make you feel better?"

Laughing softly, she shook her head. "Hell no. That would get on my nerves fast!"

Now he laughed with her. "Wow. Thanks." Pulling her in close again, he kissed her.

"Oh, stop." Sighing, Scarlett rested her head on his chest. "Are we crazy for doing this?"

"For what? For being in love? Starting a family? Planning a life?"

"Well...yeah. It is still so fast."

"Scarlett, we've been over this. We're not strangers. We've known each other since forever. It just took us a while to get here."

"I guess."

"Oh, my God, why are you always looking for problems?" he whined dramatically. "Seriously, I am a great catch and you're carrying on like I was the last guy on earth you had to choose from."

"You're not going to cry now, are you?" she teased and then squealed as Mason rolled her onto her back and tickled her. "Stop it!" she cried breathlessly, wiggling beneath him. "Stop! Uncle! Uncle!"

"Say it! Say I'm a great catch," he teased, his fingers barely touching her.

"I'm a great catch," she mimicked, sticking her tongue out at him.

And instantly regretted it when he started tickling her again. "Okay, okay, okay! You're a great catch!"

His hands stilled. "And you're lucky to have me."

"Seriously?" she deadpanned. "Someone thinks awful highly of himself."

"With good reason," he said, giving her a loud, smacking kiss on the lips.

"I've created a monster."

"Well, I wouldn't say *you* created..."

"Oh, that's right. You were a bit of an egomaniac before we met," she teased and loved the pout that crossed his face.

"I don't like this game anymore." The pout grew.

"Aww...poor baby," she said softly, moving over so she could straddle his gloriously naked body. "Does someone need me to kiss him and make him feel better?"

"Well...I wouldn't say no if you wanted to..."

"I really want to," she all but purred as she moved over him. Mason's hands came around and rested on her waist before slowly skimming around to grab her ass.

She loved when he did that.

Suddenly, playtime was over.

"I probably should let you get some sleep," he said, even as he lifted his head and began softly kissing her breasts. "But I'm not."

"Good," she said breathlessly. "Because I really love when you do that."

"I'd do this all day and all night if you'd let me."

And for some reason, she didn't doubt it.

She also tried to figure out a way to make that happen.

But once his mouth started to wander along with his hands, all thoughts of anything except wrapping herself around him escaped her. "Mason..." she panted.

Slowly, he rolled her onto her back once again and licked and kissed and touched every inch of her.

And that was okay because she was more than willing to do the same for him. Again and again.

For always.

# EPILOGUE

TWO WEEKS LATER...

"And then the doors will slide open here–I'm thinking the kind that sort of fold up against the wall so it's even more wide open–and the deck will run along the entire expanse of the back of the house. What do you think?"

Scarlett's eyes were wide and she looked at him as if he were crazy. "That sounds...it...I mean..."

"Use your words, Scarlett," Mason prompted, even though he found it adorable when she got all flustered. "Then, over here will be a set of French doors that lead to the master bedroom. You'll need to tell Jake how big of a closet you want. I know about your shoe addiction and I want you to have plenty of space for all of them."

"It's not an addiction," she argued lightly. "Not really."

"And on the lower level will be a two-car garage and a workshop for you if you want to have a space to keep building the dog houses."

Her entire face lit up with delight. "Seriously?"

He nodded. "I told you–I thought of everything." And he had. He was honestly pretty impressed with himself about how he'd sketched out a design the day after he found out about the property and even now had an architect and his cousin Mallory's fiancé, Jake, working on the blueprints.

"How long will it take to build?"

"I'd like to say it will be done by the time the baby's born, but...I can't make any guarantees. We have a meeting with Jake next week so you can ask him then."

Hand in hand, they walked through the overgrown property. It had to be cleared, permits had to be secured, and it was going to be a very lengthy process, but they had their whole lives ahead of them. They walked down closer to the water and he was careful to point out the uneven areas and for her to be careful.

"We'll build a dock down here and maybe have a gazebo down at the end so we can sit out there whenever we want and have a bit of shade."

"That would be nice."

They reached a clearing and Mason stopped to admire the view. It was perfect. The sun was just starting to set and there was something he needed to ask her before they went back to his place.

"So what do you think?"

"Hmm?" Her head was thrown back and she was smiling up at the sky.

"Do you like all of this? The plans, the property?"

"Mm-hmm...it's perfect. Absolutely perfect." Turning to him, she smiled. "I still can't believe it's yours."

"Ours," he corrected and laughed when she rolled her eyes. "What's mine is yours. You know that, right?"

She nodded.

They were silent again for a long moment, watching the boats go by on the Sound. Glancing at her, he playfully nudged her shoulder. "Hey, Scarlett," he began in a tone he knew was bound to get a reaction out of her.

"Oh, no..."

"If I had to choose between breathing or loving you, I would say 'I love you' with my last breath."

The smile she gave him was so beautiful even as she shook her head. "That one wasn't too corny."

"C'mon, you love it when I'm corny. Admit it, you wouldn't change a thing about my corniness."

"You're right. And you wouldn't change a thing about my reaction to it, right?"

"There's only one thing I want to change about you, and that's your last name." Then, dropping onto one knee, Mason pulled the ring he had purchased out of his pocket.

"Change my...oh!" she gasped, her hands instantly covering her mouth. "Oh, my gosh! What's happening?"

"Scarlett Jones, there is no one else in this world I want to have on this journey with me. You make every day better than the last. You make me strong and you inspire me. I love you and I love our baby and I love the life we are sharing. And nothing in the world would make me happier than having you as my wife. Will you marry me?"

"Of course!" she cried and as Mason stood and lifted her into his arms, they sealed it with a kiss. When they finally came up for air, she cupped his face in her hands. "Promise me one thing."

"Anything."

"Promise me this time next year we'll be standing here laughing together."

"Baby, you have my word." He put her down on her feet and placed the ring on her finger. "Forever."

"Forever," she agreed.

# A PREVIEW OF REMIND ME

Go back to where the Magnolia Sound
Series began with
Remind Me

# PROLOGUE

Mallory skipped down the steps and breathed in the ocean air and smiled. No doubt she was going to miss all of this, but it had been a good summer – a great summer! And the memories of it would get her through until she could come back.

Things between her and Jake weren't the best. After their wild romp on the boathouse roof almost a week ago, things were strained and he was distant. They said their goodbyes last night. He said it would be for the best if he didn't come by this morning.

She had to agree.

Looking over her shoulder toward the path that led to his house, she was tempted to run over and see him one last time, but she knew he wasn't there. He was going to Wilmington today to visit some friends. And again, she had to remind herself that it was for the best. She already cried all night. There was no sense in making herself cry more while she drove.

*Like that's not going to happen anyway...*

Grabbing her phone, she ran back up to the house and

straight to Pops' office. After another round of hugs, kisses, and promises to call when she got home, Mallory made her way down to her car and gave the big house one last look.

A long breath whooshed out as she started the car. "I'm coming back," she murmured. "This isn't goodbye and it isn't forever." And with those words, she slowly drove around the large, circular drive and made her way up to the road.

She hadn't gone more than a mile when she groaned.

"Dammit!" Immediately, she did a three-point turn and made her way back to Pops' house. "Darn phone charger." Berating herself for forgetting it, she shook her head. "As organized as I am, how could I have left it behind?"

The answer was simple – she'd brought it down to the boathouse yesterday and left it there by mistake. All morning she kept reminding herself to go down and get it, but between breakfast with Pops and saying goodbye, it slipped her mind.

Rather than going to the front door, Mallory pulled the car around to the Sound side of the house, since it was closer to the boathouse. No need to go inside and go through another round of goodbyes, right?

It took less than five minutes, but as she was heading back to her car, she spotted Jake walking up the back steps of the house and going into the kitchen. Was he coming to say goodbye to her before she left? Her heart skipped a beat and she giddily went after him.

*Just one more kiss*, she told herself. *One more kiss and I'll be able to handle anything.*

When she walked into the kitchen, he wasn't there.

Through the dining room, and he wasn't there.

*Nope, not in the living room. What in the world?*

In the distance, she heard voices. Jake was talking to

Pops. She heard her name mentioned and while she felt a little bad about eavesdropping, she was a little curious if Jake would profess his love for her to her great-grandfather or – at the very least – say how much he was going to miss her.

"I hate this, Zeke. You know that."

"I know you do, but you'll do it because you know it's the right thing."

Silence.

"It shouldn't be like this...I hate lying."

Lying? What was he lying about? She thought.

"You're not lying, son. You're doing what you need to do."

"Am I? Because it feels like a lie. I should have talked to Mallory..."

"Leave Mallory out of this!" Pops snapped. "This has nothing to do with her and everything to do with you and your future. And if you actually want a future – a chance to make something of your life – then you're going to take this and go." He paused. "Don't look back, Jacob. You know this is what you need to do."

Her stomach clenched and she felt like her breakfast was about to make a reappearance. What was she supposed to do? What were they talking about? What was Jake lying about?

"Take the money and go," Pops said.

Oh, God! Pops was paying Jake to go away! How...why...?!

The little voice in her head kept telling her to move – to go confront the two of them – but she couldn't move, was almost paralyzed where she stood. And just when she thought she'd go mad, Jake stormed out of Pops' office, walking right toward her. Only...he didn't see her. He was looking at the ground and it wasn't until he bumped right into her that they both seemed to snap out of their inner thoughts.

"Mallory?" he cried, seemingly horrified at seeing her there. "What...I thought you were gone."

Her throat burned and she took a step back. "I was. I...I forgot my phone charger and came back for it." She paused and glared at him. "And I thought you were going to Wilmington."

He glanced away guiltily. "Yeah, well...I had to...um..."

"You know what?" she said with disgust. "It doesn't matter. Really. Clearly you've got your secrets and I don't mean enough to you to share them."

"Mallory..." he reached for her but she moved away.

"It's better this way," she said, hating how her voice shook. "Now I finally know where I stand." Taking another step back, she gave him one last look. "I think under these circumstances it would be best if we just called this what it was – a summer fling. Nothing serious, right?"

"Mallory, just give me a minute to explain!"

But she couldn't listen. Didn't want to. She had to leave. Now. Now, before she broke down and made even more of a fool out of herself than she had all summer long. "I need to go."

Then she was running down the hall and out the front door. She heard Pops call her name as she ran by his office but she didn't stop. Down the porch steps and across the gravel driveway, she didn't stop. Even when she got in the car, she quickly started it, threw it in gear and sped away.

This time she didn't look back at the big plantation house.

This really was goodbye.

And maybe forever...

\* \* \*

THE NEXT MORNING...

"I EXPECTED MORE from you than to have you run away like that."

It was pointless to argue. Mallory had expected more from herself too. "I know," she replied softly.

"You heard a small portion of a conversation and reacted rather than getting the facts. Are you willing to sit and listen to them now?"

She nodded.

"Mallory?"

Oh, right. Pops couldn't see her nod through the phone. "I am."

"Jake didn't get his financial aid for school and he didn't want to burden his parents with helping him. I offered and he accepted," Pops explained in his usual no-nonsense way.

"Why didn't either of you tell me?" she demanded quietly, knowing better than to be disrespectful and yell at her great-grandfather.

"I can't speak for Jake, but I didn't think it was any of your business."

Yup. No-nonsense.

"Pops..."

"It's true, Mallory. If you had known there was an issue with Jake's tuition, are you telling me you wouldn't have tried to change his mind about going so far away for school?"

"Well..."

"You would," he said before she could answer. "I know how close the two of you were all summer and if you would have asked, Jake would have caved and done what you wanted to make you happy."

Was it wrong that she saw it as a good thing rather than a bad one?

"You and I both know it would have been wrong, Mallory," he said, as if reading her mind. "Jake lost out on a lot due to the financial struggles of his family. He's not a kid going away to college. He's a twenty-four-year-old man and he's waited long enough. I've offered him help in the past and he's always turned it down."

"Then why did he suddenly accept?" And yeah, her tone was a bit bratty, but she couldn't help it.

There was a weary sigh from the other end of the phone and she knew there was a bit of a lecture coming.

"The Summerfords have always been prideful, Mallory. All the years Jake's father was out of work and they hated getting a handout from anyone—no matter how much they needed it. That's what Jake learned growing up. He would have kept right on working for me at Coleman Construction and he might have even been happy doing it, but there's a lot more to that man and he deserves to discover that for himself."

"I know, Pops, I just wish..."

"No," he quickly interrupted.

"You don't even know what I was going to say!"

"You would have said how you still wished someone would have told you," he replied and dammit, he was right. That was exactly what she was going to say. "And I'm here to tell you that Jake needed to go with a clear conscience and to have his chance to finally do what he wants to do and make what he wants of his life without anyone's interference."

She was about to point out that by Pops giving Jake the financing, he was interfering.

But she didn't.

"So you can be mad and you can pout all you want, missy," he scolded, "but the only one in the wrong then is you."

Again, it was on the tip of her tongue to argue, but she didn't.

"Now the way I see it, you need to call Jake and apologize. He was a damn wreck after you left and I had to stop him from getting in his truck and chasing after you!"

"You...you did?"

"What good would it have done for him to get in the car when he was that upset? Someone would have had an accident with the way he was behaving!"

*Oh, God...what have I done?*

She'd been home for less than twelve hours and had ignored any calls and texts that came through on her cell phone for the entire eleven-hour drive back to her home on Long Island from Magnolia Sound. When she'd come downstairs this morning for breakfast, however, her mother handed her the house phone because Pops had been calling all day yesterday and all morning.

"Pops, I...I don't know what to say," she admitted, her voice small and trembly. Tears stung her eyes and she hated the whole situation.

Walking away from Jake after everything they'd shared this summer was hard enough –knowing they weren't going to see each other again until next summer was almost unbearable. But to hear him talking to Pops yesterday–especially after he had lied about where he was going to be– something had just snapped in her.

And broke.

Yeah, her heart was definitely broken.

But now she had to consider calling Jake and at least hearing his side of the story. There had been about a dozen calls and texts from him and maybe...just maybe...once she was off the phone with Pops she'd call and they could talk this out.

"Sweet pea, you know I love you," Pops said, interrupting her thoughts, "and I don't want this to come between us."

"It won't, Pops," she promised. "Nothing could ever come between us."

"Okay then," he replied, sounding pleased. "And we'll talk just like we always do and you'll come to visit next summer, right?"

Mallory smiled. "Always. You know I'd never miss a chance to come see you."

"Good. That's good." He paused. "You go and get settled in and visit with your mother and brother and we'll talk soon."

"You know it," she replied softly. "Love you, Pops."

"Love you too."

# CHAPTER 1

PRESENT DAY...

Mallory threw her satchel on the sofa as she kicked off her stilettos. It was good to be home. It had been a really long day, but it was a good one though. Great, even! After two years, she was finally getting the promotion she'd been after and a big fat raise to go with it. It felt so good to have all of her hard work recognized and a week from now, she'd have a brand-new office to go with her new executive position.

Of course, that didn't mean she wasn't going to be going out into the field and working on computer systems anymore. It just meant she would be the one overseeing a team and she wouldn't have to be pulling long hours on jobs that were technically beneath her. It was a great feeling.

There had been a cake and champagne to celebrate her new position and her co-workers all congratulated her, but she turned down their offers to go out and continue the celebration. She just wanted to come home and relax for a bit and then call her family to share the good news.

It was after seven and she was starving. The smart thing to do would have been to stop and pick up some takeout on the way home, but getting home was more of a priority. And now what did she have to show for it?

"Ugh...looks like I'm having a sandwich for dinner," she murmured, walking toward her kitchen. "Not exactly the celebratory dinner I should be having." This was becoming the norm lately–not taking enough time for herself and certainly not eating right. "Something's got to give. I can't keep living like this."

Mainly because she wasn't living–she was working long hours, coming home, sleeping, and repeating.

Definitely not the life she wanted to live.

Although, with her promotion, life should get a bit better. Just another few days and it would all kick in. Come Monday morning, there would be light at the end of the tunnel.

Off in the distance, Mallory heard her cellphone ring and sighed. It would be easy to ignore it, but what if it were something important? Making her way back to the living room, she fished her phone out of her purse and smiled when she saw her mother's name on the screen.

"Hey, Mom!"

"Hey, sweetheart! Am I catching you at a bad time?"

"Not at all," she lied. "I was just making some dinner."

"Oh, you're busy."

"No! Really, I'm not, Mom. What's going on? Everything okay?"

The first response was a sigh. "Well...we're having to evacuate."

"What?!" Mallory cried. "When? Why? I thought the hurricane was going to miss you?"

"It's one of those things...it took a turn to the west and now..." She sighed again. "I'm having a hell of a time with Pops, though. I was hoping you'd talk to him."

Two years ago, Mallory's mother had sold the home on Long Island and moved down to North Carolina's Magnolia Sound to take care of Pops. Susannah Westbrook took her responsibilities and her family seriously and after years of living so far away from her family, she'd finally made the decision to move back to her roots on the Carolina coast.

"Mom, I doubt anything I say will convince him. Surely there's enough people there who can do it. I mean, Aunt Georgia and Uncle Beau can surely talk to him. They've always been the ones to deal with him before, right?"

"In most cases, yes. Believe it or not, he's never evacuated before."

"How is that possible? Parker and Peyton have talked about those evacuations a lot over the years," Mallory argued.

"Well, your cousins–along with your aunt and uncle–always did listen to the warnings and left when they were supposed to. Your great-grandfather, however, has not, and he's refusing to do so now. Honestly, Mal, I don't know what to do. Can you talk to him? Please?"

"Of course I will." Not that it was going to do any good, Mallory already knew this. Her great-grandfather was as stubborn as they came and she knew she could talk and beg and scream and cry until she was blue in the face, but she wasn't going to change his mind. Nothing would. Still, she never turned down an opportunity to talk to him. Not since...

"Hey, sweet pea," Pops said, his voice a little weak and raspy, but that had been something she'd been noticing for some time now.

"Hey, Pops! How are you?"

"How am I? I'm fed up with everyone fussing at me!

I've lived in this house for almost a century and no storm has ever forced me out and this one won't either!"

Yup. He was stubborn.

"I know you never had to leave, but...how about just this once you do?" she suggested. "I know it would put everyone's mind at ease and...you know Mom's never gone through a hurricane there. At least, she hasn't in a really long time. She's stressing out about it and I know it would mean a lot if you would go with her."

When he didn't respond right away, Mallory was sure she had him and he was going to agree with her. She was ready to high-five herself when...

"No one's telling her she can't leave," Pops said defiantly. "Heck, it would be a lot easier if she'd go with Georgia and Beau and leave me alone! There's plenty of food here and I have a generator and if I need anything, Jake's right next door!"

Just the mention of Jake Summerford was enough to make Mallory's heart squeeze hard in her chest. It had been six years since they'd had their...what? Affair? Summer fling? Whatever it was, she had ruined it by acting immaturely and Jake hadn't hesitated to remind her of that when she tried to reconcile with him.

She'd given up after three months.

Oh, she'd still gone back to Magnolia Sound to visit Pops and her relatives, but Jake didn't come home at all during his four years of college. The first time she saw him again was two years ago when he came back to work for Coleman Construction. It had been a shock to her system to see him, but it didn't take long for her to realize she had never really meant anything to him. He'd gone back to treating her like nothing more than his neighbor's great-granddaughter.

And it hurt more than anything else ever had in her life.

"...all I'm saying is I'm a grown man who can make his own decisions and I'm tired of everyone treating me like a damn child or some sort of invalid!"

Okay, she'd lost track of the conversation and yet somehow Pops was still carrying on about not evacuating.

"Just...promise me you'll think about it," she quickly interrupted before he went on again. "You know we're all doing this because we love you, so...try not to be so angry, okay?"

"Hmph..."

"Pops..."

"Fine. I'll think about it," he said before quickly adding, "but I'm not going anywhere."

She laughed softly. "I love you, Pops."

"Love you too, sweet pea. When are you coming to visit? We missed you for Fourth of July."

"I know..."

"And you didn't come in June like you said you would..."

Yeah, life had been hectic and she was working with a company who needed a major system overhaul and she couldn't get away, so...

"I'm finishing up with a client next week so I'll look at my calendar and see if I can grab a week to come down. How does that sound?"

"Sounds like you're making excuses, but that's just me," he grumbled.

Okay, so maybe she hadn't wanted to go and visit because whenever she was there, so was Jake. It was like he was more a part of the family than she was and it was just... awkward. Mallory had considered asking her then-boyfriend Scott if he wanted to go with her for the Fourth of July celebration, but then thought better of it.

Avoidance was way better. The last time she was bold or defiant was that summer with Jake and...

"Here's your mother," Pops said, once again interrupting her thoughts. "Distract her with stories about what's going on with you so she'll leave me alone. Maybe start talking about whatever computer system you're working on. I know I find that stuff hard to follow, I'm sure she will too. And with any luck, she'll forget all about hassling me about leaving my home."

"I'll try," she said with a smile and then he was gone and she could hear him handing the phone back to her mother.

"He's exhausting, Mallory."

"I know, but...you have to see things from his point of view. That house is his whole life. It's his security. Leaving there–even if it's only for a day or two–is going to stress him out a lot."

"It's stressing us all out. Believe me, there's a lot of work that goes into evacuating. We have to secure the house and make sure we have all essential documents along with sorting through everything and just taking the necessities. I'm telling you, I'm a nervous wreck!"

"Is it really bad that he wants to stay?"

"Sweetheart, I understand why he wants to, but at his age, it's just not practical."

"Are you sure no one can stay with him?"

"Jake's offered and I have to tell you, I'm not feeling good about that either."

"Why not?"

"This storm is big. Really big. We're looking at the possibility of a Category 4 hurricane when it makes land-fall, and basically landfall is..."

"You," Mallory said sadly. "Magnolia Sound is the coast so there is no land before you."

"Exactly," Susannah said. "Georgia and Beau already have a place for us about forty miles inland. It's a townhouse they own and rent out but it happens to be vacant so we're all going there. Well...almost all of us are going."

"Mom...I really wish there were something I could do, but..."

"I know, I know. I appreciate you even trying. Georgia was here earlier having a fit and all she managed to do was make things worse. He was almost ready to pack a bag and then she came over and carried on and now he's acting like a petulant child. I tell you, it's maddening!"

"I know Aunt Georgia is not the best in these situations."

"She's not the best in any situation. Honestly, she's almost as obsessed with this house as Pops is! I think that's what got him so worked up again. He accused her of wanting him out of the house so she could somehow try and take it from him!"

"No!" Mallory cried with a small laugh. "I mean I know there's been a lot of heated discussions about her wanting the house, but...how could Pops possibly think that she could use a hurricane evacuation to take it from him?"

"At one point he accused her of being some kind of witch who caused the storm," Susannah said with a hint of amusement. "Look, Georgia is my cousin and I love her, but I swear I want to strangle her sometimes."

"As do her kids," Mallory said with a laugh.

"Oh, that reminds me! Parker's graduation party has been moved to mid-September. I have the date written down here somewhere. Georgia wants to have the party at the country club, but your cousin desperately wants to celebrate someplace fun and a lot less formal. And if I know Parker, she's going to want the kind of party that will make her mother crazy."

"That's reasonable. It's her party, right? But...wait. I didn't realize there was even going to be a party. I thought Parker wanted to go away somewhere rather than have a whole big thing."

"They're doing both, but the vacation is coming first. You know your aunt loves to throw a party, even if it's not the kind of party the guest of honor wants."

That was the truth. Her aunt was the belle of the ball of Magnolia Sound when it came to throwing parties; she lived for occasions to host one. "I'll mark my calendar but text me the date when you find it, please."

"Can do." She sighed. "Okay, I need to go pack up. We're heading out in the morning and there's still so much to do."

"You're just packing up the basics, right?"

"That was the plan, but a bunch of us are helping out the local eateries and getting as much food from them as possible to help cut their losses. Some places closed shop already, but Henderson's Bakery and Café Magnolia put the word out that they had food ready for anyone heading out of town. I'm planning on getting some things for Pops before I go."

"If he loses power, what good will it be?"

"Baked goods will keep," Susannah said. "And I just plan on getting sandwiches from the café that can go in a cooler."

"Where's Gertie? Did she leave already?"

Gertie had been Pops' housekeeper for longer than Mallory was alive. She was practically family. "She was out of town visiting her family and when the news first mentioned the storm, we told her to stay put."

"That was smart of you, but I'm sure she's worried."

"She only comes in once a week now," Susannah said. "I think she's ready to retire but she doesn't want to leave Pops."

That sounded like Gertie, all right.

"Okay, sweetie, I'll call you once we're settled."

"Be safe, Mom. And please keep talking to Pops. Maybe have...have Jake talk to him. I'm sure he'd listen to him before anyone else."

"Hmm...you may be right. I'll do that. Have a good night, sweetheart."

"You too, Mom. I'll talk to you tomorrow."

Once they hung up, Mallory's stomach growled loudly and she went back to the kitchen to make herself a sandwich. She didn't have much to choose from and ended up with ham and swiss on whole wheat. Not the most inspired dinner, but with her plate in hand, she went back to the sofa and turned on the TV, hoping to catch the weather report.

*"And now the latest on the storm that has the mid-Atlantic coast holding its breath. Hurricane Amelia has picked up strength as she seems to be heading directly toward the Carolinas. With the projected path, the storm should make landfall late Thursday night. The first evacuation orders have been issued to all coastal residents up and down the Carolina coast, with mandatory evacuation orders expected to go out within the next twelve hours. Residents on the barrier islands, Outer Banks, and Magnolia Sound areas in North Carolina look to be in the direct path of Amelia. Right now, this is a Category 2 hurricane, but predictions have it hitting Category 3 after midnight tonight with the*

*possibility of hitting Category 4 by the time it makes landfall. And we all know when winds range from 131 to 155 mph, they can cause catastrophic damage to property, humans, and animals. Severe structural damage to frame homes, apartments, and shopping centers should be expected. Category 4 hurricanes often include long-term power outages and water shortages lasting from a few weeks to a few months, so again, it's important for any remaining residents to have a significant nonperishable food and water supply at hand."*

Her appetite gone, Mallory tossed her sandwich back onto the plate and grabbed the remote to change the channel. There wasn't anything she could do from here–last she checked not only was Garden City, New York still eleven hours from Magnolia Sound, but she also had zero ability to stop a hurricane.

"Oh, but if I could," she murmured, standing and taking her sad dinner back to the kitchen and tossing it into the trash. "Now what do I do?"

Unfortunately, her first thought was to reach out to Jake and beg him to convince Pops to leave in the morning with everyone. It would be a completely legitimate reason for calling, but...

"Screw it. I don't care about how I feel or how Jake may feel about me calling. This isn't about us, so...if he doesn't like it, too bad."

Sometimes you had to put your own feelings aside and do the uncomfortable things–the things that make your heart ache and make you feel like you're going to be sick. And as she scrolled through her phone and pulled up his number, she was seriously glad she didn't take more than a couple of bites of her sandwich because...

"Hello?"

Just the sound of his voice was enough to make her want to pass out.

Buy Remind Me now!
https://www.chasing-romance.com/remind-me

## ABOUT THE AUTHOR

Samantha Chase is a New York Times and USA Today bestseller of contemporary romance. She released her debut novel in 2011 and currently has more than forty titles under her belt! When she's not working on a new story, she spends her time reading romances, playing way too many games of Scrabble or Solitaire on Facebook, wearing a tiara while playing with her sassy pug Maylene...oh, and spending time with her husband of 25 years and their two sons in North Carolina.

Where to Find Me:
Website: www.chasing-romance.com

Sign up for my mailing list and get exclusive content and chances to win members-only prizes!
http://bit.ly/1jqdxPR

 facebook.com/SamanthaChaseFanClub

twitter.com/SamanthaChase3

## ALSO BY SAMANTHA CHASE

**The Enchanted Bridal Series:**

The Wedding Season

Friday Night Brides

The Bridal Squad

Glam Squad & Groomsmen

**The Montgomery Brothers Series:**

Wait for Me

Trust in Me

Stay with Me

More of Me

Return to You

Meant for You

I'll Be There

Until There Was Us

Suddenly Mine

**The Shaughnessy Brothers Series:**

Made for Us

Love Walks In

Always My Girl

This is Our Song

Sky Full of Stars

Holiday Spice

Tangled Up in You

**Band on the Run Series:**

One More Kiss

One More Promise

One More Moment

**The Christmas Cottage Series:**

The Christmas Cottage

Ever After

Silver Bell Falls Series:

Christmas in Silver Bell Falls

Christmas On Pointe

A Very Married Christmas

A Christmas Rescue

**Life, Love & Babies Series:**

The Baby Arrangement

Baby, Be Mine

Baby, I'm Yours

**Preston's Mill Series:**

Roommating

Speed Dating

Complicating

## The Protectors Series:

Protecting His Best Friend's Sister

Protecting the Enemy

Protecting the Girl Next Door

Protecting the Movie Star

## 7 Brides for 7 Soldiers:

Ford

## Standalone Novels:

Jordan's Return

Catering to the CEO

In the Eye of the Storm

A Touch of Heaven

Moonlight in Winter Park

Wildest Dreams (currently unavailable)

Going My Way (currently unavailable)

Going to Be Yours (currently unavailable)

Waiting for Midnight

Seeking Forever (currently unavailable)

Mistletoe Between Friends

Snowflake Inn

Made in the USA
Middletown, DE
02 July 2020